"Jake and Ally
are your godparents."

Four-year-old Caleb knew that. He'd heard the word before, but he didn't like it. "Don't call them that," he said to the silver-haired priest. "God is mean. He took my mommy and daddy to heaven. Maybe He'll take Jake and Ally away, too."

Padre put down his coffee and studied the child. "Caleb, what happened to your mother and father was a really sad thing. When something bad takes place, it's natural to blame God. But He lost a son, too. He knows how you feel and He made sure that you have good people in your life to look after you. That's not mean, is it?"

Caleb was silent for moment. If Jesus was God's son, did that mean that Mary and Joseph weren't his real parents? Maybe they were his godparents—picked specially to care for him. "I don't want Jake and Ally to go to heaven," he said. "Or anywhere. I want them to stay with me."

"Have you told them how you feel?"

Caleb thought for a moment, then smiled at the priest. "I gotta go now. I gotta tell them I want them to be my mommy and daddy. Forever."

Dear Reader,

I'm often asked where I get the ideas for my stories. I've found that inspiration can come from any number of sources. The idea behind this one came from my daughter, Kelly. A casual conversation one afternoon started my mind racing with *what-ifs*. What if your best friend dies and you're the godmother to her child? And what if the god*father*—a relative stranger—wants a say in the little boy's life? I casually tossed out the idea to my editor, and she expressed an interest in seeing a proposal. That's where the "Ohmygosh, how am I going to write this?" came into play. But Caleb's story wanted to be told, and I'm glad it did. Along the way I met two dynamic, strong-willed characters who weren't the least bit intimidated by the question that set this book in motion: "How much would you do for the sake of a child?" Allison and Jake both know the answer: "As much as it takes." And if that means falling in love in the process, they're up for that, too. Well, one of them is. The other takes a little convincing. I hope you enjoy their story and come to love Caleb as much as they do.

My thanks to family friend Don Reed for filling in the gaps about life in Yosemite Lakes Park. Rose, we miss you. And to my sister, Jan, for helping me in so many ways—reading, re-reading, accompanying me to signings. Your support means so much to me.

When I'm not writing, you can find me "blogging" at my Web site, www.debrasalonen.com, or chatting on the boards at the "Let's Talk Superromance" thread at eHarlequin.com. Conventional letters will reach me at P.O. Box 322, Cathey's Valley, CA 95306. I love hearing from readers.

Happy reading,

Debra

Caleb's Christmas Wish
Debra Salonen

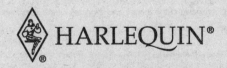

HARLEQUIN®

TORONTO • NEW YORK • LONDON
AMSTERDAM • PARIS • SYDNEY • HAMBURG
STOCKHOLM • ATHENS • TOKYO • MILAN • MADRID
PRAGUE • WARSAW • BUDAPEST • AUCKLAND

ISBN 0-373-71238-3

CALEB'S CHRISTMAS WISH

Copyright © 2004 by Debra K. Salonen.

Printed in U.S.A.

Kelly,
you inspire me in more ways than you could ever know.

And Paul,
who has always been there for me from my first book
to my tenth. I love you.

CHAPTER ONE

"HELLO? Is this Allison Jeffries?"

"Yes, this is Allison," she answered, still looking at the Gordian knot of printer, speaker, keyboard and mouse cords she'd been attempting to make sense of. "What can I do for you?"

"Ma'am, this is Officer Deese with the Madera County Sheriff's department. I'm at the home of Kenneth and Pamela Rydell in Coarsegold. Mrs. Rydell's mother asked me to give you a call. Would it be possible for you to come here right away?"

A jangle of apprehension rushed through her. She swallowed. "Why? What's happened?"

"There was a traffic accident this morning about five miles east of Shaver Lake."

"Kenny and Pam were hurt?"

"I'm sorry. They didn't make it. Black ice. A three-car pileup. The victims' car was in the middle."

Victims?

Pam and Kenny?

No!

She wanted to argue with him. To tell him he was wrong. She'd just spent yesterday—Thanksgiving—with her two closest friends. They couldn't be…

She closed her eyes and swallowed twice to keep the

contents of her stomach in her stomach. She tried to speak, but the only word that came out was, "No!"

"Allison? You're white as a sheet. What is it?"

Allison lifted her gaze from the swirling print on the carpet of Mary Zirandervon's home office and blinked to focus on the woman facing her. Her client. A job that ten seconds earlier had seemed the most important thing in her world. Making money. Meeting payroll. Worrying about the loan she owed her parents. That was Allison's life. Her narrow little life that was brightened immeasurably by her best friend and former college roommate Pam Rydell.

She shook her head to chase away what the officer had said. Pam wasn't dead. She was alive. Laughing. Teasing. Skiing. She was up on the slope at Sierra Summit right this instant. Someone else had been in that middle car. Pam was generous to a fault. Maybe she'd lent her car to someone who'd needed it.

"It's a mistake," she said, partly to Mary, partly to the man on the phone.

"The accident took place around seven," the deputy said. "It took us awhile to identify all the victims."

Holding fast to her sliver of hope, she asked, "Are you sure it was the Rydells? Kenny owns a car dealership. He sometimes drives different cars. And Pam might have lent…"

The officer didn't let her finish. His voice sounded weary. "Ma'am, the Jeep was registered to the driver. And the passenger lived long enough to give the rescuers her name."

Allison's knees buckled. She'd have dropped to the floor in a heap if Mary hadn't rushed forward and helped her onto the desk chair.

Tears swamped her vision. Her throat closed and for a minute she couldn't draw a breath. She shook her head back and forth, struggling to ward off the bad news that still rang in her ears. "No," she said again. Too loud. The word echoed in the elegantly appointed room, bouncing off the windows that were shrouded by gray fog. Up in the mountains where Pam and Kenny had been headed, the sun would be shining. The air, crisp and clean. The snow brilliant. The black ice deadly.

Mary took the phone from Allison's numb fingers and spoke in a low, urgent tone that added to Allison's turmoil. She needed to do something. Feel something. Act. But all she could do was sit in the plush leather chair and moan.

At least, she assumed the low mewling sound was coming from her. But how was that possible? She wasn't the kind of woman who fell apart in an emergency. Just ask Pam.

"You're my rock," Pam often said. "Aren't you the one who held my hand through my Cesarean after Kenny passed out?"

Allison's lips twitched at the memory. She and Pam had bonded the first day of college. Roommates as different as the worlds they'd come from—Allison, a farm girl from Minnesota, Pam a beauty queen from Detroit. But at the core, they were sisters. Allison was godmother to Pam and Kenny's son, Caleb.

"Oh, my God," Allison cried, shooting to her feet. "Caleb."

She snatched the phone away from Mary and shouted into the receiver, "Tell me their son wasn't in the car with them." Under her breath, she prayed, "Please, God, please, God, please, God." Last night,

Pam had still been undecided about whether to take the four-and-a-half year-old.

"He loves the snow," Pam had said right before Allison left. "But Kenny and I need some time together. You know how hectic the holidays get. My canned-food drive at Rydell Motors kicks off next week, and Caleb's program at preschool is coming up."

Full, fat and happy from turkey and all the trimmings, Allison hadn't paid very close attention to the final verdict. Blissfully content from a day of feasting, hiking and playing games with her best friends, Allison hadn't felt the slightest premonition that it might be the last time she'd see her friend alive.

She held her breath—frozen in agony—until the man said, "If you're referring to a cute little towhead with a big truck in his hand, he's right here with his grandmother. Mrs. Wells is…um, naturally this came as a huge shock. She should have someone with her. When I asked who to call, she gave me your number."

Caleb was okay. Relief shot Allison to a momentary crest. *Thank God. Thank you, thank you, thank you.* She tried to say the words aloud, but was too overcome to speak. A fresh rush of tears blinded her to everything but the phone she grasped. All she could do was nod in response to Mary's silent query.

"Praise the Lord," Mary said, hugging Allison. A second later, the woman dashed from the room, returning almost immediately with a fistful of tissues.

"Here," she said, forcing a wad into Allison's immobile fingers.

Allison leaned her hip against the desk to stay upright and mopped her face the best she could. "Thank you," she finally managed to choke out.

"Yes, ma'am, we can be thankful for small blessings. Now, will you be coming right away? Mrs....um Wells seems to be having a little trouble breathing. And her color isn't too good. Do you know if she has any medical condition we should be aware of?"

The question required Allison to think. To focus. Something she was said to be good at. Except when her world fell apart.

"High blood pressure maybe? Yes, I think that's right. Pam was always getting after her mother for not watching her salt intake. And I think she's borderline diabetic, too," Allison said, trying to shake off the surreal feeling of speaking about everyday things when any fool knew life would never be normal again.

"She could be in shock," the deputy said, "but I think I'd better call in the paramedics, just to be safe. How long will it take you to get here?"

It took Allison several seconds to remember where she was. From her home in Fresno, the drive to the Rydell home in Yosemite Lakes Park near the little gold rush-era town of Coarsegold took roughly forty-five minutes, but the Zirandervon home was on the northeast outskirts of town, which put Allison at least ten miles closer.

"Fifteen—twenty minutes. If casino traffic isn't bad," she said.

"I'll keep an eye on things until you get here. Are you sure you're okay to drive?"

No, Allison almost cried again. She'd never be okay again. But something in his tone when he asked about Cordelia's health problems made Allison's stomach turn over. No more, she silently pleaded. We can't handle anything else. But she knew that kind of logic was no guarantee that things wouldn't get worse. There'd been a time when she thought learning you had cancer was the worst thing that could happen to a person. But then her doctors told her that the treatment they were prescribing could only be carried out by aborting the baby she was carrying. She'd had to make a decision too horrible to imagine. A decision that had ripped her family apart, poisoned her marriage and might have killed her—if not for Pam, who'd brought Allison back to life. Pam, who'd forced Allison to re-engage in life. But now, Pam was gone.

The pain that twisted in Allison's belly might have consumed her, if not for the knowledge that Cordelia and Caleb needed her. "I'll be there as soon as I can," she said, making her vocal cords work despite the knot in her throat.

She handed the phone to Mary, who hung it up. "Are you sure you're okay to drive, Ally? I could call Ed. Or a cab…"

Allison shook her head. "I'll need my car." She spun on one heel looking for her backpack, which also served as her purse. "Mary, I'm sorry. I can't…"

"Go," Mary said with authority. "Don't worry about this. You can send Ernesto out to finish the job or Ed can set it up himself." Sniffing, she gripped Allison's arm and said, "Go. Just let me know if there's anything I can do to help. I knew Pam. Not as well as I knew Kenny. He sold me my car. Such a sweetheart. But she happened to be at the shop that day with their little boy. She was so bubbly and full of life. I can't believe this has happened."

It happened. Allison repeated the phrase over and over as she drove. Hands clenched bone-white around the steering wheel, she kept her eyes on the road, while her mind careened with "what-ifs" and "if-onlys."

"Why didn't I tell her I needed her help today?" Allison muttered, blinking away another bout of tears. Pam was hopeless around computers, but she was great in the front office. A true people person, Pam could soothe the most recalcitrant client into accepting the services of Jeffries Computing.

"Oh, Pam, what am I going to do without you?"

The pressure on her chest increased, and the dotted line down the middle of the road blurred. She blinked fiercely. She had to keep her emotions under control for Caleb's sake. And Cordelia's. The woman would be devastated. Her only child gone.

Cordelia lived in the guest house directly behind the Rydells' home. The eight-hundred-square-foot building had started life as a greenhouse, but Pam and Kenny remodeled it into a diminutive one-bed, one-bath suite after Pam's father, George Wells, passed away.

Pam had told Allison that Cordelia had been adamant about buying the empty lot next door with the intention of building a home of her own beside her daughter's. But as she became settled, the urgency to build dwindled.

Although Pam and her mother argued occasionally— they were after all, two women sharing one kitchen— the living arrangements seemed to work. Cordelia had proven to be a huge asset when it came to helping to care for Caleb. The little boy and his grandmother were close, which made the possibility of something happening to Cordelia all the more frightening. Allison stepped on the gas, pushing her Subaru wagon faster than normal.

As she neared the entrance to the housing development that Pam often called Allison's "country home," Mary Zirandervon's words came back. *Pam was a sweetheart. Bubbly. Full of life.*

"Oh, Pam," Allison cried, pounding the steering wheel with the heel of her hand. "Please let it be a mistake. I know you wouldn't just quit on me. On Caleb. Or your mother. This has to be a mistake."

She put on her blinker without thinking, turned across traffic without really looking and zoomed into the housing development. As her car soared up the slight incline past the reduced speed zone sign, Allison recalled an argument she and Pam had had about speeding.

"Loosen up, Ally," Pam had said, when Allison accused her of having a lead foot. "One might think you're an uptight nerd—which I know you're not." Allison couldn't remember the rest of the conversation, but she'd smiled. She and Pam were the kind of friends who could say things to each other that no one else could.

But all that was over. And as she slowed to maneuver past the sheriff's car that was partly blocking the driveway of the house on Sequoia Circle, Allison knew at a gut level that her best friend in the world was gone, and a part of herself was lost forever.

THE PAIN WAS MORE OF an annoyance than anything else. It prevented Cordelia from taking a full breath, which made her head feel woozy and sent flickering yellow spots across her vision.

"You silly old coot. Get a grip," Cordelia Wells wanted to tell herself, but the effort it took to speak was more than she could muster. She'd never felt so weak, so useless.

A small fear suddenly formed. What if this was a

stroke? George had had a massive stroke before he died. She'd never forgotten the agony in his eyes, days on end in a hospital bed, trapped in a useless body, mute.

Fear tightened the knot under her rib cage and the pain in the center of her chest increased. She let out a small whimper, even though she tried her best to keep it in.

Caleb, who was playing on the carpet nearby with his favorite toy, looked up at her. His big green eyes grew rounder and his bottom lip disappeared under his teeth. He had lovely teeth—just like his mother's. Kenny's mouth was generous and his smile ready, but Cordelia always wished his mother would have gotten him braces when he was younger. Even Pam, who defended her husband no matter what, agreed that Caleb would be better off with her teeth and gums.

Thinking their names brought back the dark and dangerous reality she was trying desperately to keep at bay. She bit down on the wail that threatened to erupt from the deepest corner of her soul.

"How are you doing, ma'am?" the young deputy asked. He set down the phone and returned to the couch he'd helped Cordelia onto after breaking the news of the accident. She'd been sitting up at the time, but was now lying down. She couldn't remember falling over. She sensed that one leg was hanging down in a most ignoble pose, but she didn't have the strength to move it.

"Is that pain in your arm any better?" he asked, trying to elicit a response from her.

Cordelia felt sorry for the deputy. He appeared too young for such a loathsome job—telling people their loved ones were dead.

He dropped to one knee beside her and picked up her wrist. His large square fingers pressed against her vein.

She could feel the erratic flutter as her heart did its job. Her broken heart. She'd tried to handle the news stoically when he'd first told her about the accident. Just as she had when the doctor had told her that George had passed away.

But back then, she'd been prepared for the inevitable. She'd talked with friends—other widows. Everyone told her that life and death were linked. You couldn't have one without the other. But that reasoning was easier to swallow when the person who'd died had lived his life with great verve and total disregard for the health concerns his wife had tried to alert him to. George had been seventy-two. Pam was just thirty-four.

The number jabbed Cordelia in the heart like a shard of glass. *Had Pam suffered? Had she forgotten her seat belt and hit the windshield? Had she cried out in fear? Or in pain?*

The gruesome possibilities wouldn't quit playing in her mind. Along with questions. What would become of Caleb? I'm old. How can I give him the life his parents wanted him to have? Who will take care of Kenny's business? What will we do for money?

The pressure on her chest increased; the dots were chased by black globs that terrified her. Was the blackness death?

The man at her side gripped her hand. Hard. "I've called for the paramedics. They'll be here soon. Breathe slowly. Deep, steady breaths."

Cordelia wanted to say, "Get real"—one of Pam's favorite comebacks. But she couldn't get the words out. Her mouth wasn't responding. Her voice was gone. She knew she was losing consciousness.

Was this the end? One part of her welcomed the idea. She'd been alone a long time. She was ready to join George. And, now, Pam would be there, too. The beautiful daughter, who'd brought such joy to her life. How could Cordelia go on without her?

"Cordelia. Cordelia? Can you hear me? Oh, please, don't do this."

The voice was familiar.

Pam?

Reaching deep inside, Cordelia found the strength to open her eyes, only to be engulfed by disappointment. Brown hair, not blond. Allison, not Pam. But the look of distress on Allison's face touched her.

Poor girl will be lost without Pam. That's when it hit her. If something were to happen to Cordelia, Allison would be left to care for Caleb alone. Ally, who obviously adored her godson but didn't know beans about child care. If not Allison then…Cordelia couldn't think of Caleb's godfather's name, at first. Then it came to her. Jake. Jake the Rake, as her son-in-law jokingly referred to his best friend. Jake Westin. He would be raising Cordelia's grandson.

"Cordelia, please," Allison said, leaning close, her voice a low, desperate whisper. "Please try to hang on. Caleb needs you. I need you."

In the distance, the sound of a siren grew louder. Cordelia hated hospitals, but she'd do whatever it took to be there for Caleb. He was all she had left.

FEAR AND COMPASSION WARRED inside Allison. The sound of the siren was growing closer, but Allison was afraid it wouldn't reach them in time. Beneath her perfect makeup, Cordelia's skin looked ghostly white. Her lipstick was smeared at the corner of her mouth—not something Allison had ever seen before. Her lips moved, though no sound came out. Allison squeezed the older woman's hand. "Hang on, Cordelia. Help is on the way."

She looked at the deputy for reassurance.

"Any second."

The small black box on his shoulder squawked. He stood up and hurried to the front door. One hand on the walkie-talkie, he mumbled something Allison couldn't interpret clearly. But she did hear the words "possible heart attack."

She turned her attention back to Cordelia and gripped her hand with her own. "I know this is asking a lot, Cordelia. You've just been given the most horrible news imaginable, but I'm begging you, stay with us. Caleb needs you to be here for him. You can do that, can't you?"

Tears swamped her again, choking off her words. She was failing. If Cordelia died…Allison's mind shut down. She couldn't go down that unthinkable path. She had to believe that Pam's mother would pull through.

Two strangers in black jumpsuits suddenly rushed into the room. Each carried a bulky bag of equipment. The two paramedics—a tall, thin man and a much shorter, rounder woman—advanced on the couch. Allison scrambled to get out of the way.

Cordelia's eyelids fluttered and a scary sound came from her lips. Allison couldn't bear to watch, nor could she let Caleb see whatever lifesaving procedures they needed to employ.

She looked toward the corner of the room where she'd first spotted the little boy when she'd come in.

Sure enough, a small figure peeked around the edge of the chair, small fingers gripping the polished cotton fabric as if to pull it around him for protection.

Caleb Rydell. Allison's four-year-old godson. Pam and Kenny's only child. Their *first* child, they were fond of saying. The thought hit her like a slap in the face, but she clamped down on her emotions. *Get a grip. You can do this.*

Instinct told her to pick him up and reassure him that everything was going to be okay, but she didn't want to add to his confusion by acting out of character. Pam was the touchy-feely one, Allison the reserved, analytical type. When Allison read her godson a book, he sat beside her. When Pam read to her son, the two were so entwined it was hard to see where one body quit and the other took off.

She had no idea what to do, but she had to try. The poor little kid must be scared out of his mind, she thought. She crossed the room and knelt down on one knee, peeking behind the chair. "Hi, honey. Lots of stuff happening this morning. Noisy. Kinda scary. Are you okay?"

Caleb scooted as far back as he could go. He kept his gaze on the object in his hand. His little fingers gripped the truck so tightly his knuckles showed white against his skin. But he acknowledged her question with a nod.

"I'm glad you're okay, but I'm not doing so hot. Do you suppose you could give me a hug?"

He looked at her. Suspicious or just surprised? She couldn't tell. But being the kindhearted kid his mother and father had raised him to be, he put down the metal truck so he could crawl toward her.

She opened her arms and gently hugged him, wishing she had the power to teleport them both to a place where none of this was happening.

"Thank you," she said, rising with Caleb still in her arms. He seemed far lighter than she remembered. "I needed that."

When he tried to see over her shoulder, she started toward the kitchen. "I don't know about you, but I could use something to drink."

His body craned to keep Cordelia in sight, but Allison shifted him to the other hip. "Don't worry," Allison said, trying to get him to make eye contact. "Grandma's going to be fine." *I hope.* "She was having trouble catching her breath. That's why Officer Deese came."

That seemed to make sense to him. "Policemen are good helpers," he said, as if challenging her to dispute the fact.

"Exactly. Paramedics and firefighters, too. Your mommy told me you once got to touch a real fire truck. I've never done that." Allison had no idea if her blather was helping, but when Caleb suddenly wiggled to be released, she stopped and bent over until his feet touched the tile floor.

"Did you just get up?" she asked, noticing his footed, one-piece blanket sleeper. The much-washed Spider-Man print looked a little snug on him, which reminded Allison of a conversation she'd had with Pam the day before. Apparently, his parents had been concerned that Caleb wasn't growing fast enough.

"Thank heavens for his recent growth spurt," Pam said. "I want to get him a bike for Christmas, but Kenny thinks he's still too little." She'd made a silly face and rolled her eyes. "And they say mothers are overprotective."

"Well, he is only four," Allison had replied. She often found herself siding with Kenny on parenting issues. Pam's style of mothering was far more casual than Allison's would have been. Not that Pam was anything short of wonderful as a mother, but she let Caleb explore beyond the parameters Ally would have considered safe.

"Four and a half," Pam had corrected. "And it's a teeny-weeny thing with training wheels. Metallic purple motocross. I can't wait to show it to Kenny. He'll give in eventually. He always does."

Allison had made some comment about finding it ironic that Kenny, a former rock-and-roll band member, had turned out to be the more conservative parent of the pair.

"I know. Isn't it a hoot?"

The two had laughed, but later on the drive home, Allison had wondered what kind of parent she would have made. Her child would have been nearly nine, if she'd gone ahead with the pregnancy. But instead, she'd caved to the pressure from her doctors, her husband and her family. She'd agreed to abort the fetus that was growing inside her so the doctors could start an aggressive treatment to remove the cancerous tumor they'd discovered while doing an ultrasound.

"You'll still have one ovary," the doctor had told her, as if that made the culling of one ovary and one life acceptable. "You'll still be able to bear children in the future. But if we don't operate now, there's a chance this cancer will metastasize. Both you and the baby could die."

At the time, she'd believed them, but in the dark days that followed, all Allison knew for sure was that she'd had her chance and blown it.

Now, through the worst circumstances imaginable, she was being given a second chance to step into motherhood. Only the child in question was far more real than a hazy smudge on an ultrasound image.

Allison watched Caleb climb onto one of the padded stools at the counter. "What would you like to drink?" she asked. "Chocolate milk?"

"Okay," he said.

She loved Caleb, but he seemed to reserve his effusive hugs for his mother, father and grandmother. Allison figured she was to blame for that. When he was first born, she hadn't been able to hold him without crying. Both Allison and Pam had agreed that wasn't good for a baby. So, gradually, she became the friendly aunt who brought presents and came to every family gathering but didn't kiss him too much or hug him too tight.

She walked to the refrigerator. The sight of a half-eaten, foil-wrapped turkey on the top shelf made Allison's stomach heave and her eyes fill with tears. Pam had been so proud of her perfect Thanksgiving feast.

Pretending to search high and low for the individual bottles of chocolate milk, she stalled long enough to get her emotions under control. Finally, with an artificial flourish, she handed Caleb a brown-and-white container. "Need help opening it?"

"No," he answered. Even as a toddler, he had preferred to do things himself.

"How 'bout a piece of toast?" ·

"Waffles?"

Waffles? Her heart skipped a beat as she pictured her

mother in their old farmhouse kitchen whipping up a vat of batter with a wire whisk. On the counter, their ancient electric waffle iron would sit, its thick, frayed cord plugged into a socket. Allison had unplugged it once with wet hands and received a shock she'd never forgotten. She hadn't eaten a waffle since.

Caleb slipped off the stool and walked to the freezer, which was the lower half of the refrigerator. From a pull-out basket, he withdrew a cardboard box. "Blueberry. My favorite."

Relief washed over her. "Excellent choice," she said, taking the box from his hand. "Where's the toaster?"

He looked skyward—as if asking God for patience—a gesture that was pure Pam. "In there," he said, pointing to a paneled box on the center island. The built-in unit contained a mixer, a blender and a four-piece toaster.

"Oh, yeah, I forgot."

He returned to his seat and opened his milk.

While the two little squares cooked, Allison moved from one side of the kitchen to the other trying to remember where Pam kept the plates, the silverware and the syrup. Normally, this wouldn't have been a challenge, since she knew her way around quite well. But one part of her brain was trying to decipher what was going on in the living room.

When she set the bottle of syrup on the counter, Caleb said testily, "Not syrup. Peanut butter and honey."

Allison smacked her forehead with the heel of her hand. "Of course. How silly of me to forget. And where do I find that, young master?"

Grinning, he pointed to the cupboard to the right of the gleaming six-burner gas stove.

She'd just set the plate in front of him when she noticed Officer Deese motioning to her from the hallway. The grim look on the young deputy's face didn't bring any relief.

"Caleb, I'll be right back. I'm going to see if Grandma or the officer wants coffee."

"Mrs. Wells is in cardiac arrest," the man said when she reached him. His tone was urgent, his frown grave.

Allison put her hand on the wall for support. "Is it bad?"

"Hard to say. We're transporting her to the cardiac hospital in Fresno. Could you find her doctor's name? We need to know if she has any allergies or preexisting medical conditions."

Luckily, Pam often vented about her mother's health issues—both real and imagined, so Allison knew Cordelia's primary physician's name. Officer Deese called it in on his walkie-talkie.

"As for allergies…I don't know…I'm just a friend."

"I understand. Do you know of anyone else in the family we should contact? In case…well, just in case."

In case of emergency, call Jake Westin. She'd heard Kenny say that just a few weeks ago, but she couldn't remember the circumstances behind the statement. Jake was Caleb's godfather. A man she'd never met, although she'd seen many photos of him since he either accompanied the Rydells on their annual family vacations or took Caleb off on a side trip so Pam and Kenny could have some time alone. Last August he'd taken the child to Disney World.

The Florida trip, she thought. She'd been invited, but had been called home to attend her grandfather's funeral, instead. Looking through some vacation photos that he'd just gotten developed, Kenny had remarked, "There's Jake. I'm sorry you didn't get to meet him this time. He's a helluva good guy. I'd trust him with my life. He's the brother I never had."

Allison had two sisters and a brother, and while she loved them, she was far closer to Pam than she was to any of her siblings, who still lived within five miles of the family farm.

"Cordelia is pretty much all the family Pam has... um, had," she said, trying to stay focused. "Kenny has a cousin who works for him at Rydell Motors, but I think the person they'd want notified right away is Caleb's godfather, Jake Westin. He lives in Miami. I'll call him as soon as..."

Behind them, two paramedics entered the foyer pushing a lowered gurney. The wheels made a loud, clattering sound against the rustic Mexican tile.

A second later, the ping of silverware dropping reminded her that she'd left Caleb in the kitchen. She heard the plastic soles of his sleeper shuffling against the flooring as he came to see what was happening.

Allison didn't know exactly what to tell him. How much would a four-year-old understand? She had to assume that he hadn't been told about his parents' accident, and she had no intention of bringing that up just yet.

Feeling totally out of her league, Allison decided to try honesty. "Grandma Cordelia needs to go to the hospital."

His blue eyes grew wide. "Why?"

"She was having trouble breathing. These people are going to take her in the ambulance so the doctors can make her better."

"Can I ride in it?"

"The ambulance? No. But we can follow it."

His sticky, peanut-butter-bracketed lips pouted a moment, then he asked, "Can we go fast? Jake has a fast car."

She wasn't surprised. According to Pam, Jake was living *la vida loca* in Miami. Allison was quite sure her practical station wagon wouldn't impress Caleb—even with its all-wheel-drive.

She changed the subject by telling Caleb he couldn't go anywhere if he didn't get dressed. Fast.

Allison let him select his own clothes—a bright green T-shirt with a gruesome-looking superhero on it. After a hunt that included moving his molded red race-car bed, she found a matching pair of sneakers. The socks were different colors—purple and black—but she wasn't as particular as Pam.

In fact, on those rare occasions when she went to a party, Ally had to ask for Pam's help picking something to wear. Unfortunately, they couldn't share many items because Pam was a petite blonde with a to-die-for-figure; Allison had a "utilitarian" body.

"A draft horse versus a Thoroughbred," she'd once said.

Pam had insisted that wasn't true. "I'm short and round. You're willowy and svelte, like a runway model."

The brutal reality of the enormity of her loss surged again, but Allison avoided thinking about it by scrambling to her feet to hunt for Caleb's jacket.

"Ready?" she asked, her tone bleak to her own ears.

Caleb hesitated as if waiting for her to say or do something.

"Um…you look good?" she tossed out.

He put his hands on his hips and rolled his eyes.

"You're supposed to ask if I need to go to the bathroom?" he said with an exasperated huff.

"Oh. Well, I just figured if you needed to go, you'd tell me." She waited. When he didn't move, she added, "Do you?"

He nodded, then marched off to his private bathroom. She followed but stopped short of the door, unsure whether her help was required. Did children his age prefer privacy? Why hadn't she paid closer attention to how Pam handled things these past four and a half years?

She decided to wait for his call. It didn't come. A minute or so later, he returned. And held out his hands as if she were expected to inspect them. They may not have been perfectly clean, but they looked dampish.

"Close enough. Let's go."

"Wait. My toys. And juice. And books. Mommy always takes stuff along in case. When's Mommy coming home?"

"In case of what?" Allison asked, ignoring his direct question. That avoidance strategy wouldn't work for long, but she knew she had to stall until they learned whether or not Cordelia was going to be okay. How much bad news could anyone take?

He shrugged his narrow shoulders and put out his hands. "Just in case."

While Caleb stuffed toys, books and various necessities into a small red suitcase on wheels, Allison checked on the progress of the paramedics, who were just strapping an unconscious Cordelia onto the gurney. A clear sack of fluid was attached to her arm by a needle. Thick blankets covered her lower body, but the woman's chest was exposed just short of immodesty.

An array of wires sprouted from her like something in a horror movie.

Allison guided Caleb to the garage. "We need to move your booster seat from your mother's car to mine," she said, firmly. "Can you show me how? I've never actually done this. Only watched the experts."

Doing something—anything—and knowing Caleb was watching helped Allison stave off the pain that still gnawed at her insides. The actual transfer amounted to less of an ordeal than she'd expected, but the scent of Pam's perfume was almost more than she could take. If not for Caleb's close scrutiny, she would have crawled into the back seat, closed the door and wept.

At some level, it occurred to her that Kenny's older much-loved Jeep was missing from its spot in the garage. She vaguely remembered hearing Officer Deese mention the make of the car in the accident, but it hadn't sunk in. Did a car of that age have air bags, she wondered? Or side impact protection? Both features had been of major importance to Pam when picking out their family car.

A tiny flash of anger flared. Why, she wanted to cry? *Why take the Jeep?* Allison knew why. It was a guy thing, Pam would have said, and the two friends would have laughed and shaken their heads.

Once Caleb was safely buckled in the Subaru, she backed the car up and pulled forward to the curb so they could follow the ambulance. The Rydell house was the corner lot—almost three acres—at the mouth of a cul-de-sac. Cordelia's undeveloped parcel sat to the right. Three other homes to the left made up Sequoia Circle.

Pam's immediate neighbors were a couple whom Allison had met several times. A few years older than

Pam and Kenny, the husband, Marc, was a pilot with United. Wife Gayle, a retired flight attendant, was now a stay-at-home mom of three. Their youngest son was Caleb's age, so Pam and Gayle traded baby-sitting quite a bit.

It occurred to Allison to ask Gayle to watch Caleb—until she remembered Pam saying that her neighbors had flown to Hawaii for Thanksgiving.

"They travel a lot," Pam had said a while back.

Detecting a touch of envy in her voice, Allison asked whether Pam missed the touring she and Kenny had done when he'd played in the band.

"Are you nuts," she'd exclaimed. "I love my life. Just the way it is."

Just the way it is.

A small whimper slipped past her resolve.

"Go, Aunt Allison, go," a voice prompted from the back seat.

She took her foot off the brake, but waited for a nod from Officer Deese before following the ambulance. The boxy white van maintained a safe pace, well within the legal limits, all the way to Fresno. She didn't dare question whether that was a good omen, or bad.

CHAPTER TWO

JAKE WESTIN STOOD on the balcony of his third-floor condo and watched the palm trees decorated in twinkling Christmas lights sway in the balmy Miami breeze. During the day Jake could watch throngs of sunbathers along the white sand. But now, the ocean looked like a black slate littered with neon confetti—reflections from the holiday lights of businesses that lined the boulevard.

Leaving the patio doors ajar, he walked to his kitchen and opened the Sub-Zero refrigerator, which was well stocked with healthy choices. He took a bottle of Chimay, his favorite Belgian beer, from the shelf. His first alcohol of the night. Jake's early years had been packed with substance abusers and he'd vowed never to let that kind of ugliness be part of his life.

Jake had just returned from dinner with a former colleague from the New York investment firm where he once worked. He didn't miss Wall Street. The adrenaline rush he once relied on from buying and selling stock paled in comparison to the satisfaction he got from watching a "sleeper" split and add several zeroes to a client's bottom line.

He set the portly bottle on the marble countertop and used his whimsical "talking" bottle opener to pry off the cap. "Oh, yeah, time for a beer. Heh, heh, heh," it said in a goofy voice that made him smile. A cheesy plastic gift from his godson, Caleb—the smartest, funniest, coolest child on the planet. Anything that reminded Jake of Caleb usually improved his mood.

The time they'd spent together in early August had been the best of Jake's recent memory. Not that Jake's life was anything to complain about. He did what he wanted, when he wanted and he had no one to answer to but his clients. His small, elite cadre of investors paid him obscenely large commissions to shepherd their stocks, bonds, offshore accounts and annuities. Through careful—some called it intuitive—investing, Jake was set for life. Provided he didn't do something stupid— like marry a woman who would take half when she split.

Jake had seen it happen far too often. Just as he'd witnessed older men toss away their comfortable life and comfortable wife for a handful of youth. This probably explained why he was thirty-six and still single. But life was good in Miami. If a recurrent sense of loneliness didn't clear up soon, he'd get a dog. He'd been considering the idea for some time.

Maybe I'll do a little dog shopping online, he thought, carrying his beer to his desk. He still hadn't ordered Caleb's Christmas gift, either. He'd had his mind set on a Junior Trampoline until Caleb broke a finger falling off the scooter Jake had sent as an Easter gift. Maybe a less dangerous toy. Something involving trucks and bulldozers, Kenny had suggested.

Jake sat down and clicked on his e-mail icon. He waited for Kenny's name to come up under his Instant Messaging Buddies column. Maybe they're not back yet, he decided, when the name failed to appear.

He'd talked to Kenny yesterday—about an hour before their dinner guests were due to arrive to share a Thanksgiving feast, and Ken mentioned that he and Pam were planning to go skiing today. Jake hadn't asked how far away they had to drive.

Corny though it was, Jake had long idealized the image of a white Christmas. All part of the ridiculous—utterly fictional—dad and son building a snowman in front of a Currier & Ives picket-fence-smoke-curling-out-of-a-chimney scene that seemed ingrained in his subconscious. Why this was supposed to be a good thing, he had no idea, but every year when the holidays rolled around, up popped this peculiar longing for something so far outside his realm of possibility it was almost laughable.

Besides, Jake hated snow. He'd spent four long, disgusting winters in New York. One Christmas he even flew to Switzerland when he'd mistakenly thought he was in love. The ski resort in the Alps had been romantic and expensive. He'd returned in a cast. His femur healed, but his heart was never quite the same. As a result, he'd sworn off skiing, serious relationships and cold precipitation.

Jake took a sip of his icy beer and let out a satisfied sigh. The upcoming holidays were not his favorite time of year. No family to share them with. But considering that nearly all of his contemporaries—the Rydells being the lone exception—had been through at least one divorce, Jake was content to remain single. Divorces were expensive and emotionally messy. And if there were children…

He shook his head. Nope, he thought, I'm better off with my nice, simple life. No wife. No kids. Well, except for his godson.

Jake glanced at the framed photograph on his book-shelf. Caleb Rydell—awesome *and* three thousand miles away. What could be better?

He'd balked at the idea of being anybody's godpar-ent, when Kenny called him out of the blue five years ago. "Hey, you know me, Ken. I'm more sinner than saint."

But Kenny hadn't been put off. "Don't worry, amigo. This gig is nothing that will get in trouble with your god. Pam and I have talked this over. We decided we need to have someone picked out to watch the kid's back if anything ever happens to us," Kenny had said, in a tone that got Jake's attention. Growing up the way they had, they'd learned the importance of backup—of finding that one person you could always count on. Kenny had been there for Jake when the bottom fell out of Jake's life. How could Jake refuse?

"Okay," Jake had responded.

Although Kenny's lot in life had changed after his abusive father had gone to jail and his mother had mar-ried Al Rydell—a childless man with a car lot in the mountains—Ken never flaunted his good fortune. That first year after Kenny and his mother moved, Jake took Amtrak twice to Fresno to visit his friend. Al was a big, gregarious fellow who'd adopted Kenny and given him his name. When he opened his own company, he tried to teach his new son the car business. But with typical teenage rebellion, Kenny bit the hand that fed him—skipping school, smoking pot and getting busted for drugs. He dropped out of junior college and took off for L.A. with his garage band buddies.

Jake had been on his own two years by that time. He and Kenny shared rent with about half a dozen other guys while Jake worked three jobs and went to night school. Kenny's band broke up, but he got a new gig with a group called Criminally Insane. The quartet played the L.A. scene for a couple of years before catching the eye of a promoter. The band got a recording contract about the same time Jake landed an internship with a brokerage house and moved to NYC so he could try his hand on Wall Street.

New York was a great proving ground and Jake did well. He thought on his feet and trusted his gut. But the winters sucked the life out of him. He was a southern California boy. Whatever antifreeze existed in Northerners' blood was missing from his.

When an offer came from his then-fiancée's father to work for his firm in Miami, Jake took it. Miami was hot—*cool* hot. Even though his relationship soured and he lost his job, Jake landed on his feet in the warm sand. He couldn't picture himself living anywhere else.

He shook his head and took another gulp. What was this weird depression all about? The fact that he'd eaten Thanksgiving dinner—Chinese takeout—alone? He'd been invited to dine with Matt Hughes, Jake's twenty-eight-year-old assistant, and his wife, but at the last minute Matt had called to say that their six-month old son had been throwing up all night and they were too exhausted to cook, let alone entertain.

Jake understood. His younger brother had been a sickly child. Many a night Jake had stayed up to care for the little guy when neither of their parents could be bothered. He'd sent flowers to Matt's wife, using a delivery service called 24/7, then set out to enjoy his carefree day. But Kenny's call around one in the afternoon—the chatter in the background between Pam and

Caleb, the football talk, the latest updates on Caleb's progress at preschool—had evoked a feeling of loneliness. His life seemed flat and empty by comparison.

"Shake it off, man," he muttered, sitting forward to tap his mouse. Suddenly a new image filled the wide, flat-screen monitor. A toddler in the foreground, grinning against a backdrop of sugar-white sand and aqua water. A bright pink bucket and neon green plastic shovel matched the little boy's Hawaiian print swim trunks. Caleb Rydell. Cutest kid on the planet. White blond hair cut in a spiky flat-top that reminded Jake of some cartoon character he couldn't name.

"Hey, kid, how's it hanging?" Jake said, inching his chair closer to the desk. "What's new in Preschool Land?"

He clicked on the icon to open his Internet home page and Caleb's image disappeared. He entered a Google search for Golden Retrievers and had just sat back, waiting for the list to appear when the phone rang. His private line. He glanced at the clock and frowned. Who in the hell called at this time of night?

"Hello?"

"Uh…um, is this Jake Westin?"

A woman's voice. Unfamiliar. "It is."

"I'm sorry to call so late. I forgot about the time difference. My name is Allison Jeffries. I'm a friend of Pam and Kenny Rydell."

A bad feeling took root in his belly. He knew Allison's name even though they'd never met. She was his female counterpart—as far as Caleb was concerned. The godmother.

"What's the problem?"

"Car wreck. Pam and Kenny…" Her hesitation confirmed his fear. "They were going skiing this morning. Early. Black ice. Three cars. The Jeep was caught in the middle. They…" She stopped, obviously unable to articulate what Jake knew she was going to say.

"They're dead?"

Her answer was more a tiny peep than a word, but it hit him as hard as a rogue wave that had once knocked him off his board and dragged him under water. He'd thought he was going to drown.

Kenny and Pam dead? No, it just wasn't possible.

"I…I just talked to them yesterday," he said inanely. "Thanksgiving."

The word came out as a whisper.

"I know. I was here."

She excused herself a moment and in the distance Jake could hear her blowing her nose. When she came back on the line, she swallowed loudly and took a shaky breath. "They're gone."

Jake ran his hand across his eyes. "What about…? Oh, God, please tell me Caleb wasn't in the car." The last came out as a gruff command. An order.

"No, thank heaven. He was here with Cordelia. But that's another problem. She was so stricken by the news, she suffered a heart attack. Caleb and I have been at the hospital all day."

Jake swore under his breath.

Allison went on. "She was in surgery for almost seven hours. I was afraid to leave. She doesn't have any other family. Not here, anyway. And I didn't think to take Pam's address book with me when we left the house, so I couldn't call anyone. Your number is unlisted, I was told."

Her tone seemed slightly accusatory, but Jake put it

down to stress. She must have been through hell. Losing her friends, worrying about Cordelia and entertaining a preschooler at a hospital.

"Is the little guy there?"

"He crashed—I mean, he fell asleep on the drive home. I carried him to bed. I just left his clothes on. Well, not his shoes, of course, but…"

He waited for her to finish but apparently that was all she could get out. "Does he know? About his parents?"

She started to cry again. The sound made Jake's insides twist. He ground the heel of his hand against his forehead.

"No," she said between sobs. "I…I…couldn't. I…tried, but I didn't know how. A p-pastor came by the waiting room. He said we should wait until we know for sure that C-Cordelia is out of the woods. Some good news to offset the b-bad."

"How soon will we know something?" he asked, trying to stay focused on what needed to happen, not what had happened.

"She came through surgery okay, but she's still in Intensive Care. They said they'd call if anything changed."

Jake adored Pam, but he'd never managed to win over her mother. Cordelia had joined the family several times when the Rydells came to the East Coast. And though he'd done his best to be cordial, none of his reputed charm worked where Cordelia was concerned. She was polite to him, but far from warm.

Still, she was his godson's grandmother, and Jake knew the two were close. Pam had even suggested that the reason her mother was so distant around Jake was that Cordelia felt threatened by Jake's relationship with the child. "Jake spoils Caleb," he'd once overheard Cordelia complain to Pam.

Pam had laughed off her mother's worries, saying, "It's a couple of weeks every summer, Mom. Caleb loves Jake. Let it go."

Pam. Smart. Funny. A good mother. A princess who thought nothing of keeping him and Kenny waiting an hour so she could "get beautiful," but never failed to champion his bond with Kenny and her son. "My guys need you, Jake the Rake," she'd once told him. "They'd turn into redneck mountain men if not for you." She'd laughed, and Jake had laughed, too, grateful that his best friend's wife welcomed him into their life.

Pam. Oh, God...

Allison's sniffles brought him back to the present. Action. He needed to take action. But where to start? His mind didn't seem to know how to function in the face of such loss.

"Other than waiting to hear about Cordelia, is there anything I can do?" he asked.

"You'll come, won't you?" she asked. Her voice sounded like a ten-year-old's, tremulous and fearful. He tried to picture her. Early thirties. Short dark hair. Glasses. He'd seen photos, as he was sure she'd seen shots of him, but they'd never really spoken. "I talked to my mother about what has to be done. My grandfather passed away last summer, so she's been through this. But, my father is going into the hospital for some tests and she can't come. I...I don't think I can do this alone."

If she had to ask, she sure as hell didn't know him. "Of course I'm coming. First flight out in the morning," he said, his tone sharper than he'd intended. He suddenly felt very old and tired. "I meant was there anything you needed me to do between now and when I get there."

She let out a shaky sigh. "I don't think so. There's so much…but, I guess one thing you should be thinking about is what will happen with Caleb. I had a minute alone with Cordelia's doctor, and he told me that she's going to need a lengthy rehabilitation. Several weeks, at least. I don't know how long you can be gone from—"

Jake cut her off. "I have an assistant who can handle things here. We'll worry about the long term when I get there. Okay?"

When she didn't answer right away, his temper snapped. The kid's parents weren't even in their graves and people were talking about what to do with him. As if he were a pawn in a chess game.

"If you're worried that you're going to get stuck taking care of him, don't be. If Cordelia's permanently out of the picture, he can come back to Miami with me," Jake said, flatly. "I'll adopt him."

The pause that followed seemed charged with emotion. She spoke again, her tone clipped. "That wasn't what I was getting at. Unless something has changed that I don't know about, you and I are *both* named as Caleb's guardians in Pam and Kenny's wills. But Cordelia is Caleb's only blood relative, and she's been living next door for most of his life. Caleb is very close to his grandmother." She took a deep breath. "I just wanted you to start thinking about the big picture. He's a little boy whose world has just been turned upside down. There are no simple solutions here, Jake."

She was right, of course. They had to put Caleb first.

But Jake would make certain she—and Cordelia when she was well enough—understood that he planned to be a part of Caleb's life. Not just because he'd given his word to his best friend five years ago, but because he knew all too well how devastating it was to lose your family.

"So, we'll talk more when you get here, right?" Her question was conciliatory. "Do you want us to pick you up at the airport?"

"I'll rent a car. Let me give you my cell phone number and e-mail. I'll have my BlackBerry in case something comes up while I'm in the air."

She, in turn, gave him all the numbers and addresses he needed to stay in touch. After an awkward goodbye, he hung up the phone and sat without moving for several minutes.

Finally, he gave himself a mental shake and backed out of his dog search. It only took him a few minutes to book a flight and arrange for a rental car, then he clicked off the Internet. On his screen, Caleb's grinning face made him pause. In the far background of the shot, a couple stood, arms around each other. The robust, dark-haired man with shoulders developed from years of drumming and lifting weights was hugging a petite blonde in a sexy swimsuit that showed off her voluptuous curves.

Happy, relaxed vacationers celebrating their son's birthday at the beach. Just four months earlier.

Shoving the keyboard out of his way, Jake lowered his head to the desk. And wept.

ALLISON MANAGED to fall asleep for a couple of hours after talking to Jake. Pure exhaustion, she figured. Which might account for why Caleb was still in bed at…she craned her neck to get a clear look at the clock above the stove…*Noon?* She hadn't realized it was so late.

She'd had a busy morning fielding calls from friends of the Rydells and members of Cordelia's bridge club. Allison's mother and sisters had called, too. Each sympathetic and full of advice, but each, for various reasons, unable to make the trip west.

She wasn't surprised. Or disappointed. She loved her sisters, but their way of dealing with painful situations was radically different from how she dealt with crises. They cooked and prayed. Allison's culinary skills were dubious at best, and her relationship with God was strained. She could have used her mother's help, but her dad was scheduled for a new test, which required him to be admitted to the hospital overnight, next week.

"I should be there for you, honey. I know how close you and Pam were. But I can't be two places at once," Janet Jeffries had repeated this morning.

"I know, Mom. Don't worry. Kenny's best friend, Jake Westin, is coming from Florida. He'll be a big help. He and Caleb are really close. Much more than Caleb and I are."

And whose fault is that, she asked herself, knowing her mother wouldn't. *Mine. I'm the one who kept my distance. Kids pick up on things. And Caleb was a smart little twerp. He read her like an ABC book.*

Allison refreshed her cup of coffee and returned to the window where she'd been standing. The view from the window was glorious—winter's dormancy in the fields and forest around the house, but up close, Pam had planted flats of marigolds and mums. The backyard was awash in color.

Everywhere she looked were reminders of the husband and wife who'd made this house such an attractive and well-lived-in home. A garden statue of a little boy, who looked so much like Caleb. It reminded her of the day Pam had towed Allison across traffic in San Francisco to buy it. "It'll be perfect in the garden," Pam had cried in triumph. "You should get one, too."

Pam was always prompting Allison to spend money. Unfortunately, Ally's budget didn't come close to Pam's—a disparity Pam conveniently forgot. Not surprising, Allison figured, since Pam was a princess—who'd taken a lost and miserable commoner under her wing.

When they'd met in college, Allison had been sure the two had nothing in common. Pam dressed better than Allison, had a limitless allowance from her parents and moved in a social circle that included pledging for a sorority. But, Pam was more than her fancy trappings and background suggested. Once she made up her mind to be your friend, that was it. Friends for life. Sisters linked by something stronger than blood—secrets.

Allison knew Pam's secrets—the craziness of life on the road with a rock band, and Pam was privy to the intimate details of Allison's most harrowing episode in life—her cancer and the abortion. Wandering aimlessly, she paused in front of the refrigerator. A dozen or so photographs made up a collage held in place by an assortment of magnets ranging from a wedge of pizza with Mountain Pizza's number in red to a tiger-shaped sculpture from the San Diego Zoo.

A goofy shot of Pam in bunny ears caught her eye. Rydell Motors hosted a canned food drive for the needy in December and an Easter egg hunt for underprivileged children every spring, both of which Allison was happy to help with.

In the photo, Pam was holding two toddlers with big chocolate grins while in the background Kenny tried to round up a flock of baby ducklings that he'd bought for the occasion. Was Allison the only one who knew Pam was afraid of fowl? The result of a traumatic encounter with an aggressive gander at a petting zoo.

Later, Allison and Pam had laughed themselves silly recalling Kenny's helpless efforts, and Pam's frantic attempts to evade the baby ducks.

Allison blinked away the tears that threatened. She was afraid to give in to the grief that followed her around like a stalker. She had to be strong. There was so much to do.

As if on cue, the phone rang. She walked to the small desk area near the door that led to the garage and sat down. "Hello?"

"Ally? It's Ernesto. *¿Cómo estás?*"

How am I? I wish I knew. "Fine," she told her assistant manager. "At least, I will be when you tell me you completed the Zirandervon job."

"All done. No *problema.* But this is such a tragedy. Everyone at the shop wants to help. Tell us what to do."

Allison didn't even know where to begin. Despite the few hours of sleep that came after talking to Jake Westin, she felt like a zombie. At the moment, she had two priorities: Caleb and her cats. Caleb was still asleep or she'd have driven into town to feed her pets.

"Could somebody check on my cats?" Allison asked.

"Of course. I have a key. I'll run over there right away. What else?"

Keep my business from disintegrating. "You know which work orders need parts. Get them ordered and check on the technicians. We can't afford to lose a single client." That was an understatement. Her company's future depended on how well they did this quarter. Without her to keep her technicians fired up and overseeing the job orders, Jeffries Computing was likely to wind up in bankruptcy.

"I'm sorry to put this extra work on you at this time of year, Ernesto, but I think I'm going to be tied up here for a while."

"Don't worry. We will handle everything the best we can."

Allison believed him. A five-year citizen of the United States, Ernesto Flores gave a hundred-and-ten-percent effort to every job. His drive and attention to detail had proven itself within weeks of starting at Jeffries Computing. He was her right-hand man, but he was still learning the computer business and lacked confidence in his language skills.

Each of her six employees needed the job her company provided. Ally just prayed they'd survive this crisis and make it through to the next year.

They talked for a few minutes, and then Allison hung up. Instead of rising, she looked at the odds and ends on the desk. A few Rydell Motors pens stuck in a coffee mug that was missing its handle. Pam's day-planner sat open—her full, rich life waiting for her to step back into it.

Allison thumbed through a couple of pages. Next week alone, Pam had four appointments scheduled: two doctors—hers and Caleb's, the dentist and a pedicure. Two sticky notes in Pam's handwriting forewarned of a Christmas party at Caleb's preschool on the seventeenth and the upcoming canned food drive at Rydell Motors.

A postcard fell to the desk. Allison turned it over and read a notice reminding Pam that it was time to have the oil changed in her car.

The word car triggered a question. *I wonder where the Jeep is at. Do I need to do something about it?*

When she first closed her eyes last night, all she could see were images of the boxy black vehicle squashed between two other cars. She cursed her imagination and pleaded with her subconscious to leave her alone. Oddly, her escape came from rehashing her conversation with Jake. He was an enigma that she both welcomed and worried about.

Ally pushed herself to her feet. The house was too quiet—oppressively so, but she was afraid to turn on the stereo. Afraid the six compact discs in the changer would remind her too much of Pam.

With a sigh, she dumped the dregs of her coffee into the sink. After she'd washed and dried the cup, she walked around the counter and sat down on a stool, drawing the yellow legal pad she'd found in Kenny's desk closer. A venerable list-maker, Allison always felt more in control of a situation when she could consult a written hierarchy of steps. Last night, before calling Jake, she'd sat down and tried to organize her thoughts. She studied the two columns entitled: *Now* and *Soon*.

According to her mother, the first thing Allison needed to do was notify family and close friends.

"Done," Allison said, drawing a line through the words *Call Jake.*

Second, she needed to find out what was happening at Rydell Motors. Would they close the doors or keep the place open? Third, the lawyer. Who did Kenny use? What provisions had been made for Caleb? Who was executor of the estate?

Allison's pen hovered above the Rydell Motors entry. At seven-fifty-five this morning, she'd reached Richard Marques—Kenny's cousin, who was second in command at the car dealership. Richard, though shocked by her news, rose to the challenge. "I'll call a company meeting right away. We'll figure out how to proceed," he'd told her. Not half an hour later, Richard informed her that every Rydell Motors' employee had voted to keep the business up and running with no interruption of service.

"We're doing this for Kenny and Pam," he'd said.

"I don't know exactly what will happen after the dust settles," he'd added, "but I'd like an opportunity to buy the business. Kenny and I discussed the possibility of letting me join him as a partner a few months ago. This isn't exactly what I had in mind, but I might be able to raise the money with some investors, if you can give me a few weeks. A month tops."

"Me?" Allison had almost choked on the bite of leftover pumpkin pie she'd finally made herself eat.

She told Kenny's cousin that any business discussion would need to include Jake. She firmly marked a big bold *J* beside point number two. Kenny always seemed to respect Jake's ability to handle money. He could figure out what to do with Rydell Motors.

Allison glanced at the clock. "Twelve-forty-three."

Caleb had been asleep since around ten last night. Was that normal? Was he ill? Maybe he had something. Meningitis? Mononucleosis?

Allison slipped off the stool, made a quick dash down the hall to Caleb's room, then hurried back to the desk. A slate beside the phone included a list of frequently called numbers. She found the line for Pediatrician. If the doctor wasn't in on Saturdays, maybe his service would tell her who to call.

"Hello, my name is Allison Jeffries. I'm caring for Caleb Rydell, a patient of yours, and I'm concerned that he's been asleep for almost fourteen hours. Is that normal? Should I be worried?"

She was transferred to a nurse who asked questions about when he went to bed and whether or not he was breathing. "Yes, I just checked, but…"

"Then he's probably just fine," the nurse interrupted. "Toddlers sometimes sleep twelve to fourteen hours straight, then go to bed at their regular time without a problem. It's what their bodies need."

Feeling a bit foolish but relieved, Allison thanked the woman and hung up. She probably should have called her mother or one of her sisters instead of bothering a nurse, but Allison hated to ask her siblings parenting questions. Invariably, one of them would say something that would remind her of that day in hospital when she'd made the decision to end her baby's life. Her sisters had played a role in that choice. Each had called and begged her to do the right thing. "God will forgive you," Liz, the oldest, had told her.

Yeah, but will I ever forgive God? Allison had wondered at the time. And now, He had even more to answer for in Allison's book.

Restless, she paced from one end of the kitchen to the other. Since rising at dawn, she'd straightened the house. Taken a roast from the freezer—in case Jake was a big meat eater. And visited ten or twelve websites devoted to childhood trauma and grief. She knew all the current theories on how to help Caleb through this horrible period. Unfortunately, as her mother liked to say, "The problem with manuals on how to raise children, is that children can't read."

Luckily, according to Pam herself, Jake was surprisingly good with kids. "Jake is the only man I know who will change a diaper without making a big production about it," Pam once told her. "Even Kenny balks at the task."

Jake was just a man in a photograph with a charismatic smile as far as Allison was concerned, but she was certain he'd make a better *mother* to Caleb than she could. Yesterday's fiasco at the hospital was proof of her ineptitude. The first waiting room near the emergency room had been filled with kids, so the hours passed with relative ease. But when a nurse asked Allison and Caleb to follow her to the surgical floor, they were ushered into a tiny cubicle with a mute television perched on a shelf high in one corner. Allison knew without being told that she'd just entered purgatory.

Caleb's bag of toys suddenly became "boring." A trip to the gift shop on the first floor bought fifteen minutes of diversion. Her one break came in the form of an angel—a visiting chaplain, who apparently heard Caleb complaining and came to the rescue.

Father Raymund Avila, or "Padre," as he asked to be called, sat with them for over an hour, engaging Caleb in a game of cards and carefully questioning Allison about the nature of their visit to the hospital. When Caleb finally dozed off, she explained about the accident and Cordelia's heart attack.

"When do you plan to tell him about his parents?" the silver-haired priest had asked.

"I don't know. What do you suggest? I'd hoped to put it off until his godfather arrives. They're close."

Padre Avila hadn't called her a coward as she'd expected. Instead, he'd agreed that it was best to wait until a time when they could sit down with the child and help him understand that although his life had irrevocably changed, they would continue to care for him and support him until his grandmother was better.

"This will be a difficult time for you all. If you need my help, please call," he'd told her, passing his card with a pager number on it.

Not long after that a nurse came with news that Cordelia had made it through surgery. "Why don't you two go get something to eat," the woman had suggested. "You won't be able to see her until she's out of recovery."

Allison had taken Caleb to a nearby fast-food chain even though she knew his mother would have had a fit. Pam always tried to provide nutritious, balanced meals for her son. But the respite gave Ally time to think while Caleb happily expended his pent-up energy in the fun room.

After a quick check on her cats—neither of whom would come near the eager child, Allison and Caleb returned to the hospital. A nurse watched Caleb while Allison spent a few minutes with Cordelia, who was too groggy to talk. Allison had promised to return today.

She added: *number four: go to hospital* on her list.

She glanced at the clock again. Jake's plane should be landing soon. Maybe she should try calling him.

She scrolled down on her notes to the numbers

he'd given her last night. As she reached for the phone, a movement to one side made her heart leap. A ghost?

No. A half-awake child in rumpled clothes and bare feet.

Her heart thudded against her chest. Her best friend's son was so small, so vulnerable, so dependent on Allison. She couldn't look at the little boy without feeling panicky and overwhelmed. She wanted to do the best for him, but what if she blew it?

"Good morning, Caleb," she said, getting up. "Or should I say afternoon? I thought you were going to sleep all day."

His white-blond hair stuck out every which way with several errant locks falling across his forehead.

"How do you feel?" she asked, with forced brightness. "Are you hungry? Do you want pancakes?"

He looked around. "Where's Mommy? I want waffles."

Caleb had asked about his parents a dozen or more times yesterday—even asking her to call them. Allison had made flimsy excuses for not doing so. Finally, she put him off by saying they were too far away for cellular service, and he'd just have to wait for their call.

"Again?" she asked, pouncing on the easier question. "You had them yesterday. How 'bout scrambled eggs?"

He made a face. "Dunkin'."

"Duncan? Duncan who?"

He blinked once, then laughed, a bright sound that seemed to dispel some of the gloom in the kitchen. "Not a person," he said. "Mommy cooks the eggs so I can dunk my toast in them."

Realization hit. "Oh, over easy. I can do that."

No girl grows up on a farm without learning to cook. Allison had had the basics down years before for her senior Home Economics class. She was grateful for that skill now.

"Where's Mommy?" Caleb asked again.

Oh, God, how do I tell him? I can't. I just can't say the words.

"She's not here. I'm filling in. Do you want toast or an English muffin?" Allison asked. "Pick whichever you prefer from the pantry."

Deflect and divert. A method of dealing with the public that Pam had perfected during the summer she and Allison worked at the information booth in Union Square.

When a tourist asked a question they couldn't answer, Pam would flash her sweetest smile and point toward one of the older women behind the souvenir counter. "Well, now, that *is* a good question," Pam would say. "And I'm certain that lovely gray-haired lady right over there can answer it for you. But if you'd like a trolley car schedule, I'm your girl."

Caleb hesitated just a second then walked to the door where Allison knew he'd find a selection of healthy bread choices. He picked the bag that appeared the least healthful. Allison didn't blame him. White bread was a standard at her house.

He handed her the bag like a dead fish on a line. "Thank you," she said. "Have you brushed your teeth?"

"*Before* breakfast?" His tone implied that she was the stupidest person on the planet. Which, when it came to mothering, she probably was.

"Good point. Sorry I mentioned it. Why don't you pull up a chair? This won't take long."

Was she blathering, again? No doubt. Anything to

avoid a repeat of the where's-mommy question. Where's Jake? That's what she wanted to know. Let him divert and deflect scary questions. Let him make a parenting faux pax so obvious even a four-year-old caught it.

"Can I have cereal instead?"

She looked at the eggs sizzling in butter. What would Pam want her to do—give in or stick to her guns? Stick to her guns. Kenny was the pushover, not Pam. "Maybe for a snack later. You need protein. It'll give you energy."

His skinny blond brow lifted—in a manner identical to his father. Allison's throat tightened as she turned to the refrigerator, cutting off the question she knew was coming. "Juice or milk?"

"Milk."

"Smart choice." She poured a glass. Too full, she realized and had to surreptitiously slurp off the excess. The cold beverage instantly curdled when it met the acid in her stomach.

Pivoting, she placed the glass in front of Caleb who eyed it suspiciously. He didn't reach for it.

The clack of the toast popping up provided another diversion. She buttered the golden square and placed it whole on the waiting plate, but Caleb made a squawking sound. "You gotta cut it in angels."

"Angels?" Allison stared at the bread. Was she going to fail another test? How did one make angels out of toast?

Caleb rose up on his knees and reached across the counter for the knife she'd used. With two fairly smooth passes he managed to cut the bread diagonally from corner to corner. The result was four small triangles.

"Oh, angles," she said, with a sigh of relief. This was short-lived when she realized she'd probably over-cooked his eggs.

She quickly slid the white-capped domes on his plate. "Bon appetit."

"You talk funny."

If Pam were here, she'd probably have retorted, "Oh, yeah, well you smell funny." That kind of nonsense had kept their friendship alive through distance, separation, silly spats, respective marriages, Allison's divorce and Pam's pregnancy.

And now that rare bond would be gone from Ally's life forever. She didn't know what she was going to do without her best friend.

CHAPTER THREE

JAKE DECIDED HE HATED electronic maps. And Fresno. And lawyers. Not necessarily in that order.

He'd arrived at the Fresno-Yosemite International Airport ahead of schedule, but the time he'd saved in flight had been eaten up by the inept agent at the car rental office. Then, following the directions Jake had printed from his computer, he managed to become resoundingly lost.

A bright green road sign announced that he'd arrived in the town of Coarsegold. "Damn," he muttered, pulling to a stop across the street from a row of buildings that looked like a facade of an old west town from the movies. "I've come too far."

Not that his map told him this. But he remembered Kenny mentioning that Coarsegold was the closest hamlet to his subdivision. The name was so odd that Jake had asked about it. "It's named after the kind of gold that was found here in the 1850s," Kenny had said. "It was a booming place at one time."

Jake rolled down his window and took a deep breath. The air was brisk. Vastly different from the warm humidity he'd left behind. He thought about turning around and trying to figure out where he'd gone wrong, but his growling stomach made him pick up his cell phone, instead.

He punched in the Rydells' home number.

A busy signal.

Jake's stomach made another noise, but he knew the difference between hunger and worry. The acid in his belly had been churning like crazy ever since talking to Kenny's lawyer, whose name had suddenly come to him while in flight somewhere over Texas.

Jake had reached him by phone while waiting for his rental car.

"Mr. Fenniman, this is Jake Westin. I'm a friend of Kenny Rydell's. We did a little business a couple of years ago. I just got to town."

Fenniman hadn't heard about the accident. He was full of sympathy when Jake told him. He agreed to go to his office and look at Kenny's will to see whether the couple had left instructions for their funeral.

"I seem to recall that you and another person—a friend of Pam's, I believe—were named as the child's guardians. Or was the grandmother the legal guardian and you two were the co-executors of the will? I'm sorry I can't remember the specifics, but I will check on it right away."

Jake knew he wasn't going to be able to breathe easily until he learned that his godson wasn't in some kind of legal limbo. With Cordelia in the hospital, they might run into some overeager social worker who could recommend the orphaned child become a ward of the state.

And Jake wasn't about to let that happen. Neither did he plan to let Allison have the final say. If she thought that her sex automatically meant she would make the better parent, she was in for a surprise. Jake was prepared to do battle.

He watched a steady stream of cars and vacation vehicles rumble past. "One more try," he muttered and punched redial.

The call went through.

"Hello." In the background a loud crashing sound made him sit up and look around, as if he could see what had happened.

"Wait, Caleb. I'll help you," he heard a woman say.

"Allison? Is everything okay?"

After a muffled pause—he imagined the phone being pressed to her bosom—she was back on the line. "Are you here?" she asked.

"Close. I think I missed a turn."

"That happens to everybody the first time. Are you in Coarsegold?"

"Yes."

"Well, don't give up. I'll talk you through this."

Jake followed her instructions, switching to hands-free so he could stay on the line as he drove. "What was the crash I heard?"

"Caleb was helping me clean up after breakfast."

"Don't you mean lunch?"

Allison's small chuckle made him wish he could picture her better. None of the photos he'd looked at after her call last night had given him much to go on. Tall, willowy, short auburn hair. Thick glasses. Never as stylish as Pam. But then, few women dressed with as much flair as Pam Rydell.

"No. I mean breakfast. The kid slept fourteen hours. I was searching for a stethoscope to check his heart when he finally got up."

Jake smiled for the first time in twelve hours. "He did that one day last summer when we were in Orlando. Pam called it catch-up sleep."

"That's what the nurse in his pediatrician's office said, too, when I called." Her tone held a quiver of chagrin, as if she were embarrassed to admit that she'd consulted a professional for something so trivial.

"You should be coming up to a sign on your right that says Yosemite Lakes Park," she said. "Turn in and stay on that road through two stop signs. At the next intersection, pull over and wait. Caleb and I will walk down and find you."

"That seems like a waste of effort. Why don't you just tell me which streets to take?"

"Because I don't know their names, and if you make a hard left instead of a soft left, you'll wind up in the lake."

He closed his eyes and stifled a groan. She must have sensed it because she said a tad defensively, "This isn't my home, you know."

"Gotcha."

"I'm hanging up now. We'll be there in a minute."

Frustration combined with hunger and lack of sleep made him ready to snap, but he couldn't let his emotions take over. He remembered all too well what it was like to live in a place where angry voices were the norm.

As he drove, Jake looked around with interest. Kenny and Pam had spoken highly of the place. Jake had always planned to visit, but had somehow never found the time. Or so he told himself. He and Kenny both knew the real reason for Jake's reticence to return to his home state. Memories. Bad ones. It was easier to meet his friends on neutral turf. Fun places, like Disney World, the Kennedy Space Center and Key West.

The size and magnitude of the planned community

surprised him. Yosemite Lakes Park had its own supermarket, stable and service station. He passed at least two churches. Road signs warned him to be on the lookout for equestrians. Off to one side was a golf and tennis club. And ahead he spotted a small, almost dry pond surrounded by thick clumps of cattails—some shedding their fluffy white seeds.

At the crossroad, Jake pulled to one side and shifted to Park. Fortunately, there wasn't any traffic, but he wasn't a patient man. He was just about to put the car in gear and go in search of his godson when a knock on the passenger side took him by surprise. He pushed the power lever to open the window so he could get a better look at the two faces staring at him.

"Jake, Jake, Jake," Caleb cried, squirming in the arms of the woman who'd lifted him to see. "We found you, Jake. Me 'n Ally."

"Ally," he repeated. The nickname changed her somehow.

The woman in question put her hand in the window and said, "Hello, Jake. I'm Allison Jeffries. It's good to finally meet you, although, of course, I wish it were under different circumstances."

Jake could only see her from the waist up. She was dressed casually in a gray, hooded sweatshirt and fleece vest. He shook her hand. "Me, too."

Caleb used the opportunity to lever himself through the window. Jake could see Allison struggling to keep her balance. "Hey, bud, wait a second and let me open the door so you don't hurt…"

Too late. The little guy wiggled free and tumbled butt over head into the bucket seat. Seconds later a small projectile flung against him with the force of a rip wave.

"Whoa, kiddo, let's not kill…" He swallowed. "Crush your old buddy."

"Did you bring me something, Jake?"

"As a matter of fact I did, but first I get a big hug, right?"

Caleb obliged. His little arms squeezed Jake's neck so hard the pressure triggered tears that had been threatening all morning. Feeling embarrassed, he glanced at the woman who was watching. Her eyes were dewy, too. Her very pretty eyes, he noticed—despite the dark circles. *Where are her glasses?*

Before he could ask, she opened the door and picked up the map, cell phone and brief case on the seat. She glanced at him as if to ask permission to join them. "The house is just up the hill and around the bend."

He nodded. "Hop in."

Before she sat down, he hefted Caleb over the seat into the tiny cavern the car manufacturer euphemistically called a back seat. "Stay put, squirt." Then he glanced sideways and said, "Seems weird that we've never met. I thought you wore glasses."

She touched her fingers to her gracefully curved cheekbone. Her skin was pink from the chilly breeze. Jake pushed the button on the armrest to roll up the passenger window.

"I had eye surgery. My gift to myself last Christmas."

"Do you like it?"

"Definitely. In my business, I'm always under desks looking up. The dust made it impossible to wear contacts and my glasses were always getting scratched or broken. I raved about the end result so much, Kenny was thinking about getting it. He said…" Her voice trailed off.

Jake glanced in the rearview mirror. In a hushed voice, he asked, "Have you told—?"

She answered him with a vehement shake of her head. "I thought that was something we should do together. Besides, I ... well, I couldn't."

"You didn't bring your neat car, Jake," Caleb said, flopping over the seat. "I like it better."

Jake tousled the child's soft blond locks. His hair had grown a lot since they were together in August. Caleb looked an inch or two taller, too. Still a little boy, but less a toddler. "Sorry, pal. The airlines wouldn't let it through security. But do you know what's cool about this car?"

Caleb shook his head.

"Four-year-olds can drive it."

"Really?" The little boy's eyes went round. He glanced at Allison for confirmation.

"No," she said with a high-pitched croak. "He's kidding, Caleb."

Jake watched Caleb's expression go from joy to pouting. "Hey, loosen up a bit. I know what I'm doing." Jake regretted his words the moment he saw the serious frown on her face. Surely she didn't honestly believe he'd let a kid drive, did she? Or was her reaction tied to Pam and Kenny's accident?

Suddenly Jake felt like a heel. What had started out as an impulse to give his godson a little pleasure had turned into a skirmish that had made him look stupid.

Swallowing his pride, he turned to look at his godson and said, "How 'bout a rain check, buddy? We can show Allison what a great driver you are another time. I'm so hungry, my stomach's ready to cave in. Okay?"

"O...kay," he said, drawing out the word. The shoulders of his hooded fleece jacket rose and fell with an exaggerated shrug, but despite the show of being a good sport, he was obviously disappointed. And Jake could tell by the scowl he sent Allison that he blamed her for his missing out on a special treat.

Jake felt badly about that since this little fracas was his fault. The last thing he wanted was to let Caleb think he could play one adult against the other. And Jake couldn't expect a complete stranger to understand he'd never do anything that would endanger his godson. A quick glance to his right revealed another scowl, albeit a lovely one. She was far prettier than he'd expected. But the look in her eyes told him they were on different wavelengths when it came to making decisions regarding Caleb.

"Sit down, kiddo," he said, tweaking his godson's nose. "And, um, put on your seat belt," he added, hoping Allison would give him points for being safety-conscious.

The arch in her eyebrow indicated she'd seen through his lame effort completely, but she made a show of complying as well. Jake wasn't certain, but he thought he caught a glimpse of a smile just before she looked down to snap the belt in place.

Five minutes later, they were parked in front of a house Jake had seen only in photos. He looked around, unprepared for the sudden, immobilizing sadness that swamped him. Kenny should have been standing at his side. Waiting to welcome his closest friend into his home.

Caleb hopped out of the car when Allison reached across the seat to unlock the door. Her arm brushed Jake's shoulder, shaking him out of his melancholy thoughts. He got out, too, and was immediately engulfed in a thigh-high hug. "Come see my room, Jake."

Jake's heart melted in his chest. "Let me grab my bags, kiddo," he said, barely managing to get the words out.

Together, they unlocked the trunk. "Where is my present?"

Jake realized Allison was standing beside them—apparently waiting to help. He saw her frown, no doubt appalled by Caleb's lack of manners. But Jake was to blame for this breach of etiquette, too. Since Jake saw his godson so seldom, he tended to spoil the little boy.

Instead of making excuses, he focused on Caleb, letting him carry the lightest bag—a carry-on that held the gifts Jake had purchased at the airport. Jake handled the rest of the luggage himself, letting Allison close the trunk and lead the way into the house.

Jake spent almost half an hour playing with his godson. Then, leaving Caleb with his new toys, he returned to the kitchen-cum-family room, where he found Allison sitting in front of a computer at a built-in desk.

"I made you a sandwich," she said glancing over her shoulder as he stepped into the open, spacious room. "Leftover turkey."

The way she dropped the last word made him realize the meat was from the last holiday dinner she'd shared with their friends. He was too hungry to pass it up. "Thanks. I'm famished."

The plate, covered with a sage-green cloth napkin, sat on the counter beside a glass of milk and a bag of potato chips—the kind that went in lunch boxes. A designated eating area was marked by three padded stools, each different. A captain's chair with padded arms and a back. A stool topped with a tufted pad in some springy print fabric. And a similar stool wearing a plastic cover that resembled a shower cap.

"Papa Bear, Mama Bear, and Baby Bear," he said, drawing out the largest of the three.

"Pardon?" Allison said, looking up from whatever it was she was working on. He found it hard to believe that she could concentrate on work at a time like this, but he kept his opinion to himself.

"Oh, nothing. Just muttering to myself."

She gave a puzzled half smile and returned to her task.

Jake folded the napkin in his lap and picked up the sandwich. Firm, sourdough bread, slightly toasted. Leafy lettuce stuck out around the edges. A good inch and a half of meat. He bit down and closed his eyes with pleasure. As he chewed, a tangy flavor caught his attention. "Umm, good," he said, washing it down with a gulp of milk. "Different."

"In my family, we always make our leftover turkey sandwiches with cranberry sauce and mayo," she said without turning around.

Fabulous, he thought, but he was too busy devouring it to say so.

A few minutes later, Allison closed off the screen she'd been reading—it was too far away for Jake to make out, pushed the keyboard back into its compartment and stood up. In a long-sleeve, hunter-green T-shirt tucked in the waistband of her snug jeans and a pair of black sneakers, she looked years younger than her age.

"There's fresh coffee in the pot," she said picking up the mug beside the workstation. "Would you like a cup?"

"Please," he said, wiping the corners of his mouth.

She walked to the counter and filled a large navy blue Rydell Motors mug. "Black?"

"Yes, thanks."

As she set it down on the marble counter in front of him, her head cocked to one side, obviously listening to an unusual sound coming from deep in the bowels of the house. "Is that gunfire?"

Jake winced. *"Mea culpa,"* he said, shoveling chips into his mouth. He chewed fast. "I know. I know. Totally un-politically correct, but I was in a hurry. The box said ages four and up. Nowhere did it say 'Makes annoying sound that will drive adults mad.'"

Her frown made her look older. Weary. He suddenly regretted the impulsive buy. Which was odd. He didn't regret much.

"Don't worry," he said after guzzling the last of his milk. "At the rate he's using it, the batteries will wear down before our hearing goes."

She didn't smile at his jest. Instead, she said, "Pam didn't like guns. Kenny was the only man at the volunteer fire department who doesn't hunt. I know he got razzed about that, but he said he didn't want his son to think guns were cool."

Jake eyed the last bite of the delicious sandwich and decided his hunger had disappeared. He obviously couldn't do anything right in this woman's eyes.

Instead of trying to defend his choice of toy—one gun wasn't going to turn Caleb into a mass murderer—he posed the question that had been bothering him ever since he arrived. "How come he hasn't asked about his parents?"

A dark cloud passed over her features. He reminded himself that she was hurting—just as bad as he was. Worse, probably, since she'd been here from the first. "He has," she said, fiddling with the handle of her coffee mug. "When they didn't return last night as expected, I told him they'd extended their ski trip. But he's a smart kid. I'm pretty sure he knows something is up."

"How's Cordelia?"

"As good as can be expected, I guess. I talked to her on the phone shortly before you called. I gather she had a rough night. A lot of pain. They upped her drugs and she was pretty groggy when we spoke."

Jake could only imagine the horror of losing a daughter, a son-in-law and one's health all in the same morning. "And things are going to get worse before they get better," he predicted.

She sat down on the "baby" stool, leaving the "mama" stool between them. "Do you mean the funeral? Because I've started a list." She reached across the counter to grab a yellow legal-sized tablet. "My mother handled the arrangements last summer after my grandfather passed away. But Grandpa had left specific instructions. He'd been planning on dying for years."

A faint glimmer tickled his memory. "I think Pam mentioned that when we were together in August. I'm sorry for your loss."

"Thank you," she said somberly. "But he was ninety-four. He'd led a long, industrious life and was ready to go. Not the same as—" She took a drink from her mug. Jake could tell she was holding back her grief through sheer willpower.

"Anyway," she said, after clearing her throat, "Mom said the first thing we need to do is get in touch with the family lawyer. I found his name in Kenny's files and left a message on his machine. He hasn't—"

Jake interrupted. "I talked to him this morning."

Her left brow shot upward.

"Kenny referred him to me on an investment matter a few years ago. He's not one of my regular clients, but I had his name and number on file. He hadn't heard about the accident, but he told me he'd call here as soon as possible. He couldn't recall whether they'd made any specific last wishes."

Her gaze dropped to the tablet. "Last wishes," she repeated. "Who does that? Who plans for death at our age? I don't have any idea where I want to be buried. Do you?" Jake could tell she was remembering something sad. Something from her past, maybe?

"Actually, Kenny and I talked about this a couple of years ago," he said, striving for a more upbeat tone. "On Caleb's second birthday to be exact. I'd just set up my will and made Kenny executor. I told him that after he paid off all my bills, I wanted him to use whatever was left to fund a party on the beach. Champagne. A band. Then afterward, he could kick the tin can with my ashes into the sand. Period."

She didn't say anything, but Jake sensed that she thought he was an ass. Before he could add that the bulk of his substantial estate was set up as a trust for Caleb, the doorbell rang.

"Somebody's here," a youthful voice rang out—followed by the rat-a-tat-tat of a plastic machine gun.

Jake winced. The gun was definitely a mistake. Maybe he'd have to help those batteries disappear.

Allison started toward the foyer with Jake behind her. Caleb beat them to the door but didn't open it. Jake unlatched the deadbolt, and two strangers—a man and a woman—entered. The woman, who was wearing a Hawaiian print dress under her black wool coat, carried a covered casserole dish that smelled delicious.

"May I help with that?" Jake asked.

The woman gave him a startled look. "No, that's okay. I know my way around Pam's kitchen like it was my own. I'm going to put this in the oven on warm, Allison."

Jake thought that rather presumptuous of her, but Allison shrugged as if to say "whatever."

The man put out his hand in greeting. "Marc Mason. Neighbor across the fence. That was my wife, Gayle."

Allison introduced Jake before he could do it himself. "Jake is Kenny's best friend from way back. He just flew in from Miami."

"Really, which flight?" the man asked. "I'm a pilot with United. I was off this past week. We just got back from Hawaii and heard the news. Gayle had to make food." He gave a sheepish smile. "Must be her midwestern roots. Giving casseroles is how you show respect to the family, I guess. You understand, don't you, Ally?"

Jake didn't like the tall, handsome man calling Allison by her nickname. The familiarity made him feel like the odd man out.

"Gayle was one of the first people I called," Allison said. "But I had to leave a message because your cell number isn't in Pam's book, Marc, and Gayle's phone wasn't on."

"It would have been on," the woman said returning to the foyer. "But someone forgot to include my charger when we switched cars." She gave her husband a pointed look.

"Where's Bradley?" Caleb asked, squeezing off a few rounds. "Can he come play with my new gun?"

Gayle discreetly wiped a tear from her eye and said, "Sorry, sweetie. He's taking a nap. He had to get up very early this morning to catch our flight, but you could come over later, if your…um, if Allison says it's okay."

"Can I bring the gun Jake gave me?"

The woman gave Jake a severe look that said only an idiot would buy a four-year-old a gun. "We'll see."

Jake put his hands on his godson's shoulders and pointed him in the direction of his room. "Why don't you read that new book I brought you, buddy? Save some ammo for later."

The child glanced over his shoulder at the ring of adults for a brief moment then dashed down the hall, spraying bullets in every direction.

Allison gave a small sigh and pointed toward the living room. "Can you come in? I made a fresh pot of coffee."

Jake hadn't been in this room, but he recognized it from the photos Pam sent him every year after Christmas. He knew right where the tree traditionally stood—in the middle of the bank of windows that framed the pond in the distance. The mantel of the whitewashed brick fireplace would be trimmed in greenery and candles. Pam always went all out for the holiday. Jake hated to think what this place would be like without her.

The Masons declined Allison's offer of refreshments. "We can't stay," Gayle said, choosing to sit on the red leather sofa. Marc sat beside her, leaving Jake and Allison to take the overstuffed chairs. Jake liked Pam's decorating style—modern and fun, yet stylish. He wished he'd been able to tell her so.

"We just came by to drop off the hot dish. And I thought you might need our help with Caleb, but it's clear you haven't told him yet."

Jake wondered if he detected a hint of reproach in

her tone or was he projecting? She seemed like a kind and neighborly person. Just because he didn't live in a small town, didn't mean he couldn't appreciate gestures of goodwill.

"Allison and I decided to hold off until I got here," he said. That wasn't completely true, but he wanted to portray a united front to these people.

"Makes sense," Marc said. "Kenny told me you and Caleb were pretty close."

"Well, I'm no expert," Gayle said, "but I do have three kids. And last year, my daughter's friend's mother passed away from breast cancer. She's fourteen, not four, but it was still very, very traumatic. She's seeing a therapist, who has helped a lot. I could get you the woman's name."

Jake wanted to say, "Hold on. Let us tell the boy, and then find out what he needs." But Allison answered before he could find a diplomatic way of declining Gayle's offer.

"Thank you. I'd appreciate that. I was online checking out sites that dealt with helping children facing tragic losses. From what I read, children of Caleb's age might not fully comprehend the concept of death, but they understand that their world has changed irrevocably. Our job is to reassure Caleb that he'll always be loved and safe."

Jake kept his mouth shut. How could he argue with that kind of logic? Still, it irked him slightly that he hadn't thought to do some research himself last night.

"I know we all want what's best for Caleb," Gayle said. "Pam was one of my dearest friends. Our little boys have been practically inseparable since they were infants. So if we can help, please don't hesitate to call."

"Thank you," Allison said. "As a matter of fact, I need to go home to get some clothes. I completely forgot about that when I was there last night. And I want to stop by and see Cordelia. If Jake is tired—"

Gayle interrupted with a loud, huffing sound. "I can't believe Cordelia had a heart attack. Talk about bad timing."

Allison frowned. "It's not like she did it on purpose."

The woman reached out and squeezed her hand. "I know. I'm being totally unreasonable, but when I heard what happened, and thought about you trying to handle all this and Caleb by yourself…well, it just seemed so unfair."

"Death is unfair," Jake said. "Just ask Kenny and Pam."

Gayle suddenly collapsed against her husband. Loud, wet sobs filled the room. Her shoulders shook. While trying to console his wife, Marc told them, "I've never seen her so rattled. This came as a real shock. You never appreciate how precarious life is until someone close to you dies."

Jake was sorry he'd said anything. He glanced at Allison. Her top teeth worried her bottom lip and she blinked rapidly as if trying to keep her tears at bay. Jake braced for her to start crying, too. Then what would he do? Touch her? Offer his shoulder, as Marc had? That didn't seem right. They barely knew each other.

Fortunately, Gayle suddenly sat up straight and took a deep breath. "I'm sorry," she said. "I'll be better soon. I promise."

Following her lead, they all rose. Marc stood awkwardly for a moment, then took a step forward and gave Allison a hug. Jake could tell she was surprised.

"Jake," the man said, shaking Jake's hand again. "Good of you to come so far. If you need anything, holler."

Gayle sniffled, patting her nose with a tissue she'd withdrawn from the pocket of her coat. "Give Caleb a big hug for me. It breaks my heart to think of him… alone…motherless…" The tears started again, but this time she turned away and dashed out the door, leaving her husband to follow.

Jake closed the door behind them. He knew this was only the beginning of what they'd soon have to face. Pam and Kenny had been young, friendly and well-known in their community. The outpouring of grief would start soon. He only hoped he could shield Caleb from some of it.

When he turned around, he saw Caleb standing a few feet away. The toy gun dangled from one finger. His little face was etched in worry.

"Why was Bradley's mommy crying?" he asked.

Jake looked at Allison. She nodded, then closed her eyes and took a breath.

He walked to his godson and picked him up, discarding the gun discreetly behind a large potted palm. "She's sad, Caleb."

"Why?" Caleb's thumb went into his mouth—a habit Jake hadn't seen for two years.

"Because something happened that you should know about."

Caleb looked at Allison who tried to smile reassuringly. When she glanced at Jake, he read the look in her eyes: resolve, fear, heartbreak. He felt the same, along with an overwhelming sense of responsibility. *Please let us do this right.*

Allison gently touched Caleb's arm and said, "Let's sit down. Jake and I need to tell you something, honey."

As soon they were seated on the sofa, Caleb between them, Allison said, "Remember when the policeman came to the house yesterday?"

He nodded. "Policemen are our friends," he told Jake.

Allison nodded. "That's true, but one part of their job is telling family members bad news when something happens to someone they love."

Caleb twisted his thumb back and forth. He looked so very small and scared Jake wanted to snatch him up in his arms and run away.

Allison put one hand flat to his back and rubbed in circles—something Jake had seen Pam do. "There was a car accident, honey. On the way to the ski place. Your daddy's Jeep was in it."

Caleb looked at Jake to confirm what she said. Jake nodded.

"Mommy got hurt?"

Allison cleared her throat. "Yes."

"Is she in the hospital? Like Gramma? Can I go see her?"

Allison looked at Jake. *Now what?*

"I'm afraid not, Caleb," he said, shifting the boy to his knee, using his left arm to keep him snug.

"How come?"

Jake could barely draw a breath past the weight on his chest. "Because she died, champ. Do you know what that means?"

Caleb frowned. "You ain't got no more lives left. You can't play the game no more."

Allison moved to her knees in front of them. Her

eyes level with her godson's, she said, "Caleb, sweetie, do you remember Grandma's dog Geisha?"

Caleb nodded, "Uh-huh."

Allison took Caleb's hand. "When Geisha died, your daddy buried her down by the pond. Remember?"

Caleb didn't answer, but Jake felt the little boy stiffen. His eyes grew wide, and he leaned against his godfather, who tightened his hold.

"Grandma cried," Caleb mumbled.

Allison's lips trembled and she blinked back tears of her own. "It's not easy to say goodbye to someone you love, but sometimes that's what you have to do. When bodies get old—like Geisha's, or when something bad happens, like an accident, and doctors can't make them better, they die."

Caleb looked up at Jake, silently pleading for his godfather to tell him this wasn't true. Jake's heart felt as if someone were ripping it out of his body, one inch at a time. He took a shallow breath and said, "This isn't easy to say, champ, but your mommy and daddy died in the accident."

"They're in heaven now," Allison added.

Jake didn't know how much religious training Kenny and Pam had given their son, but his personal bias made him wish Allison hadn't said that. Well-intentioned people had tried to console Jake after his brother passed away by assuring Jake that Phillip was "in God's hands." Jake hadn't believed them. If God hadn't lifted a finger to help Phillip on earth, why should Jake believe the deity would care about him in the afterlife?

Caleb's bottom lip trembled. "When are they coming back?"

"They can't come back, Caleb," Jake said.

Jake felt the alarm that passed through the child's body. Caleb's grip on Jake's forearm intensified. "Can I go there?"

Jake shook his head.

"I want to go," Caleb cried. "I want my daddy. I want my mommy. Now." His high, thin wail pierced the air. Without warning, he erupted in a fury of arms, legs and flailing punches. Allison tried to help and took a blow to the cheek that knocked her backward.

Jake locked his arms around the little boy and jumped to his feet. Rocking, cooing, smothering the violence as gently as possible, he paced back and forth, like a father with a colicky infant. "It's gonna be okay, buddy. Allison and I are here for you. I know you're sad. So are we. We loved your mom and dad and we love you. And we're going to be here to take care of you until your grandma gets home. We promise."

"And it's okay to be mad, Caleb," Allison added. "This shouldn't have happened. Not to them."

The tantrum ended as abruptly as it began. Caleb went limp and formless as a wet beach towel slung over Jake's shoulder. His crying continued nonstop but he seemed oblivious to either of his godparents.

"What now?" Jake mouthed to Allison.

She stepped close and pressed her lips to the little boy's convulsing back. Her eyes pooled with tears, she looked at Jake and whispered, "I don't know."

Without thinking, Jake used his free arm to pull her closer and the three of them huddled together and wept.

CHAPTER FOUR

ALLISON EYED THE dozen or so neighbors and friends who had begun to congregate at the Rydell home. Most brought food and drink. The women were grouped in the kitchen and dining room. The men either outside where they could smoke or in the living room.

Ally recognized a handful of familiar faces. Some she'd met a few months earlier at Pam and Kenny's Labor Day barbecue. Others she knew, but couldn't immediately place—including the man making his way across the room toward her.

Kenny's cousin. *Rick? Roger?* Although she'd talked to him that morning, his name escaped her. Her mind seemed to have developed an insulated coating like the plastic wrap around wires that kept them from shorting out. She'd survived telling Caleb about his parents two hours earlier, but wasn't sure how much more she could take.

Thank God Jake was here, she thought. His affable manner instantly put people at ease, welcoming them to share their common grief. Allison wasn't that generous. She wanted to lock the door. Keep the world at bay—as she had after her personal tragedy. Until Pam had dragged her back into the world.

Oh, Pam, who's going to do that for me now?

"Hi, Allison," the man greeted her.

She lifted her hand mechanically. "Hello. Good to see you. How did it go at the car lot today?"

"Busy. Sympathy or curiosity. Can't say which," he said with a shrug. A few years younger than her, he might have been handsome if not for the scars left behind from a bad case of acne.

He enfolded her hand between his. "I was just talking to Jake. Nice guy. I told him what we talked about on the phone this morning, and you don't have to worry about the business. I took a straw poll among the salesmen, and they unanimously voted to stay open. We're going to buy some black bunting and wreaths to honor Kenny and Pam. I know my cousin would want us to carry on."

A straw poll. She'd heard the phrase but had no idea what it meant.

She cleared her throat and gently extracted her hands. "I'm sorry. My brain is mush. Is it Rick? Roger?"

"I understand completely." He clamped one hand on her shoulder and squeezed. "I'm Richard. Kenny's stepdad and my father were cousins. I've been working for Kenny for about five years. He was a great guy. I can't believe something like this has happened. The good die young, don't they?"

Allison's stomach heaved. *The good…die…* Desperate for a distraction, she leaned over to pick up an empty glass from the end table. Unfortunately, her hand shook so badly she was forced to stuff her fist in the pocket of her sweater, where a wad of wet tissues reminded her of all the tears she'd shed.

Richard was still speaking. "…Kenny had just added

the Subaru dealership and expanded his sales team when I came on board. I used to work in Sonora. How's the car running?"

"Uhh....great." *How's the weather? The Bulldogs look good, don't you think? What about those Niners?* Was small talk a defense mechanism? she wondered. Or are we all so egocentric we can only talk about other people for a few short minutes before the topic reverts back to what's important to us?

"My Outback has over two hundred thousand miles on it," he boasted. "My wife says she'll trade me in before she gets rid of that car."

Cars. Hers was just outside. She could hop in it and disappear. No one would miss her. Jake could handle the funeral. Funerals. Plural.

Her gaze found him without effort. Of course, it was hard to miss his six-foot-two-inch body. His smoky gray-blue silk turtleneck draped across his broad shoulders and was tucked into black jeans. No love handles at that waist, she thought. A simple belt with a plain silver buckle was the only ornamentation.

Allison put a hand to her cheek. Her skin felt flushed. No doubt her hormones were as screwed up as her emotions. Otherwise, she wouldn't be standing in the middle of a wake admiring her co-godparent's great body.

Thank goodness he wasn't her type. She traditionally went for the quiet, academic types—like her ex-husband, Dean. An Albert Einstein hairdo and thick glasses might not appeal to some women, but Allison had fallen in love with Dean in their senior year. Unfortunately, the qualities that had drawn her to him in the first place—his intellect and logic—had contributed to the demise of their marriage. When tragedy struck,

Dean turned to his work for solace, not realizing until too late that Allison was floundering in a sea of guilt.

"Oh, my," Richard exclaimed. "There's the fellow who was in the shop last week looking at a new pickup truck." He cuffed her upper arm lightly in what was undoubtedly intended as a supportive gesture and started to leave. "We'll talk soon, Ally, but in the meantime you can rest easy knowing we have things under control at the car lot. The only thing I need from you is a decision on the canned food drive. But that can wait until after…well, you know."

The food drive? Oh, God. Pam's baby. Rydell Motors' "A Truckload of Cans" consumed her time and attention from the Monday after Thanksgiving till the Saturday before Christmas, when the cash contributions were used to buy turkeys and the mountain of donations was hauled to the local food bank.

With a weighty sigh, Allison leaned against the wall. One more thing to add to the list. Of course, the smart thing would be to cancel it. Everyone would understand. But when she closed her eyes she could see Pam's euphoric smile as she handed a check to the food bank personnel last year. "You should have enough here to buy at least sixty turkeys," she'd crowed. "If that isn't enough to give everyone on your list a great dinner, send them to my house. We always have too much. Right, Ally?"

Allison pressed her forehead against the painted wall. Tears burned against her eyelids. Her neck felt wrapped in barbed wire.

"How are you holding up?" a deep voice asked.

She froze. Jake. Quickly wiping her eyes with her sleeve, she stood up straight. "I'm surviving," she said, trying for a smile. "I really appreciate all that you're doing. You're a natural with people. As soon as someone looks at me and says, 'What a tragedy!' I either want to run the other way or hit them. Crazy, huh?"

He turned so his back rested against the wall. He took a deep breath and let it out in a long, continuous sigh. "Not at all. What you see is an act. Perfected at the age of ten when I learned that you can get away with just about anything as long as you show people what they want to see."

Allison was shocked by his candor, and her expression must have shown it because he straightened, put on the same warm and empathic smile she'd seen for the past hour and shook her hand. "Thank you for coming. A tragedy, yes, that's it exactly," he said, nodding soberly.

Her eyes filled with tears again, and he looked chagrined. "Sorry," he said, dropping her hand. "I'm doing what has to be done. But inside, I feel just like you do."

The doorbell chimed before she could reply. He gave her a small, self-deprecating smile then walked away. He'd taken on this responsibility because he'd somehow sensed that she was uncomfortable in the role of hostess.

Suddenly, Allison felt ashamed. She'd abdicated her part of this job because he made what he was doing look effortless. But it wasn't. And she needed to dig deep and be part of the team.

She started by picking up used glasses and cups, which she carried to the sink. As she loaded them into the dishwasher, a voice called out, "Leave the dishes for us, Ally. You shouldn't have to do that. This wake was my idea."

Allison located Gayle in the group of eight women sitting around the dining room table. All in their early-to midthirties, they were friends of Pam's. Most were mothers whose children attended the same preschool as Caleb.

"It's okay," she said. "I need to keep busy. Go on talking."

Allison always had been a loner. Her sisters—seven and eight years older than her but just a year apart in age, were like twins. Her brother, the eldest, was too busy preparing to take the family farm into the twenty-first century to have time for his baby sister. Growing up on a farm with no playmates her age, Allison never developed the social skills it took to make friends.

Until Pam rescued her. Pam—one of the most popular girls on campus—had reached out to befriend Allison. She'd taught her how to dress, how to dance, how to flirt. Pam had made Ally attend college functions. She was the one who'd told Allison about birth control and what a lover should do for a woman. She'd also held Allison's head the first time she came home drunk and, at the lowest time in her life, Pam had forced Allison to keep going when all Ally had wanted to do was die.

And now she was gone. Allison felt like kicking and screaming—just as Caleb had earlier. A question entered her mind. *Would Jake hold me until my sobs subsided then rock me in his arms till I fell asleep?* A second question followed on the heels of the first. *Could I be any more depraved and needy?*

With a muffled groan, she opened the cupboard by her knee and took out the big green jug of dishwasher soap. Jake was a nice man, and very kind, but this attraction she felt toward him had to be denied. She'd read about survivors' guilt and what happened to people who turned to each other in times of great emotional upheaval. Nothing good or lasting ever came from it.

As she gave the big container a vicious squeeze, a thick white stream burped into the machine—followed by an embarrassingly gross sound that made the whole room go silent.

Cheeks burning, Allison peeked above the counter. Everyone was looking her way. Including Jake, who smiled and winked.

Allison quickly closed the hatch on the soap container and locked the latch on the dishwasher. *A wink. Good heavens, the man* is *a rake.* But try as she might, Allison couldn't keep from smiling.

As she carried the empty detergent container to the recycling bin in the garage, Allison recalled a recent conversation with Pam. "You're a beautiful, sexy woman, Ally, and instead of dating, you spend all your time and energy on USB plugs and DSL modems," Pam had scolded. "You need a man, girl. And I'm gonna find you one."

Allison placed the jug in the appropriate receptacle then walked to Pam's car. She leaned down, placing her cheek flat to the cold hood. "Oh, Pam, I miss you so much already." She cried softly. "You were always in my corner. Setting up blind dates. Encouraging me to go out with guys my mother would never have chosen." She tried to smile, but half her face was frozen and the other half wouldn't work.

Pushing upright, she glared at the car and said, "If I die an old maid, it's all your fault." She kicked the car's tire because she'd been longing to kick something all day then walked inside.

The first thing she noticed was the heightened noise. More people had arrived, including several children— one that she recognized. Gayle's son, Bradley.

"Hi, Ally," Marc called when he spotted her. "More food."

He nodded toward the teenage girl at his side. A blond clone of his wife. In her hands rested a glass cake pan, which Gayle quickly took. "Thanks for making this, sweetheart. You're a peach."

She gave her daughter a peck on the cheek then carried the cake to the counter. Allison hurried over to make room for it. "Where did all this come from?" she asked.

"People want to help," Gayle said. "I guess food is the way we comfort ourselves. We can't do anything else, so we eat. And drink," she added, watching her husband pour a measure of bourbon into a glass.

Allison didn't know Gayle well. And she'd certainly never seen this sensitive side of the woman before. She began to understand why Pam had liked the woman. Allison wondered if her own shyness and even a little jealousy of the friendship the two had shared had kept her from getting to know Gayle better.

"How are you holding up?" Gayle asked. "Is this too much? I thought about telling people to come to my house, instead. But, somehow, I felt Pam would want them here. To be closer to her spirit. To say goodbye."

"I think you made the right call, Gayle. It's a good diversion for Caleb, too, having other children around."

Gayle's lips compressed together in a frown. "I thought Marc would bring the kids over sooner, but he said Bradley was reluctant to come. We told them what happened, of course. Bradley was terribly upset. Marc's father passed away last spring, and we took the kids to Boston for the funeral. Not the smartest move, I'm afraid. Brad had nightmares for weeks."

She lowered her voice and added, "I think it was the open casket that did it. At least, Caleb won't have to deal with that. He'll only have positive images of his parents to remember them by."

Open or closed casket. Cremation or traditional burial. All items on her list. All decisions awaiting a discussion with the lawyer.

Gayle dished up a piece of cake on a small paper plate and reached for a plastic fork in a box of mixed dinnerware. "But Bradley did seem to perk up when I told him that Caleb might be spending a lot more time with us—after the funeral and after Jake leaves, I mean," she qualified when Allison gave her a questioning look.

"I know how crazy it's going to get for you, Ally, with Cordelia in the hospital and the demands of your business. This time of year is chaotic anyway—even without dealing with a grieving youngster. Marc and I both want you to know you can lean on us as much as you need to."

Allison couldn't speak. Her mind was still struggling over "...after Jake leaves." He would, of course. She knew that. But the idea of being left alone in this big house to care for Caleb made her head spin. "I...I need to sit down."

"Oh, you poor thing," Gayle said, dropping her cake plate to grab Allison's shoulders. "Come over here to the family room sofa. You look ready to pass out."

Allison was too dizzy to resist. She let Gayle lead her to the big L-shaped sofa that faced the new plasma television Pam bought her husband for Christmas last year. "Kenny-vision," she'd called it.

At the moment, the wide, crystal-clear screen was filled with undersea creatures in a Disney video—one of Caleb's favorites, Pam told her. Gayle's older son was sitting in the recliner across from the sofa while Caleb and Bradley played with the new Matchbox cars Jake had brought, driving the die-cast autos up and over magazines that were grouped on the coffee table.

Just as Allison's vision cleared, she witnessed Caleb grab Bradley's car from him. "Mine," Caleb snapped.

Bradley tried to take it back and a scuffle ensued.

Gayle turned toward the boys and said, "Stop it, you two. This isn't the time to be fighting. We need to co-operate and get along."

Bradley looked at her, mouth agape at the obvious injustice. "But, Mommy—"

"No, buts, young man," Gayle said sternly. "Remember what I said. You have to be very kind to Caleb right now. If he needs all the cars, then let him have them."

Allison wasn't comfortable with that attitude. Pam was a stickler for good manners. She'd never have let her son get away with being greedy. Allison sat forward and held out her hand. "May I see the car, Caleb?"

Caleb's triumph turned to rebellion. "No," he said, crossing his arms so the cars were tucked under his armpits. "Mine."

"That's true. But Bradley is your guest. He shares his toys when you're at his house, doesn't he?"

The child's slim shoulders lifted and fell.

Allison could feel Gayle watching her. She wished she'd stayed out of the argument entirely. "Do you want him to go into your bedroom and get another car from your toy box?"

"No," Caleb said, but Allison could tell he was wavering. He was such a good kid. One of the most generous Allison had ever been around.

Before he could say anything else, Gayle suddenly dropped to a seated position and pulled Caleb into her lap. "Oh, honey, it's okay to want to keep things. We understand. You just lost the most important things in the world, so it's natural to be angry about that. Bradley understands, don't you, sweetheart?"

Bradley nodded but Allison could tell he was just as confused as Caleb, who looked tense and uncomfortable in Gayle's arms.

"Hey, what's going on?" Jake asked, dropping to an easy squat beside the couch next to Allison. "Caleb, could I see you a minute, bud? I need to make an ice run and I thought you and Brad could come along so I don't get lost."

Caleb dropped both cars on the floor and sprang into Jake's arms, nearly knocking him over. Allison was close enough to see Jake fight for his balance and, without thinking, she put a hand on his shoulder to steady him.

The contact sent a weird jolt through her arm and upper torso—something that had never happened to her before. She snatched back her hand and shoved it between her thigh and the cushion.

"Me, too?" Bradley asked, looking to his mother for permission.

She glanced at Allison then nodded. "Sure. If you're not gone too long."

Jake rose, still carrying Caleb, and extended his

index finger to Bradley. Then he looked at Allison. "Do you want to come? I promise to do all the driving."

The little inside joke brought a smile to her lips, but Gayle's scrutiny made her shake her head. "I'd better stay. In case the lawyer calls. Thanks, though. Don't forget their coats."

He looked at his charges. "You heard the lady. Let's get our jackets." To Gayle, he said, "Back in a flash."

When they were gone, Gayle shifted to her knees. "He's a natural, isn't he? With kids, I mean. My brother is the same way—my children's favorite uncle. But when it comes to the tough stuff, like discipline and following through? Nada. Zip. He's outta here."

She stood up and walked back to the counter. But her words hung in the air like an ominous prediction.

Half an hour later, Allison was still sitting in the same spot. She might have dozed off for a minute or two, she wasn't sure. But the little fish on the screen was safely reunited with his father, and she couldn't say how that had happened. So she must have missed something.

Feeling guilty about not being a better hostess, she started to get up just as the phone rang. Gayle motioned for her to stay put and hurried to the small desk to answer it. Jake apparently beat her to it because he walked into the kitchen with the portable phone to his ear. They'd had dozens of calls from concerned friends and people wanting to inquire about Cordelia, but from the expression on his face, Allison knew this call was different.

She couldn't catch his reply, but a moment later, he pressed a button on the unit and walked to where she was sitting. Without invitation, Gayle joined them.

"That was Dick Fenniman—Kenny's lawyer. He'll be at his office in half an hour. Do you want to go? Or should I?"

Before Allison could answer, Gayle said, "Why don't you both go? I'd be happy to hold down the fort."

"Good idea. It'll save repeating everything later. Thanks very much." Jake turned. "I'll go get Caleb."

Caleb? Allison tried to keep her reaction from showing, but Jake must have sensed something. He looked at her and said, "What?"

"Nothing."

His eyes narrowed, giving her a piercing look that made her confess, "Yesterday at the hospital was really hard on him. On us both. Waiting rooms generally aren't fun places for little kids. Plus, the lawyer might have things to tell us that Caleb isn't ready to hear."

"Ally's right," Gayle said authoritatively. "Leave him here. He'll be fine. He has Bradley to keep him company."

Jake frowned. "I understand what you mean, but I don't want him to think we abandoned him."

"You won't be gone long," Gayle argued. "Two, three hours. And you have a cell phone. I'll call if there's any problem.

"You might even have time to visit Cordelia," she added. "Didn't you say you wanted to see her, Allison? And when I called down there, they told me no visitors in Intensive Care under the age of eighteen."

Jake looked at Allison. His frown told her he wasn't wild about leaving Caleb. But Allison knew that Pam and Gayle had traded baby-sitting all the time. She stood up. "I'm sure they'd make an exception under the circumstances, but we should probably see her first. We don't want to scare him, and, frankly, she looked pretty bad last night."

Jake turned up his hands to signify his capitulation. "Fine. I'll go tell him what's going down. The boys are playing in Caleb's room. I helped them set up his race track."

Allison followed. "I need my jacket. It's in my room," she said, referring to the guest room that she and Pam had decorated together. *This is your room, Ally. Any time you need to get away from the valley, you come here. This is your home, too.*

"Speaking of rooms," Gayle said, trailing after them. "Are you both staying here?"

Allison looked at Jake. "We haven't discussed arrangements, but I assumed you'd want to stay here."

"Absolutely," Jake said. "I want to be where Caleb is. Is there any reason that's a problem?"

Allison shrugged. "Not as far as I'm concerned. It's a four-bedroom house, but Kenny converted one room into his home office, and I usually stay in the guest room. So, you either have to take the master bedroom or go over to Cordelia's."

He glanced from her to Gayle and said, "We'll figure that out when we get back. I can sleep on the couch for all I care. Right now, we have to get to the lawyer so we can start making some decisions about the funeral. But first, I'm going to tell Caleb what's happening. And if he wants to go with us, we take him."

His tone held an air of challenge, but he'd get no argument from Allison. She wasn't confident enough in her parenting skills to put her foot down one way or the other.

"Fine with me. I'll warm up the car."

As she walked away, she heard Jake tell the gathering, "Everyone, help yourself to food and drink. Gayle will be filling in while Allison and I run to town. We truly appreciate your support and I promise to let you know the day and time of the funeral as soon as the plans are finalized."

Plans. Whenever Pam had accused Allison of being too "anal" about her neat lists and five-year business plan, Allison had countered that establishing a plan and sticking to it meant you'd have something to show for your life someday. And while Pam preferred to live life spontaneously, she did plan some things—like asking Allison and Jake to be Caleb's godparents.

"IF YOU WON'T take me home, I'll call a taxi," Cordelia told her two visitors. "I need to see my grandson."

"Oh, Cordelia," Allison said stepping closer to the bed. "You will. Soon. But the most important thing at the moment is for you to recuperate."

"But how can I help Caleb if I'm chained to this bed?" Cordelia cried, trying to lift her right arm, which was hooked up to tubes that the nurses fiddled with every hour or so—even in the middle of the night when they told her she was supposed to be asleep. How could a person sleep knowing her daughter was dead and her grandson was alone?

Just thinking about it made her start to cry again.

Allison leaned down and tried to give Cordelia a hug, but the little plastic breathing tubes under her nose made it awkward. "You can help by getting well," Allison said, standing up straight again. "In the meantime, don't worry about Caleb. He's fine. Well, as fine as can be expected."

"You told him about his parents?"

Allison nodded. "This afternoon. Shortly after Jake got here."

Cordelia closed her eyes. She couldn't imagine how hard that must have been. She should have been the one. She should have been stronger.

"Cordelia," Jake said, touching her hand. "This isn't easy for any of us, and I know it's got to be even worse for you. But I promised Kenny I'd be here for his son, and I want you to know I'm here for you, too."

Cordelia felt ashamed. She'd never thought too highly of Jake. A wastrel, she'd called him. Wasting his life on surfing, of all things. But she could tell he meant what he said.

Suddenly terribly weary, she sighed. "It…should… have…been…me."

Allison patted her shoulder. "We can't change what happened, Cordelia. All we can do is try to make the best of things."

Jake nodded. "As soon as you're up to it, you can talk to Caleb on the phone. He's worried about you, too. It would help put his mind at ease."

"When can I see him?"

Jake looked at the floor. "Well, um, Allison said it might scare him to see you hooked up to all these monitors."

Cordelia looked at Allison whose cheeks blushed bright red. "Do I look that bad?"

The answer was in her eyes. The girl couldn't lie for spit. "No. Not at all. You look great. So much better than yesterday. But, it's all this stuff," she said, motioning toward the monitors. "It scares me, so I thought it might scare Caleb. But what do I know?"

Cordelia frowned. Allison was a smart girl, very accomplished when it came to computers, but she didn't have much confidence when it came to taking care of children. Pam used to say the reason Ally didn't have a family of her own was because she was doing penance. Cordelia hadn't asked for details. Maybe she should have.

"We'll bring him soon, Cordelia," Jake said. "But first we have to get past the funeral. That's what Allison and I came to talk to you about."

Funeral? She'd already planned two—George's and her own. No mother should have to plan her child's, too.

"We just left the lawyer's office. Pam and Kenny were very specific about how to handle the estate and anything affecting Caleb, but there's no mention of any preference for burial or cremation. And if we go with a burial, where do we do it? Here? Or back in Detroit?"

Jake pulled up a chair and sat down. "Sorry," he said. "Jet lag is catching up with me. Can I give you my opinion without sounding too insensitive?" He took a breath. "I think cremation would be the best route. Then we can hold a memorial service when you're up and about."

"Postpone it?" Allison asked, sounding horrified. She turned away and started pawing through the lumpy backpack she always carried.

Even though his words were blunt, they helped Cordelia sharpen her focus. "I remember hearing the kids talk about this after your grandfather passed away, Ally. Kenny mentioned that his stepfather had six extra spaces in the cemetery where Mr. Rydell and Kenny's mother are buried. Pam said she liked the idea of being buried in the town where they started their family together. I believe there's even a large marble headstone with the name Rydell already in place. All you'd have to buy is the little markers with their names and dates…" She couldn't go on.

Jake slapped his knee as if sealing the deal. "Perfect. Kenny loved getting a bargain. And what's better than free?"

Allison wiped her eyes and tried to smile, but Cordelia could tell she was barely hanging on by a thread. "Then you won't mind if we go ahead with the services right away? Even though you won't be there?"

Cordelia sank back against the hard pillow. She missed her bed. Her life. Her daughter. She closed her eyes to keep from crying, but the tears slipped from beneath the lids and slid down her cheeks—just as they had all day. "It's the way it has to be," she finally said.

A warm hand gripped hers. "Pam will understand."

Cordelia blinked. Jake. Jake the Rake was gently squeezing her hand. She tried to squeeze back but couldn't find the strength.

Allison touched her shoulder and said, "You rest now. I'll talk to you tomorrow and let you know what we've decided. Thank you."

After they left, Cordelia dozed fitfully. She ached in places the doctor hadn't touched with his scalpel. Bone deep. Soul deep.

She'd failed at so much in her life. She hadn't been the best wife she could have been. She hadn't been able to keep George from eating and drinking like there was no tomorrow—and there hadn't been, for him. She never put her foot down and told Pam to stay home when she should have. Pam did too much—always on the go. But Cordelia hadn't said a word. And now, she wasn't even going to be at her own daughter's funeral.

JAKE FELT UTTERLY DRAINED by the time they left the hospital. Cordelia Wells might not have been his favorite person in the past, but seeing her so small and fragile in the stark surroundings brought fresh pain to his already broken heart. Was any step of this going to get easier? Somehow, he doubted it.

Allison started the car and backed it out of the parking space, but instead of going forward, she said, "I know you're exhausted, but would you mind if we swing by my house? I need a change of clothes, and I'd like to check on my cats."

She looked so sincerely apologetic, Jake couldn't say no. "Can you make it quick? I'm really starting to feel uneasy about having left Caleb. Is that crazy? Have I turned into an overprotective father?"

He said the last as a joke, but Allison didn't smile. "You mean like Kenny?"

Jake startled. "I beg your pardon?"

She stepped on the gas and drove toward the busy street. "Pam used to complain that, as a father, Kenny was too restrictive. She attributed it to his mother being too permissive when he was young and his stepfather trying so hard to be a buddy when Kenny was a teenage that neither set down any rules."

Jake frowned. Pam had never mentioned that to him. On the other hand, Kenny had had plenty to say about Pam's permissive style of parenting. "Maybe he was trying to take up the slack because Pam was too lax. No set bedtime. No routine of any kind that I ever saw."

Allison stepped on the brake. Hard. "She wanted her son to experience life—the good and the bad."

"Even if he got hurt."

"Accidents happen."

They looked at each other until a horn sounded behind them. "Oh, for heaven's sake," Allison said, putting on her blinker and pulling into traffic. "I can't believe we're arguing about this. Not now."

Jake stared out the window. "You're right. I apologize. I don't know why I said that. I loved Pam. She was a great mother. I guess I just listened to Kenny blow off steam and… Well, he thought Pam should be a bit more cautious with Caleb."

As they waited for a traffic light, Allison said, "This might not be the right time to ask, but do you know what your plans are? How long you'll be here?"

Jake had projected several different scenarios in his head on the flight west—one week, two weeks, maybe sticking it out through the holidays, but everything had changed the minute he'd held his godson in his arms. An unexpected feeling had surfaced the moment Caleb's arms had closed around his neck. Something so powerful and familiar it had left him shaken.

He slumped down in the seat and closed his eyes. "I don't know and, frankly, I'm too damn wiped to give you an exact agenda, but I'll stay as long as I can. I understand you'd like me to be more specific but I can't be right now."

Allison realized she was being unreasonable, but she needed reassurance, needed to know that she could count on his help. But then who could predict what the future would bring? Certainly not Pam and Kenny—or they'd have left more explicit instructions for their friends to follow.

Tears flooded Allison's eyes without warning. A rough sob escaped.

"Ally?" Jake said, turning toward her. "I didn't mean to be short with you."

She blinked frantically to clear her vision. "It's not that. The pain just hits sometimes."

He put his hand on her shoulder. "Parking lot. Just ahead. Take it." His tone brooked no resistance. Allison put on her blinker and quickly escaped the traffic. The brick and stucco building adjacent to the paved lot was one she didn't recognize.

She put the car in Park and closed her eyes. "Sorry about that," she said. "All we need is another wreck."

Both were silent a moment—the only sound the muted roar of traffic and the hum of the engine until Jake heaved a sigh and said, "Do you believe in Fate?"

She found a tissue and blew her nose. "I don't know. Is Fate to blame for what happened to Kenny and Pam?"

"Possibly," Jake said. "Or poor judgment. Wasn't the ski trip Pam's idea?"

Allison's teeth ground together and she let out a low warning sound. "The only way Pam could have avoided dying would have been not to get into the car that morning. Nobody knew there'd be black ice on the road. She and Kenny had made that trip dozens of times without a problem. So be careful when assigning blame."

Even in the dim light, she could see the look of surprise in his eyes.

"You can rail at Fate," she went on. "Or take a potshot at God—heaven knows, He and I aren't on the best of terms. But don't for a second imply that Pam was a risktaker who should have known better than to plan a trip that might put them in harm's way."

He whistled softly. "Whoa. For a person who doesn't like to argue, you nailed that one pretty impressively."

She drew a deep breath to get her emotions under control. "Who says I don't argue?"

"Pam. She once bragged that she taught you the fine art of social debate. She said you were the youngest in your family and never got a word in edgewise."

Allison exhaled. After a pause, she smiled. "That's true. I was the odd man out in my family. Nobody really listened to me even if I did voice an opinion, so after a while, I just shut up. Pam would intentionally say things to rattle me. We were known to argue for hours over politics, fashion, movies." She smiled at the memory. "Pam kept me from being a total pushover."

He shifted in the seat to face her. "For the record, Allison, I don't blame Kenny or Pam for what happened. I believe with all my being that Kenny did everything in his power to avoid that collision. What happened was just damn bad luck. But if I ever find out that Fate or God had a hand in it, they'll have to answer to me."

Allison's tension abated. But she had to ask him something—a question she'd been holding in all day. "Jake, do you know where they are?"

He looked away. "Their bodies were taken to the morgue. An autopsy was performed. It's SOP…um, standard operating procedure. As soon as we've decided on a mortuary to handle the funeral, they'll be released."

Neither said anything for a few minutes as the hum of traffic passed by outside the car. People rushing about their lives as normal, oblivious to the fact that two wonderful people were dead and for those who had loved them, the world would never be normal again.

"So," Allison said, "the sooner we choose a place, the better, right?"

"Right."

She stretched laterally to reach behind his seat and came back with a phone book. "It's only four-thirty. Maybe we can talk to someone today," she said, handing him the two-inch-thick directory.

His right brow arched in question.

Allison felt her face grow warm. "This is my mobile office."

He didn't say anything but continued to stare at her a few seconds longer before opening the book to the business listings. She punched the map light, which drew her gaze to his hands. One of her mentors in college believed you could tell a lot about a person by his or her hands. Allison's were square and utilitarian; Jake's elegant, yet masculine.

"There are two funeral homes listed," he said. "How do we pick? Rock, paper, scissors?"

Allison startled, thrown by his flip comment.

Immediately contrite, he said, "I'm sorry. That was stupid. I'm a little punchy from lack of sleep. Which should we go with?"

Allison pulled her phone from her bag and hit the first number on her autodial. "Gayle? This is Allison. Jake and I have a question about mortuaries. You've lived here a long time. What's your opinion?"

She watched Jake's face as she listened to Gayle lay out the pros and cons of each facility. Head tilted back against the headrest. Eyes closed. He appeared utterly exhausted. Just as his godson looked last night.

"Okay. Thanks. How's Caleb? Does he need to talk to us?"

Jake turned his face toward her, his expression etched with concern.

"Got it. We'll be there soon."

She ended the call. "Caleb's playing a game with Bradley at the moment, and she didn't want to disturb them, but she said he's been asking about us. Maybe…"

"We should go back and pick him up," he finished.

He was right, but they were so close. "My house is just a mile or so away. It won't take me long to pack. And my cats—"

"We'll come back later. With the kid. Kids like cats, right?"

Pam would probably think Jake was overreacting—just the way Kenny tended to. And as usual—although she rarely told Pam how she felt—Allison was tempted to side with caution. Gayle was a good mother and perfectly capable of caring for Caleb, but what if Caleb was afraid that yet another set of adults had skipped out on him?

"Right," she said. "Let's go get our godson."

CHAPTER FIVE

CALEB DIDN'T UNDERSTAND why there was a party at his house when his mommy and daddy weren't there. Ally and Jake told him about a car wreck. They said his mommy and daddy had to leave and go to heaven. He didn't want to think about that. It made him sad, and he didn't really believe it was true. His mommy wouldn't leave for good. She once forgot to pick him up from preschool when he was little, but his teacher told him not to worry because mommies sometimes ran late.

That's what happened this time, too, he figured. She was running late. Real late.

He decided to ask Jake if maybe he knew when she'd come back.

"I gotta ask Jake somethin'," Caleb told his friend Bradley. "You stay here."

"Okay," Bradley said.

Bradley took the car Caleb had been racing and put it on his side of the track. Caleb didn't care. He needed to find Jake.

Jake lived a long ways away. He told Caleb he came here because he'd promised Caleb's daddy to look after Caleb if anything bad ever happened. Caleb liked Jake. A lot. He was fun to be with. Ally wasn't as much fun, but he knew his mommy loved her. They always hugged when they saw each other. Ally didn't hug Caleb much, but that was okay. Sometimes people hugged him too much.

Like Bradley's mother. She was always picking him up and squeezing him. Caleb peeked around the wall to make sure she wasn't close by. He wanted Jake, not her.

That's when he remembered that Jake told him he had to go to town with Ally. But they were coming right back.

Caleb couldn't tell time, yet, but he figured they should be back by now so he stealthily maneuvered past a group of adults into the living room. Nope, no Jake.

Darting behind the big chair where he'd hidden yesterday when the policeman came, he paused. A loud voice said, "We're not equipped to understand God's will, but we can take solace in knowing that heaven opens its doors to good Christian souls like Ken and Pamela."

Caleb grinned. His mother hated to be called Pamela. "Pam. Just Pam," she used to say when meeting someone new. "Like the nonstick cooking spray."

"They were good people," another person said. "What a tragedy! You just never know when your time is up."

Caleb frowned. Sometimes adults sounded so serious it made his stomach hurt. He wanted Jake to make them leave. He was tired of all these people. Maybe if they left, his parents would come home.

"And that poor little boy," a woman said. "It just breaks my heart. After I heard the news, I picked up Tyson out of his crib and held him. Weeping like a baby. God, it's just so wrong."

Caleb's stomach hurt worse. He wanted to escape so he didn't have to listen anymore, but he was afraid they'd see him.

"Are the godparents back yet?" someone asked.

Caleb knew that word. Ally and Jake were his godparents. His mommy once explained that they were like super-duper aunts and uncles who loved a kid just as much as his parents did, only they didn't have to do any of the dirty work—like change diapers. Caleb hadn't worn diapers for a long time. That was for babies.

"They're on the way," another person said. Caleb recognized the voice—Brad's mommy. He hunkered down, trying to stay out of sight. She added, "They've picked out a mortuary and will be meeting with the director in the morning to finalize plans. The funeral will probably be on Wednesday or Thursday."

Funeral. Caleb knew that word, too. Brad had had to go on an airplane when his grandpa died because they had a funeral for him. Brad said it was icky. His grandpa was in a box, and they put it in the ground.

Caleb's heart started beating faster. They did that to old people, but not to people like his mommy and daddy. Right?

He needed to ask somebody. Someone he trusted.

Jake. He needed Jake.

Unable to control his fear any longer, Caleb shot from behind the chair and raced into the kitchen. He could hear the people behind him talking and moving around. They might try to stop him, but he had to find Jake. Or Ally. Jake said they were both going to be here for him any time he needed them. And he needed them now.

"Jake," he cried, knocking over a stool at the counter. It made a loud clattering sound.

The ladies at the table stopped talking to look at him. Two got up and came toward him, but Caleb whirled around and dashed down the hall. He checked his parents' room, and the bedroom where Ally slept when she stayed with them. His daddy's office.

They were gone.

Frantic and breathless, Caleb ran into his room and jumped up on his bed. He grabbed the first thing he saw to hold on to—the toy gun Jake had given him.

Bradley looked up. "What's wrong?" he asked.

Caleb didn't answer. He couldn't. His throat hurt and tears were coming out of his eyes. Like a baby. *A baby.* He pictured his mommy telling him a few days ago, "Daddy and I are thinking about having a new baby. Would you like a new baby brother or sister, Caleb?"

"No," he'd said.

His mommy had looked sad. And disappointed.

Was that why she left? Because he didn't want another baby in his world? Because he didn't want to share her and Daddy?

Bradley got up and walked to the red race-car bed. "Wanna play a game?" Brad asked.

Caleb shook his head.

The door opened and Brad's mother stepped in. "Caleb, honey, are you okay? Jake and Allison will be here soon. I promise."

Caleb turned his back to her. He didn't believe her. He didn't believe anybody. He wanted his mommy.

"Can I play with your gun?" Brad asked, reaching for the plastic toy.

Caleb looked down at the oval race track where Brad

had caused a pileup of cars. Right in the middle of the tangled mess was a black one that looked like his father's Jeep. His heart thudded harder. Tears bubbled up. Anger surged through his veins.

All of a sudden, Caleb was mad. Very mad. He pulled back on the gun, ripping it from his friend's fingers, and used it to whack Bradley over the head.

Bradley let out a horrible wail that seemed to shake the walls.

Caleb started sobbing, too. He hadn't meant to hurt his friend, but he felt a little bit better knowing he wasn't the only one in pain.

"I'VE BEEN CHECKING some Internet sites on loss and young children," Allison told Jake the next morning when he finally dragged himself out of bed. He couldn't believe his internal clock was so messed up. Here it was nearly ten, and he was barely awake. "Violent outbursts are not uncommon. Lashing out when in pain is typical of young children."

Was it typical of sleep-deprived men, he almost asked? Fortunately, he remembered that Allison wasn't thrilled by his quirky sense of humor.

"Is Bradley going to live?" he asked, stumbling toward the coffeepot.

"Yes. He's fine. No stitches, although Gayle did take him to the emergency room to have him checked out."

Jake rolled his eyes. "The skin wasn't even broken," he said. "Well, maybe a little, but not much."

He and Allison had returned to utter chaos—one screaming child, another sobbing under the covers of his bed, well-meaning parents all trying to give advice and at the center, a plastic gun that everyone agreed had no business being in the hands of a distraught child. Great, Jake thought. He flunked Parenting 101 on the first day.

He poured a cup of coffee and took a long pull, enjoying the burn as it slid down his throat. When the stimulant jump-started his mind enough to think, he looked at Allison, who was watching him from the little desk.

Dressed in the same outfit she'd worn the day before—they'd never gotten around to driving back to town for her things—she said, "We need to talk."

"I know. I'm sorry I pooped out on you last night."

"You were exhausted. And Caleb wasn't in any shape to go anywhere, either. Don't worry. I'm sure the cats are fine, but I do have to get home sometime today." She pulled at her sweater. "This outfit is getting old."

He was about to say that he didn't know a single woman, Pam included, who could wear the same clothes for three days, but she didn't give him a chance. Instead, she said, "According to this Internet site on grief, children should be included in the planning of a funeral of a loved one. Depending on their age, of course. What do you think?"

That perky people should be outlawed before noon? Jake mumbled something that sounded like "I dunno" and went in search of food. Dozens of containers were strewn about the counter. He found a particularly delicious-looking cake and dug in using a plastic fork that he found nearby.

"Would you like a plate?" Allison asked, getting up from the desk.

He shook his head. "No. I feel like a barbarian this morning."

Allison carried her cup to the coffeemaker. "Are you okay? I take it you didn't sleep well?"

"Just peachy," he growled. "Nothing I like more than sleeping in my dead friend's bed."

Tears filled her eyes and she turned away.

Jake felt like a heel. "Sorry. I'm not really myself until I've ridden a couple of waves." A surge of homesickness hit swiftly, suddenly. In Miami, he would have been up before dawn, out in the surf on his board. Instead, he'd tossed and turned in a bed that didn't belong to him, in a house that wasn't his, in a world where he didn't want to be.

Allison walked to the refrigerator and took out a carton of milk. "Cream?" she asked.

"No, thank you. Black is good. Just please tell me this is the real stuff and not decaf."

She snickered softly. "As real as it gets. I ground the beans myself. And I like it strong, so you ought to be coming out of your stupor in a minute or two."

Her friendly grin seemed too contrary to his sullen mood so he dropped his eyes to the steam rising from his mug. The aroma held a scent he couldn't quite discern. *Vanilla?*

"Butterscotch," Allison said, apparently reading his mind. Jake had always prided himself on being inscrutable.

"It doesn't change the flavor," she added, "but I like the smell. After all, isn't that what draws us to the stuff in the first place? Sure can't be the taste."

Jake lifted the cup and breathed deeply. He liked the smell, and she was right about the flavor. The bitter taste was part of his routine—his midmorning break at the tiny pastry shop around the corner from his condo. Sitting at an outside table gave him time to plan his day, organize his thoughts.

He could use a little of that organization now. Unfortunately, his current goals and objectives were tied to other people. And he was willing to bet that the woman watching him from across the counter had a long list of things for him to do today. "So, what's our agenda?" he asked.

She returned to the desk where she picked up the legal pad he'd seen earlier. "Well, I have to go home to pack and pick up my cats," she said, emphasizing the word *have*. "My assistant manager fed them yesterday, but they can't stay there alone forever. Would you and Caleb like to come or stay here? Your call."

Jake's first thought was to stay put, but maybe Caleb would benefit from an outing. One thing was certain, wherever they went—the kid went, too. Apparently, the hullabaloo last night stemmed from Caleb thinking his godparents had deserted him.

"And I changed our appointment with the mortuary guy till two," Allison said. "Since that's up here, I thought we could arrange for Caleb to stay with Gayle. He needs to apologize to Brad; maybe take him a little present or something."

Jake hesitated. "If he's not cool with that, do you have a Plan B?"

"Well, our other option is to split up. One of us stays with him, the other makes all the funeral arrangements."

Jake could tell she wasn't thrilled about that idea, but he'd do just about anything to avoid seeing the look of heartbreak that had greeted him when he peeked under Caleb's blanket last night.

"Speaking of Caleb, where is he?"

"In the bathtub."

Something in her tone made Jake look at her closely. Her cheeks were a dull red. "What's wrong with that?"

"Nothing. Except that a four-year-old had to tell me that he needed a bath. What kind of mother doesn't know that?"

He didn't understand why she cut herself so little slack when it came to parenting. Last night, she'd tried to blame herself for Caleb's meltdown because she'd wanted to stop by her house after visiting Cordelia. "The kind that's only been a mother for thirty-six hours?" he asked. "Did you hear me suggest a bath last night? No. Because number one, the kid was a basket case by the time we got home, and number two, it never crossed my mind."

"Well, he must have been awfully dirty because he's been in there for over half an hour," she said. "I kept pacing between the door and the kitchen. Finally, I slipped that baby monitor in the room. I figure as long as I can hear him splashing, he's okay. Right?"

Jake reached across the counter for the small white plastic unit with the puny antennae. He examined the little buttons on the side and pushed the volume higher and brought it to his ear. Other than a mechanical hum, he didn't hear anything. Then suddenly, a deafening splash and squeal of pleasure made him jump back.

"Wow, where'd you get this? It's powerful."

"I gave it to Pam as a shower gift before Caleb was born. I spotted it on a shelf in the linen closet last night when I got the sheets for your bed."

"How'd you sleep?" he asked.

"An hour or two more than the previous night. Progress, I guess."

He held the receiver in both hands. The child's chatter was too garbled to make out distinctly, but it seemed as if Caleb was telling a story. "What's he saying?"

Allison shrugged. "I heard something that sounded like "The Itsy Bitsy Spider" a few minutes ago, but your guess is as good as mine."

Jake knew the tune. He'd heard Pam sing it to her son on several occasions. A sudden pressure squeezed his heart. When would the pain quit? he wondered.

"Oh, and I just talked to Cordelia," Allison said. "They're moving her into a regular room later today. We might think about taking Caleb down—even if it means a second trip to Fresno."

"Are children Caleb's age allowed to visit?"

Her eyes went wide. The color brought to mind periwinkle—a word he didn't even know was part of his vocabulary.

"If not, they should be. I think we can make the case that these are special circumstances, don't you?"

She grabbed a pen from a Mickey Mouse mug by the computer, then hurried around the counter to stand beside him. Her fresh, outdoorsy scent wrapped around his senses. She didn't actually touch him but was close enough for him to see the faint smudges of purple under her eyes and the chafed cracks in her bottom lip.

She pointed to the top item on her list. "We don't have to do this today, but we'll need to pick out flowers as soon as we have the exact date and time. This is the florist in Oakhurst that Gayle recommended."

"Oakhurst. That's where Rydell Motors is, right?"

She seemed to weigh the motivation behind his question. "Yes. Do you want a new car?"

"I can't drive a pint-sized rental forever."

"What about using Pam's? It's practically brand new."

"I thought you might want to drive it. Instead of putting miles on your station wagon."

She shook her head. "No, thanks. Red isn't my color. I don't need to catch the eye of every cop on the road."

Her halfhearted grin told him that wasn't the real reason, but he didn't push it. "Well, I don't suppose there's any sense buying another when I have a perfectly good one sitting in a garage in Florida."

"A fast one, I heard," she said, nodding toward the little receiver.

As if on cue, Caleb's voice filled the room. "Mommy, I'm ready to get out."

Allison flinched as if struck. "He called me that by mistake this morning when he woke up. I almost lost it."

She started to move away, but Jake caught her elbow. The muscles beneath his fingers felt strong, but there was a fragility about her, too. "I'll get him," he told her.

She blushed a sweet shade of rose, loosening his grip on her sleeve without making a fuss about it. "Great. Little boys aren't all that modest, I noticed, but I'm sure he'd be more comfortable with your help. I laid out some clothes on his bed."

Jake was just about to the doorway when she said, "The neighbor across the street brought over an egg dish that looks delicious. I thought I'd warm it up before we go." Her lips curved in a playful smile. "Unless the cake was enough for you."

Jake shook his head. "Heck no. That was just to tide me over until real food showed up."

"Smart choice. You'll need your strength."

"Oh, really? Why is that?"

As she opened the door of the refrigerator a second time, she shot him a mischievous look. "I take it you've never tried herding cats."

"Herding cats?"

"Ask Caleb. He'll tell you all about it." Her chuckle got him wondering—and not about cats.

AN HOUR LATER, the Subaru wagon pulled up in front of a smallish, but quaint circa 1940 bungalow on a tree-lined street. Like the houses on either side of it, the siding was a combination of stucco and wood. Allison's home was a light tan with dark trim. The front lawns ran together and were neatly mowed with divots Jake remembered concealed in-ground sprinklers. As a teen, he'd mowed more than his share of lawns just like this one.

Chest-high bushes with a shiny leaf that he recognized but couldn't name encircled the building's bay window. As she pulled into the driveway that ran alongside the house, Jake spotted a detached one-stall garage.

She nosed the car close to the rear porch. "I'll pack a few things while you guys bring in the cat carrier, okay? It's somewhere in the garage. You might have to dig under some computer boxes," she warned.

Jake looked at his godson in the back seat. "We can handle that, can't we, Caleb?"

Caleb had a petulant look on his face. "Her cats don't like me."

Allison spun in her seat. "Oh, honey, that's not true. Cleo and Rom are a little shy, but if you let them warm up to you, everything will go smoothly."

Jake smiled as his keen hearing picked up the whispered addendum, "I hope."

Allison got out, raced to unlock the door and returned to hand him the keys before he'd even gotten Caleb out of his booster seat. After she disappeared inside, he and Caleb went hunting.

The garage was presumably the same age as the house. The heavy-duty padlock seemed overkill for such an unpretentious little building. He opened the door and looked inside. Dark, unfinished walls with one small window made it seem dungeon-like. Stacks of boxes—as if the homeowner never got around to unpacking—took up most of the space.

"Are there spiders?" Caleb asked. "I don't like spiders. 'Cept t'rantulas. I like them. We had one at preschool last year. His name was Leggy."

Jake smiled. This was more like the chatterbox he'd spent a week with in August. He flicked on the light switch and surprise made his breath catch. The boxes bore the names of leading computer manufacturers. She was sitting on some pretty expensive inventory.

Locating the cat carrier didn't take long. Caleb helped by carrying a bag of kitty litter that he insisted must go, too. "Hellooo…" Jake called opening the back door. "Cat Herders Limited, at your service."

Allison waved him in. "Just set it on the washing machine. If Cleo and Rom see it, they'll disappear. Caleb said he was thirsty. I think there are soft drinks and juice in the fridge. Help yourself."

She was gone before Jake could reply. He thought it odd that she entrusted free rein of her personal space to a perfect stranger, but perhaps their situation required thinking outside the box.

Her kitchen was small and easy to negotiate. He couldn't help noticing that Allison's home lacked the profuse clutter—however charming—found in Pam's very large, airy kitchen. He opened a can of root beer for Caleb and poured half a glass. He'd learned his lesson about overfilling cups several summers ago.

He turned to put the can in the refrigerator and caught a fleeting glimpse of a fuzzy gold snake that disappeared behind the stove. His heart made a funny shift. He'd never felt any affinity for felines. He didn't dislike cats, he simply didn't care whether they existed or not.

Allison appeared a moment later with a cloth satchel in one hand and a garment bag tossed over the opposite shoulder. Squeezed under her arm was a small cosmetic bag.

"You call that moving?"

His shock must have been obvious because she blushed. "I'm a simple girl. Clean jeans and a toothbrush and I'm good to go," she mumbled and shot out the back door just as Caleb sang out, "I seen one. I seen a cat."

Jake hurried toward the living room and missed seeing the white tail in his path until it was too late. A loud screech of outrage coupled with the piercing barbs of an irate paw sent him airborne. He crashed into a low table and knocked over a brass lamp which he managed to catch but only by falling into an overstuffed chair.

Caleb's eyes were wide and his thumb popped into his mouth. Before Jake could reassure the little boy that everything was fine, two cats—one a golden tiger, one white—shot in opposite directions. Jake could have sworn they scaled the walls as adroitly as Spider-man before vanishing like ghosts.

He started to holler for help, but as if reading his

mind, his savior appeared. "What did you do to my cat?"

Jake answered with a curse too low for Caleb to hear, but Allison's brows lifted. Certain his calf would need stitches to staunch the flow of blood, he set the lamp back on the wicker end table and hiked up his pant leg.

Thick blond hair obscured his search for the damage. Out of the corner of his eye, he spotted Allison's sneakers and looked up. "Your cat scratched me," he said.

"Which one?"

"The left, obviously."

"Which cat?"

Humor. Definite traces of humor in her tone.

"The white one," he grumbled.

She bent forward. "I don't see any blood."

Her tone wasn't as sympathetic as he felt the situation warranted.

"Well, it hurt like he...ck," he grumbled, changing his word choice at the last second when he noticed his godson standing a few feet away.

Allison's lips pursed as if trying not to smile. "I'm sorry. Maybe Cleo will apologize personally, but I wouldn't count on it. She's as regal as her namesake and just as temperamental. Wasn't Cleopatra the one with an affinity for poisonous snakes?"

She straightened and walked to the table. Obviously, she expected Jake to suck it up and join them.

Heaving a sigh, he pushed the denim back down and rose. He had a bad feeling about this cat business, but what could he say? Allison was living up to her part of the bargain—changing her life to help a friend. He could certainly be man enough to do the same—bloodthirsty cats or no bloodthirsty cats. Maybe he'd buy boots.

Caleb sipped his soda and fidgeted in the chair while Jake carried a dress bag and two lumpy totes filled with what Allison called "work stuff" to the car. She was just starting to hunt for the cats when her cell phone rang. She retrieved it from her backpack, which Jake gathered doubled as a purse. Most of the women he knew carried handbags that cost more than dinner at a fine restaurant. Not Allison. Practical, efficient Allison.

Jake caught bits and pieces of her one-sided conversation as she transferred the few perishable items in her refrigerator into a paper sack. From the serious frown on her face, he gathered something had gone wrong at her job site and someone wasn't happy.

"I know that handling personnel is a little outside your experience, Ernesto," she said, her voice rising. "But I'm going to have my hands full with the funeral this week. You'll have to take charge, but I promise if you can keep us afloat until I get back, there'll be a bonus in it for you. Whether we go belly up or not.".

Belly up? That didn't sound very good, Jake thought.

She clicked off the phone and put it back in the bag. Returning to the table, she said, "Sorry about that. My employees are used to having me around, but they'll just have to handle things, won't they?"

He gave her credit for trying to sound optimistic, but as a hands-on type of boss, Jake understood what it meant to give up control. Which explained why he seldom managed to keep an assistant longer than a year or two. His latest protégé was constantly chafing under Jake's reluctance to delegate, but Matt's eyes and ears on the East Coast would come in handy while Jake was tied up here.

"Are you done with your drink, Caleb?" Allison asked. "If you are, why don't you go to the bathroom then I'll call my c.a.t.s and get them ready to g.o."

Jake's heart did a funny pirouette, which made no sense at all. He wasn't the type to fall for a woman who spelled words in front of animals. He just wasn't. But something about her serious look made him want to kiss her.

Damn. Any kind of attraction—especially at such an inappropriate time as this—was ludicrous. He'd just have to do his best to avoid her quirky, endearing little habits.

He made room for Allison's bags in the chaotic mess of her rear storage compartment, then started the car and turned on the heater. The outside temperature was far chillier than he'd expected it to be, but he should have remembered. His little brother had spent every winter battling one kind of illness or another contracted on the damp, dank playgrounds near their southern California home.

Caleb climbed into his booster seat. He appeared pretty subdued compared to the child Jake was used to seeing. He was probably tired—it had taken a long time for him to fall asleep last night. Jake fastened the safety belt and gave him a quick kiss on the forehead then walked to the back door and peered through the window to check on Allison's progress. He could see all the way into the dining room where Allison was on her hands and knees coaxing two very large, very sleek cats to come to her. The animals approached cautiously, probably because they expected the strangers to return.

He rested his forehead on the cold glass and watched. He had to say Allison's derriere, which was facing him, was in mighty fine shape for a thirty-something computer geek, as Kenny had once described her. Butts were a fairly common sight in Miami. Naked, bronzed, firm, flabby, male and female. Jake was certain he'd grown inured to the sight. This made it all the more baffling that he now found himself mesmerized by the denim-clad bottom wiggling back and forth like a tail-twitching feline.

She moved as stealthily and gracefully as the animals she was trying to catch. He'd already noticed that quiet watchfulness about her. No doubt she was coaxing her pets in the low, firm voice he'd heard her use with Caleb. He smiled when she slipped first one, then the second animal into the cargo box without a fuss.

She rose and turned around, brushing off her knees unnecessarily. Her house might be small, but it was tidy—unlike the rear compartment of her car. She gave a start when she spotted him. He opened the door but didn't walk inside. He was reluctant to leave Caleb alone—even though he could tell at a glance the little boy had nodded off.

"Just about ready," she said. "Could you grab my backpack? I'll carry the cats."

"They look heavy. Shouldn't it be the other way around?"

Her smile was the first honest grin he'd seen. And he liked it. A lot.

"I'm stronger than I look. Besides, you haven't picked up my purse."

He did her bidding and let out an unplanned grunt when he hefted the webbed strap over one shoulder. "What's in here? Lead weights?"

"My life," she said simply. "Quick fix stuff for my business. A book I need to read. My PalmPilot. My phone. Keys—some that I can't remember what they unlock but I'm afraid to throw away. That kind of stuff."

She carried the rose-colored carrier quite effortlessly. "Ready?"

"Yes, please," Jake said. "Let's go home."

It wasn't until he followed her down the steps that his words sank in. *Home.* Kenny's home. Kenny who didn't live there anymore. The thought was almost too much to bear, but Jake had learned years earlier that when faced with paralyzing loss, you put one foot in front of the other and kept moving forward. It was the only way to keep the pain at bay.

CLEO AND ROM WERE surprisingly quiet on the drive back up the hill. They weren't experienced travelers, except for the requisite trips to the vet for neutering and shots. But this time, they were together in one box, so perhaps that helped, Allison thought.

Which also meant they had time to plot revenge. Allison had no doubt whatsoever that cats possessed superior intellect and a long memory. She only hoped that Pam's sofa wouldn't be their victim.

Pam had loved that sofa. She'd pestered Allison with half a dozen calls to make sure she was buying the right one.

A sudden, sharp arc of grief swept through Allison's mid-section. Only iron will and prayer kept her from vomiting. Or weeping. She was afraid if she started crying she might not be able to stop.

"You're going to want to turn left—"Allison started to say, but Jake cut her off. "Would you mind if I gave it a try without help?" he asked politely.

Allison had been only too glad to let him drive. Her eyelids felt gritty with exhaustion and unshed tears.

"No problem." Well, one small problem. Riding versus driving freed up the brain to think about things she really didn't want to think about. Like funerals. And eulogies. And obituaries.

"I like your house," Jake said, breaking the silence. "Those older homes have a lot of charm."

"Thank you. I think so, too."

"I didn't notice any Christmas decorations. Too early for you or not your thing?"

"Way too early," she admitted, grateful to have something neutral to think about. "I usually buy one of those little tabletop-size living spruce trees a few days before the twenty-fifth. Kenny always plants it for me, but I've yet to get one that survives past SuperBowl."

His low chuckle felt surprisingly intimate. Yes, the guy was gorgeous, but that was a pretty lousy reason for thinking improper thoughts when your best friends in the world weren't even buried.

Sitting up a little straighter, she said, "Although my house may look Grinchy, I've got all my Christmas shopping done."

"That's impressive."

"Not really. I ordered online and sent everything directly to Minnesota. That's where my family lives. We drew names this year. I got my brother. And I bought things for my parents, of course."

"What did you buy?"

She looked at him, wondering about the reason behind his curiosity. Was he looking for ideas for his family? Did he have family somewhere? Why didn't she know the answer to that question?

"Well, let's see…a CD wallet and a book about Lewis and Clark. Both were items on my brother's list. For my dad, a flannel shirt and sheared fleece slippers and for Mother, I ordered an antique cookbook off eBay and a new robe from JCPenney that she'll probably never wear."

"Why won't she wear it?"

"She'll say it's too pretty and she's saving it for good. I never knew what constituted *good.* Your honeymoon? Gallbladder surgery? What?"

"Are those the only people you buy for?"

"I give my employees gift baskets." *When I can afford to.* "And Pam, and Kenny and Caleb," she added softly, glancing over the seat.

She felt another twist of the knife in her belly. What would the holidays be like without Pam—the woman who regarded the other eleven months of the year as a prologue to December?

"You know, Pam and Kenny almost didn't go skiing," she said. "Pam usually makes him hang up the outside lights. But Kenny told her he'd take off a day midweek and do it for her."

Neither spoke for a minute, then Jake said, "Pam really got into the holidays, didn't she?"

"You have no idea. She firmly believed that it was sacrilegious to decorate for Christmas before Thanksgiving, but once turkey day was over, she went into full Christmas mode."

"I've seen pictures."

"Which can't truly capture the depth and breadth of her holiday depravity. I used to accuse her of being a shill for Hallmark. She has dated ornaments ranging back to the Baroque period."

Her teasing was the kind of thing Pam took in stride,

but Allison bit down on her lip. Jake might misunderstand. What if he thought—?

His chuckle eased her worry. "So I gathered. She made us go into a Christmas-Around-the-Year store in some Podunk town in Florida last summer. Here we are in shorts and flip-flops and she's oohing and aahing over tiny snow-covered ornaments."

Allison smiled. "I bought her a bumper sticker one year that read I Brake For Christmas."

Jake glanced in the rearview mirror, then cleared his throat. Something about his body language told her whatever he planned to say was going to be serious.

"I've been trying to picture what life is going to be like after the funeral," he said keeping his voice low. "Especially with the holidays coming up."

"To be perfectly honest," she said, "my biggest fear—after breaking the news to Caleb—was trying to imagine how I'd handle the holidays alone."

"You say that like you expected me to leave right after the funeral."

"Well…I didn't know what to expect. Don't you have a round-trip ticket?"

"No. I bought a one-way."

"Really? You can take five weeks off from your business?"

He made a so-so gesture with his hand. "As long as I make my clients money, they're happy. I'm not looking forward to dealing with the three-hour time difference, but I'll figure it out. Is the house wired for high-speed Internet?"

"Of course."

"Then I'll be fine. Unless you'd prefer I stayed somewhere else after things settle down?"

"No, not at all. I want what's best for Caleb. It's a big house. We'll each have plenty of personal space. And as long as you're okay staying in Kenny and Pam's room, then Cordelia's little house will be there for her when she's able to come home."

He glanced sideways. "I peeked in the window this morning. It reminds me of a dollhouse."

Allison smiled. "That's exactly what Pam asked from the contractor who remodeled it. It was originally a greenhouse, but after her dad passed away Pam invited Cordelia to move out here. Technically, it's a guest house—it has everything except a kitchen. Kenny once told me he'd lucked out there. Although he'd never have admitted this to Pam, he loved Cordelia's cooking."

"The arrangement seemed to be working for them," Jake said.

Allison nodded. "They'd have a little friction now and then—mostly between Cordelia and Pam. Cordelia didn't always approve of Pam's choices where Caleb was concerned and Pam used to tell me that her mother was critical of her spending habits, but, all in all, they got along well."

"Did you visit often?"

"Not really. Holidays, birthdays. And I'd baby-sit every once in a while when Cordelia was busy. Mostly Pam and I got together in town."

Allison decided now was as good a time as any to make her confession. "For the record, when I promised Pam that I'd be here for Caleb if anything ever happened to her, neither of us really thought anything would happen. She'd never admit it, but Pam knew I wasn't exactly the maternal type."

His expression looked baffled. "What does that mean?"

"I lack whatever gene makes people like Pam and Gayle great mothers. Kids can sense this. You've seen it yourself. If Caleb has a choice of turning to you or me, he automatically picks you."

"Because I'm a guy. And he just spent some one-on-one time with me in August. We hung out."

Allison didn't know how to explain something so personal. She'd felt that way all her life. And look what had happened the one time she'd tried to go against her predisposition? Her ovary had developed a cancerous cyst and she'd had to abort the baby she was carrying.

"I'll give you an example," she told him. "I was the first non-family member to hold Caleb after he was born. He didn't cry a peep until I picked him up. Then he howled. What does that tell you?"

"You're paranoid?"

He said it jokingly, and she actually smiled. "That's what Pam said, too. She always insisted I'd make a good mother if I loosened up a bit, but that's not in my nature." She couldn't keep her voice from cracking a little. "I truly agonized over accepting her request to be Caleb's godparent. I wouldn't have, but Pam promised not to die."

Neither spoke for a few miles, then Jake said, "So what you're saying is that you plan to honor Pam's request—even though you think you're not the right person for the job."

"Well…yes. I'm pretty sure I can handle the actual care and feeding of a child, but meeting his emotional needs has me worried. Since that seems to be your forte, we might actually make a good team, except for logistics. We live on opposite sides of the country."

He gave an abrupt snort. "When Kenny asked me to watch Caleb's back, I figured that meant setting up a trust fund, taking the kid to fun spots, giving him a chance to stretch his wings when his parents became overprotective. Does that sound emotionally supportive?"

"But Caleb likes you better than me," she argued. "That has to count for something. He's a very astute little boy."

"He likes me because I spoil him rotten. You think I'm father material? Ha! Yesterday's gun fiasco should have told you something." He shook his head. "At least, you're reliable and kid savvy."

"Reliable? Hardly. When I get caught up in a complex installation or repair, I can lose all track of time. What if I forgot to pick up Caleb at preschool or something? Aren't we trying to avoid abandonment issues?"

Jake heaved a long sigh. "Good Lord, we're pathetic. I'm not sure that even *together* we make one parental unit. Maybe we should ask Gayle to take him."

Allison knew he was joking, but the suggestion made her furious. "If this decision were based on logic, you might be right. But unless you're blind, Caleb loves you. He needs you—not your money. And whether you intended it to happen or not, the two of you share a bond that I can't touch."

He was silent a moment, then asked, "Why is that, Allison? You obviously love the little guy."

"I...I don't know," she said, unwilling to tell him about her shattering experience with motherhood. "But I do know that once the funeral is over, I'm going to need to focus on my business or the six families that depend on me for their livelihood will be at risk of losing their jobs—just in time for the holidays."

They'd reached the intersection where she and Caleb had met him. Yesterday, she realized. How could that be? Surely they'd been together more than twenty-four hours. She felt she'd known him for months.

She held her tongue, waiting to see if he would miss the turn. He put on the blinker and said, "So, what I'm hearing is that, one, your presence is required at Jeffries Computing on a regular basis, and, two, you don't think of yourself as a warm, fuzzy type of caregiver, right?"

"Pretty much, yes."

"But you are honest with Caleb. And direct. I know he trusts you because I've seen him turn to you for answers."

"And to you for comfort."

He reached overhead for the garage door opener she'd taken from Pam's car. "Sounds as if you're the 1950s father—going off to work, remaining slightly less engaged emotionally, while I'm the stay-at-home mom."

Allison couldn't help but smile. "I might not have put it that way, but, yeah, I guess so." His chuckle produced an odd shiver she wished she could put down to chill, but the toasty heater robbed her of the excuse.

"I can live with that, but I do have one question?"

Allison spotted his mischievous grin as the car pulled into the garage. "Who cooks?"

CHAPTER SIX

"GRAMMA," Caleb cried, shaking off Jake's hold on his hand to race across the brightly lit room to the bed where his grandmother was lying.

Allison's breath caught in her throat. They'd put off this visit another day after Cordelia called and said she was too tired from the move to have visitors. Now, it was Monday, and Caleb was impatient to see his grandmother.

Allison hurried after him, fearful that in his exuberance, he might inflict more pain on his grandmother who looked wan, but better than when Allison had last seen her.

Cordelia managed to move over on the mattress to give the child room to climb up beside her. "Oh, honey boy, I missed you so much. Are you okay? Give Gramma a big hug."

The little boy flung himself against her chest, and Allison saw Cordelia flinch before she wrapped her arms around him and hugged him, too.

Allison looked at Jake, who was watching the scene intently. He glanced sideways. Go or stay, he seemed to ask with his eyes.

She made an "I don't know" gesture.

"Sit down, you two," Cordelia said, motioning toward the lone chair by the window.

Jake gestured for Allison to take it. "I'll go borrow another from the nurses' station. And get a vase for these," he said, indicating the bouquet he carried.

"I picked them out for you, Gramma," Caleb said. "This morning. When Jake and I went to the flower place. I picked out all Mommy's favorite flowers, too."

Cordelia looked up sharply. Allison nodded at the question she read in the woman's eyes. The funeral director had encouraged Jake and Allison to include Caleb in the process of arranging the funeral, although whether he'd understood the purpose of the shopping expedition was another matter.

"That was so smart of you," Cordelia said, kissing his forehead. "I'm sure she would have been very proud of you."

"She went away," Caleb said, seriously. "Daddy, too."

Cordelia's lips quivered. "I know, dear. Not because she wanted to, though. You understand that, don't you? Some times things happen that we can't control. Your mother and father never would have left us if they could have helped it."

Allison wiped the tears from her eyes and dug in her bag for the card Caleb had made for his grandmother that morning. "Here, Caleb. Don't forget this."

His face lit up. "I drew this just for you, Gramma. Ally helped. Jake would have, but he was on the phone talking to his office. Back in Flor… Flor…"

"Florida," Jake supplied, rejoining them. He carried a large vase filled with Bird of Paradise in one hand and a straight-back chair in the other. "Where should I put these?"

Allison stood and cleared a spot for them amongst

the numerous baskets of plants and cut flowers that occupied the window ledge. "These are beautiful," Allison said, glancing at the cards attached to them. The largest arrangements were from Cordelia's bridge club and bunco group. "You're obviously missed."

Allison knew Pam had been extremely proud of how well her mother had blended into the community.

"So, what are you doing today?" Cordelia asked her grandson.

He shrugged. "We hafta go to the car lot. Not Daddy's. Some other one. Jake is taking back his car. He doesn't like it."

Cordelia looked at Jake who said, "Rental. Allison suggested I use Pam's while I'm here."

A look of despair crossed the woman's face but she rallied after a few seconds. "Of course. Too bad mine isn't available. It needed a major overhaul so Kenny sold it to some dealer. He was going to order me a new car—one of those hybrids. I'm on a waiting list, I think."

Allison tuned out the car talk that followed. She was just happy to see Caleb looking engaged and spunky. The past two days had been difficult. He'd slept fitfully the night before and hadn't eaten more than a few bites at a time. Plus, he seemed whiny and far more demanding than usual. When she expressed her concerns to Gayle, the more experienced mother had downplayed Allison's concerns. "He's adjusting. Give him time."

That was probably true, but the more she read about childhood grief, the more Allison wondered if some kind of professional therapy might be in order. She hadn't broached the topic with Jake—certain he'd think she was overreacting. But, she'd hoped they might bump into the pastor she'd met at the hospital that first day. According to his card, he was a counselor as well.

"Did they fix your heart, Gramma?" Caleb asked. He sat cross-legged, his stubby athletic shoes leaving bits of leaves on the pristine cotton blanket.

"Yes, love, the doctor put in some new parts. He says I'll be good as new in a few months. Then I can come back home."

Caleb nodded. "We got two cats, now." He held up his fingers in a peace sign. "Cleo and Rom."

"Really?" Cordelia exclaimed. Something in her tone said she didn't approve. Allison started to defend her decision, but Jake cut her off.

"I'm not a cat lover, but I have to say, these guys are pretty amazing. Rom has decided Caleb is the coolest person on the planet. He even slept on Caleb's bed last night. Right, buddy?"

Caleb nodded with more enthusiasm than Allison had seen all day. "His whiskers tickled my face this morning and his breath smells like fish, but he's nice. Cleo hides most of the time. Ally says she's not ac..acl…"

"Acclimated," Allison supplied. She didn't think Caleb had been listening when she explained why the white cat was so shy.

"Well, it's good that you can help Allison take care of them since she couldn't leave them alone until I—" her voice dropped "—get home."

Jake got up and walked to the bed. "The nurse said we should only stay a few minutes. She doesn't want you to get tired, but we'll try to come back tomorrow."

"When is the—"

"Thursday," Allison said, jumping to her feet. "And there's a visitation the night before."

Jake held out his arms to Caleb who clambered to his feet and leapt. Allison hurried closer and brushed the little bits of debris off the pale pink blanket. "Do you have a list for me?" she asked, noticing that Cordelia's color had faded.

"List?"

"You said on the phone there were some things you needed from home. Are you sure you wouldn't prefer I just bought them instead of poking around in your things?"

Cordelia let out a harsh laugh. "If you knew how much poking they do around here, you wouldn't ask that question. I…I think the list is on that tablet."

Allison found it. Denture cleaner, tweezers, a hand mirror, a hairbrush. "No problem. I'll get this stuff together and bring it down tomorrow."

"Whenever," Cordelia said her tone flat.

Allison looked at Jake and saw the same concern she felt. The last thing they needed was for Cordelia to give up. She moved to the bed and gave Pam's mother a hug. "Be strong, Cordelia," she whispered. "Caleb needs you. This is the perkiest I've seen him since we told him the news. You have to get better— for his sake."

CORDELIA DOZED FITFULLY after her grandson left. She felt so useless—a burden, instead of the vital, active woman she'd always prided herself on being.

"Mom never slows down," she'd once heard Pam tell a friend. "She's afraid old age will catch up with her."

Pam had been proud of her, but she wouldn't be proud now. Lying here too weak to get out of bed, let alone play with Caleb. Even making conversation with him for a short time had left her winded. A part of her wanted to give up, but she couldn't do that.

If she did, Caleb would wind up with Allison and Jake. Both were good people, but they weren't family. Ally was too wrapped up in her business to be a good mother. Shaking her head, Cordelia corrected herself, to be as good a mother as Pam was. Pam could have worked outside the home. She was a dynamo—intelligent and friendly. Her charity drive at the car lot got a good write-up in the paper every year. But she chose to stay home with Caleb.

"He'll only be this age once, and I need to be a part of that," she'd told Cordelia more than once.

Allison didn't understand that. Her business was her baby, Pam often said. And Jake? Who knew about him? He seemed to have turned into a truly compassionate man but eventually he'd have to go back to his life in Miami. If Cordelia gave up, what would happen to Caleb? Would they put him up for adoption or try to share custody on opposite sides of the country? What kind of life would that be?

No, she thought, I have to get well. That's all there is to it.

"THAT WAS SIMPLY AMAZING," Jake said as he helped Allison clean up after dinner. They'd considered getting takeout while they were in town visiting Cordelia, but Gayle had called to tell them the neighbors were bringing in a four-course meal. A pot roast the likes of which Jake had never tasted. He'd eaten far more than he should have. Allison and Caleb on the other hand, had barely picked at the food on their plates.

"A farm meal," Ally said. "Made me quite homesick."

"Is that why you didn't eat more?" he asked.

She shook her head and scraped the remains of the meal into the sink. "No. Just not hungry, I guess. Lack of sleep is catching up on me. But I'm glad to see one of us had an appetite."

"One is right. I don't think Caleb took more than ten bites. Should we be worried?"

Allison stopped what she was doing and looked across the room where Caleb was sitting in a beanbag chair in front of the TV. Rom was on his lap, curled up as if he'd been born there. "I called my mother this afternoon after we got back from the hospital to ask her what she thought. She said one of my nieces went through a real rough time last summer after Grandpa died. They'd been close. She wouldn't eat, had bad dreams and even stopped talking for a while."

Jake had been reading online about children's reaction to great loss and knew things could be a lot worse than what they were experiencing with Caleb. "What did your family do?"

"Took her to see a therapist."

"Really? How old is she?"

"Ten."

Jake studied his godson from a distance. He was pale and wan but he deserved to be, didn't he? "Well, I think he's doing pretty well considering."

Allison's bottom lip disappeared. "Maybe."

"You disagree?"

"I don't know, but I am worried. He's so little. And he's never been a picky eater."

Jake frowned. That was true. "How about we give him until after the funeral? If nothing changes, then we try to find someone who specializes in helping young children."

Allison looked as though she wanted to say something but instead she shrugged and finished putting the dishes in the dishwasher. After she pushed the button to start the wash cycle, she straightened and let out a sigh. "I suppose there's no more putting it off."

He didn't know what she meant.

"Picking out clothes."

Jake still missed the meaning for a couple of heartbeats. Then it hit him. She'd asked him earlier in the day to go through Kenny's closet and select something for him to wear. In the casket. Something that would molder and rot in the ground for all of eternity.

She must have seen him shudder because she drew back defensively. "It was on our checklist from the mortuary."

"The caskets will be closed," he said. "What does it matter what they're wearing?"

"I don't know. Maybe it doesn't apply to us. I..." She spun on one heel and left the room.

Jake drove his right fist into the palm of his left hand. He felt like a jerk. He hadn't meant to upset Allison. But the underlying truth was Kenny's and Pam's deaths brought back memories he'd worked twenty years to keep out of his mind.

The phone rang. Jake looked at his godson expecting to hear him cry, "I'll get it."

The little boy's head never moved. His attention remained glued to the screen and the Muppet show Allison had let him watch after dinner.

Jake finished wiping down the counter then poured himself a second glass of wine. Allison walked into the room, carrying the cordless phone. "It's Gayle," she said, holding the phone to her chest. She still wore jeans and a sweater, but this sweater was a velvety shade of sage. "She's offered to let Caleb stay with Bradley during the funeral. Apparently her mother will be baby-sitting, and Caleb knows her."

Jake took a large swallow of burgundy liquid but it lodged sideways in his throat and nearly strangled him. He'd known this issue was coming. He'd fully expected someone to suggest that Caleb was too young to attend the service, but he was determined to argue the opposite. He knew from experience that being excluded from something as important as this could produce a very unwelcome backlash. Twenty-odd years ago his brother died and their father decided that Jake was "too young" to participate in Phillip's burial.

"Funerals aren't for children," Rod Westin had decreed.

Jake, who had been living in a group home for boys at the time, had been furious. In retaliation, he'd set fire to some papers and if it hadn't been for a compassionate juvenile court judge, he might have been locked up for years. Instead, he'd managed to earn his high school equivalency certificate and enroll in community college.

But Jake had been fourteen when Phillip died, not four. What would Caleb remember of this time? What impact would this decision have on the little boy in later life? Questions without answers, but he did have an opinion.

"I think he should go to the funeral," Jake stated, bracing for her argument.

Allison flashed a quick smile and mouthed the words, *Me, too.*

Into the receiver, she said, "Thank your mother for

offering, Gayle, but Jake and I both think Caleb would benefit from the kind of closure that comes from participating in the whole grieving process. We're going to take him with us."

Jake tried to hide his shock by taking another sip of wine. As he watched, she said goodbye, set the phone on the counter and then turned to face him. "Why do you really think he should go with us?"

It wasn't the question he was expecting. Jake closed his eyes and let out a sigh. "I was excluded from my brother's funeral because my father thought I was too young. I'm still ticked off about it."

"I'm sorry. That must have been rough. How old were you?"

"Fourteen. Phillip was ten."

Her expressive face crumpled. Jake didn't want to cause her any more pain, so he quickly added, "It was a long time ago. My point is that what we decide could impact Caleb for years to come. He's a smart kid. Maybe we should let him decide. If he doesn't want to go, I'll stay home with him."

She smiled suddenly, and Jake's bluster left him. There were times when she glowed, and he had no business in the world noticing such things.

"Wow," she said with a little wink. "That's the best cop-out yet. Wish I'd thought of it."

Her grin told him she was teasing. And oddly, he didn't feel quite as depressed as he had a few minutes earlier.

ALLISON STOOPED to pick up Cleo, who lingered beside Caleb's door but had yet to venture inside the little boy's bedroom. Rom had no such reservations. He'd attached himself to the child in a complete reversal of attitude from the first time she introduced her cats to her godson. Ally didn't know why the change of heart, but she was grateful for it.

"Why are you still so standoffish?" she asked, nuzzling the large cat's tattered right ear. Cleo and Rom were both foundlings—abandoned pets who'd adopted her.

Allison continued to pet the cat a moment before heading to her room, but the sound of voices caught her attention. She stepped closer to the doorway and saw Jake sitting on the edge of the race-car bed—one hand brushing back Caleb's errant cowlick.

"Jake, is Gramma gonna die?" the little boy asked.

Allison's heart stopped.

"No, Caleb. You saw her today. She looked good, didn't she?"

Caleb made a face.

"Well, maybe not as good as you're used to seeing her, but she's been sick. Her heart had a problem and the doctors fixed it."

"How come the doctors couldn't fix Mommy's heart?"

Allison squeezed Cleo a bit too hard and got a warning bite on the hand. She put the animal down and grabbed the wooden frame of the door instead. She could tell that Jake was searching for the right answer. "I don't know, kiddo. I'm sure they tried."

Caleb gnawed on his cuticle—a new habit that alternated with thumb-sucking. "Bradley said people die in the hosp'tal."

Jake frowned. "Well, I was at a baseball game last summer and a man who was sitting a few rows over from me had a real bad asthma attack. That means he couldn't breathe. The paramedics came—just like they did when your grandmother needed help. They took him to the hospital and I saw him back in his seat a few games later. Hospitals and doctors fix a lot of people."

Caleb took a moment to consider the idea, and then nodded.

"Jake, why did Daddy die?"

Allison's stomach clenched. When her grandfather passed away last summer, people shook her hand and said, "It was his time." "He's in a better place." "He won't suffer any more." The platitudes seemed appropriate, but none of those applied to Kenny.

"I don't know, buddy. I wish I did. As far as I'm concerned, there isn't one good reason why they're gone. But no matter how much we want it to be different, we can't change what happened. Do you understand?"

Caleb nodded again.

But Allison knew he didn't. How could a child make sense of something that even adults found unfathomable? She suddenly understood why people spouted platitudes at times like this. A little comfort was better than nothing.

CHAPTER SEVEN

"THIS WAS A GOOD IDEA," Jake said, joining Allison on the park bench facing the public playground. A six-foot tall, impossibly bright orange plastic fish provided a climbing obstacle to the second level of the jungle gym from which Caleb sped down a spiral slide with a loud "Whee."

They'd left the cemetery a few minutes earlier, Allison behind the wheel. To his surprise, she'd cut across traffic to the opposite side of the highway and parked in an unpaved lot adjacent to the county library. "How 'bout we stop at the park for a while, Caleb?" she'd asked the little boy who had a somewhat dazed look on his face.

Her suggestion had earned a half smile, and by the time they'd crossed the wooden footbridge to the park, an open grassy area with an impressive view of the surrounding mountains, he'd perked up considerably.

"It never would have occurred to me to stop and let Caleb race off some of that pent-up energy," Jake said, hunching forward. His suit coat wasn't the best protection for the wind that seemed to come straight off the white capped peaks he could see in the distance. "I'm glad you suggested it."

"He was getting pretty antsy by the end of the service," she said, her tone flat. "And then the inter-ment…" Her voice disappeared, and Jake understood completely.

Two graves. Side by side. The earth hard and cold. Six or more tripods supported huge sprays of flowers—unnaturally bright against the winter landscape. The cemetery, located on a knoll in the heart of the community, was dotted with stately pines, but the many oaks and other deciduous trees were stark, leafless silhouettes against a pewter sky. As the minister voiced the last goodbyes, traffic sounds—horns honking, engines revving—provided a dose of reality. Life did go on.

Jake looked at Allison sitting beside him on the plastic-coated metal mesh bench. Her hands were pushed deep in the pockets of her black wool coat. A multi-colored knitted scarf looped around her neck and provided enough of a cowl that she could shelter her nose but still keep an eye on Caleb.

"I'm so glad that's over," he admitted. "I wasn't sure I'd get through it." He kept his voice low.

She nodded but didn't look at him. "By the time we got to the cemetery, I was too numb to think. The music and that video did me in," she said, giving him a sideways, thanks-for-nothing frown.

Jake settled one ankle on his knee. A gust of dampish air shot past his sock and made him shiver. "Hey, that wasn't my idea," he said, sounding far more defensive than was necessary. "The guys from the band handed me the DVD. I just gave it to the music director."

Although Kenny's band had broken up shortly after he'd left the group, two former members of Criminally

Insane had remained in touch with Kenny and Pam over the years. Both had arrived early that morning from southern California and had presented Jake with a video collage set to a few of the group's mellower songs.

"They must have worked day and night to get it done in time," Allison said, sounding less put out. "I know Caleb will treasure it someday."

The images had shown a much younger, more devil-may-care side of their friends. Jake had lived through those wild years with Kenny, and he'd known Pam, too, after she'd impulsively dropped out of college to travel with Kenny. Her parents had been against the relationship from day one, but that hadn't kept the two young lovers apart.

"I just wish someone had warned me," Allison said with a sigh. "I think my crying upset Caleb."

Jake looked at the little boy in question. He was about ten yards away scaling a wall embedded with projecting footholds. "Caleb," Allison called, sitting forward. "Are you sure you should be climbing that?" To Jake she said, "It looks dangerous and he doesn't have his sneakers on."

As Jake watched, the boy scrambled hand-over-hand up the five-foot tall challenge like a veteran rock climber. "Way to go, Caleb," he called, applauding.

Allison let out the breath she'd been holding. Her concern was touching, but Jake worried that her fears might be limiting to his godson in the long run. He kept his opinion to himself. Just as he hadn't said anything when Kenny had fretted that Pam was too lax with Caleb.

Caleb slid down the slide again—headfirst this time,

winding up on his belly in the tan-colored sand. Allison groaned softly. "His suit."

Jake shrugged. "He's almost outgrown it. Might as well let him play."

Caleb started running in his choppy, stiff-legged gait, toward a four-seated teeter-totter on springs. The molded yellow seats and handholds resembled a headless duck. "Watch me, Jake," Caleb cried, kicking up sand as he ran.

Two other youngsters—boys, one a couple of years older than Caleb and the second a bit younger, were already seated opposite each other. The pair wore sweats, athletic shoes and down coats that looked far cozier than what Caleb was wearing.

"Do you think he's warm enough?" Allison asked. "Maybe this wasn't such a great idea. I should have brought play clothes."

Jake let out an exasperated breath. "Will you quit second-guessing yourself? He's hopping around like a cricket on speed. He's warm. We're cold because we're sitting still."

She didn't say anything, but she didn't take her eyes off her godson as he interacted with the other children. The two children continued bouncing on the contraption as Caleb boldly climbed aboard and started rocking back and forth with a frenzied zeal.

Allison let out a long, heartfelt sigh and sank back against the metal bench. "I feel like Wile E. Coyote when he chases Road Runner off a cliff and finds himself standing in midair, waiting to fall," she said. "Are we going to hit bottom soon?"

Jake gave his head a little shake. She had a habit of putting his feelings into words. It bothered him.

"I lost track of how many people came up to me today and said, 'Now the healing can begin.' How do they know this?" she asked, her tone bitter. "Because I'm sure not feeling it."

Jake had heard the same rhetoric when Phillip died. "He's in a better place," people would say. Screw that, Jake remembered thinking, if I have to stick around this lousy world, then Phillip sure the hell should, too.

She turned her chin to look at him. "Is it me or has Caleb gotten progressively more belligerent all week?"

"Gayle says it's natural for a child his age to act out," Jake said.

"*Acting out.* I've heard that expression a dozen times—first from my mother and sisters, and then from the articles I've read online. But what does it mean, exactly? Should we send him to preschool on Monday or not? What if he whacks another kid with a toy?"

She shifted sideways to face him. Her eyes were reddened from crying, her nose and cheeks pink from the cold, hair tousled about her forehead and ears. Despite nearly a week of contact, Jake couldn't remember sitting this close to her before. But it felt natural, somehow.

"I hope this doesn't make me sound as if I'm overreacting," she said in a hushed tone, "but I think we should take Caleb to see a grief therapist before we send him back to school."

Her near-whisper had brought him closer, but her opinion wasn't anything he wanted to think about. The counselors from his youth had been overworked and impotent when it came to helping him or his brother. "I don't agree. I think he's doing pretty well."

She swallowed. "I promised him I wouldn't tell you,

but…he…wet the bed last night." She checked to make sure the subject of their conversation was out of range. "He's very embarrassed. And I don't think he needs another source of stress at the moment."

Jake wondered if talking to a counselor after his brother's death would have disarmed some of the animosity he felt toward his father. Before he could speak, Caleb called out, "Jake, push me on the swing."

Jake stood and extended a hand to Allison. Her fingers were like Popsicles. Without thinking, he briskly chafed them between his palms. "You're not dressed for this. We should go."

She stood still as a statue watching him warm her hands. Suddenly, she stepped back. "No. You go play with him. I'll wait in the car with the heater on. Caleb shouldn't miss out because I'm wearing a dress."

She turned on one heel and walked unsteadily across the grassy strip leading to the bridge. From the back, she looked less like a mourner than an elegantly dressed woman ready for a dinner date. Her calves and ankles could have belonged to a model. *I wonder what she'd look like in a bikini,* Jake thought before he could stop himself.

The totally inappropriate line of thinking shook Jake. He was known for his ability to stay focused. Relationships were pleasant interludes he allowed in his life when time permitted. This was not the time.

He jogged the last few feet to where his godson was standing. "Push me," Caleb demanded, pointing to a swing, which by that time was occupied. Another group of children of varying ages had arrived with their parents.

"There's an empty one over here," Jake said, placing his hand on the top of Caleb's head.

Caleb crossed his arms at his chest and shook his head. "No," he said stubbornly. "Those are baby swings. I'm not a baby."

Jake lowered his hand to the boy's shoulder when Caleb started to walk toward the swing, obviously intending to knock the other child off. Jake tightened his grip a bit, and to his complete shock, Caleb twisted just enough to lean down and bite his hand. Hard.

"Ouch. Son of a…gun." Jake caught the curse in time. "You bit me."

The other child slipped off the swing and ran toward the orange fish jungle gym. Caleb ignored Jake and climbed up on the plastic plank. "Push. Push," he demanded.

Jake stared at the imprint of small, sharp teeth on his skin. No blood, but the mark made it clear this was no accident. Taking a deep breath, he walked to the front of the swing to face Caleb. He grabbed the ice-cold links of chain and lowered himself to one knee.

Eyes level with his godson, Jake said, "Caleb, you bit me. That was wrong. We don't bite people."

The belligerent look in Caleb's eyes dissolved into tears. His bottom lip popped out, and he started to cry so hard he nearly toppled off the swing.

Jake swept him into his arms and rose. "It's okay, buddy. I'm not mad, but I want you to promise you won't do that again. My skin is tough, but if you chomp down on someone else, like Allison or Bradley, you'll hurt them. A person doesn't go around biting people just to get their way."

"But…but…" Whatever he wanted to say was lost in brokenhearted sobs and Jake knew it was time to go home.

As soon as he turned toward the car, Caleb let out a loud wail and tried to throw himself from Jake's arms. "Swing. Swing. You p…p…promised."

Jake tightened his hold and walked faster. He could feel the other parents looking his way. "We'll come back tomorrow if the weather is clear. It's been a long day and we're all tired. And we have to check on the cats to see if they're okay. We've been gone a long time."

ALLISON WAITED IN THE CAR, the heater on full blast. She was pretty sure she'd never been more exhausted in her life. Her shoulders ached. Her hips hurt from sitting in the church pew. Her toes throbbed from the shiny black shoes that she'd never really liked.

Each was minor compared to the pain in her chest. It had started the moment she'd walked into the church and seen the two caskets bedecked with flowers. It had increased when the minister, an elegant woman with long silver hair and a warm smile, had spoken of God's plan for Kenny and Pam. But the worst moment came when the lights dimmed and a screen lowered from the ceiling so the audience could watch a video of the young couple, so much in love you could almost touch the emotion.

She'd been helpless to prevent the wracking sobs that seemed to come from the bottom of her soul. Then Caleb, who'd been sitting between her and Jake, crawled up on her lap. The look of worry on his face had forced her to stifle her sobs, but the pain had stayed.

Resting her head against the seatback, she wondered how much of today Caleb would remember. So many glowing tributes were made about two people he would never really know. Maybe my goal should be to make sure Caleb never forgets the amazing people who gave him life, she thought.

She was considering how she would do this when she spotted Jake and Caleb walking toward the car.

Caleb looked upset. Jake, too. "What happened?" she asked. But Caleb simply hid his face against Jake's jacket.

"I'll tell you when we get home," Jake said softly.

"Oh, no," Allison said, a short while later as the car pulled into the cul-de-sac. Four other vehicle were parked in front of the Rydell home—Gayle's in the lead. "I thought you made it clear that we were in no condition to socialize."

"I guess she didn't catch my hint," Jake muttered as they parked in the garage beside Pam's car.

"Hint?" Allison asked. "I believe the exact phrase was 'Now is not a good time, Gayle.' I could have kissed you for that."

She'd spoken in jest, but the way he turned his chin sharply to look at her made Allison regret her quip. Quickly exiting the close space, she retrieved her purse and Caleb's tote bag from behind her seat. The boy was fast asleep. Dirty smudges from dried tears mixed with dust made his cheeks look bruised. His nose was crusty. "I hate to wake him up, but he needs a bath."

"I'll take care of it," Jake said opening the passenger door. "He and I can use the time to talk about inappropriate behavior," he said cryptically. Before unsnapping the safety harness, he looked at her and said, "I've changed my mind. I think we should make an appointment with a counselor, but I'd appreciate it if you didn't mention this to the neighbors."

Allison shut the door with more force than needed. "You don't need to tell me that. Caleb's problems are a family matter."

He picked up the boy, who drooped like a rolled-up rug across his shoulder, then closed his door soundly, too. Allison's brief burst of temper faded as quickly as it materialized, leaving her drained. She looked at Jake carrying Caleb's dead weight as if it were nothing and knew without a doubt she couldn't manage to care for the little boy alone. Thank God Jake had agreed to stick around until Cordelia was released from the hospital.

She passed Caleb's tote bag to Jake as he slipped into the hallway leading to the bedroom wing. Bracing herself, Allison followed the sound of women's voices. She found the five friends—each with a wineglass and a stack of unopened envelopes in front of them—grouped around the dining table. The overhead chandelier cast a falsely cheerful glow.

"Hi," she said, noticing the piles of discarded envelopes on the floor.

"Ally," Gayle cried. "We were starting to worry. Come join the Thank-You crew. There are plenty of cards to go around if you want to pull up a chair. Pam and Kenny were obviously well loved."

Allison had planned to tackle this chore over time, maybe after the holidays. "Are you making some kind of master list?" she asked, grateful for the help but at the same time irritated. Sometimes Gayle was just too perky. Apparently she wasn't the type to wallow in her grief as Allison wanted to do.

"Of course," Gayle said as she ripped open another envelope. A slim piece of paper fell to the table. "My sisters and I did this for Marc's mother last year after his father died. Addressing thank-you notes can be an arduous, time-consuming chore, and I know you have to get back to your job."

True, Allison thought, suddenly sorry she'd reacted so negatively to the offer of help. "This is very nice of you. I appreciate it, but I'm emotionally spent. I don't think I could stand to look at those right now."

"Understood," Gayle said. "That's why we're here. I know Jake was concerned about the timing, but with this many hands, it's going fast. Right, girls?" Her friends nodded, several sniffling. "We have a system. Cash donations in one column, cards-only in another."

She extended a flowery card toward Allison. "Look at this one. A hundred dollars to the volunteer fire department's emergency fund."

Just the glint off the shiny card brought tears to Allison's eyes. "Nice," she said, turning away. "I need to change then I'll come back and help."

"No problem," Gayle said. "By the way, I put the cats in your room. Jen's allergic."

Allison didn't know which of the women was named Jen, so she gave a wave to encompass them all then stumbled down the hall. Tears of relief filled her eyes when she dropped fully clothed on the bed. Her cats pounced in greeting.

"Hi, kids," she said. "I missed you. How was your day? Mine was pretty horrible. Okay, really, really horrible." And it's not done, a small voice reminded her.

After dutifully petting and praising her feline friends, she heaved a sigh and rolled to her side. She sat up and loosened the top buttons on her dress. Probably terribly outdated style-wise, the belted shirtwaist was black with long sleeves—the only criteria she'd felt was truly important. But the length was a little short and the fabric too clingy.

She'd just kicked off her pumps and removed her panty hose when a knock sounded.

"Come in."

Jake popped his head around the door. "I need your help. Right away."

Panic made her toss the suntan colored, nude-toe nylons on the floor and dash to Caleb's room. The NASCAR night-light was burning and the covers were turned back, but Caleb wasn't in bed.

"Where are you?" she called, her bare toes gripping the plush carpet.

"In here," a muted voice answered.

Like the other bedrooms of the Rydell house, Caleb's had a walk-in closet. Not as large as the one in his parents' suite, but bigger than the bathroom in Allison's house. She peeked inside.

Caleb lay curled in a fetal position on the floor, facing the wall. He was dressed in the top of his two-piece flannel pajamas and a pair of Spider-Man underpants. The outfit's bottom half was draped across Jake's knees.

Jake was sitting perpendicular to Caleb, his back against the wall, legs splayed in defeat. "I give up," he said, passing her the size-four bottoms like a white flag of surrender.

"What should I do?"

He shrugged. "I don't know. He freaks out whenever I touch him."

"What happened?"

"Beats me. I thought a shower in the master bedroom would be faster than a tub bath. He was in the bathroom dressing when he suddenly went ballistic and tore past me. By the time I caught up with him he was hiding in here. He won't let me finish dressing him and he refuses to go to bed."

Jake closed his eyes and ran his hand over his face. He looked as tired as Allison felt. Reaching deep into her reserves, she dropped to her knees and moved on all fours toward her godson. Progress was slow given the hem of her dress, which she kept kneeling on, but when she was close enough to peer over Caleb's shoulder, she saw that he was curled around something. At first, she thought it was a stuffed animal. Then, she recognized the bright orange object—Pam's sweater.

Rocking back, she closed her eyes and drew a deep breath to quell the rush of emotions that threatened to swamp her. "What is it?" a soft voice asked by her ear. He'd moved to his knees beside her.

Jake's presence helped Allison find the control she needed. Turning her chin slightly, she whispered, "The sweater Pam wore on Thanksgiving. Was it in the bathroom?"

"Maybe. There were some clothes beside the hamper. I figured we'd get around to the wash this weekend."

"The fabric probably still has her smell." Her voice broke with the last word. A comforting hand touched the small of her back.

Steadying herself, Allison inched closer until she could see Caleb's face. His eyes were open but his gaze seemed fixed, like a person in a comatose state. "Hello, sweetie," she said. "I see you found your mommy's sweater. It was one of her favorites. I bet she left it right where you could find it so you'd be able to hold it any time you wanted."

He didn't give any indication that he heard her.

"You probably don't remember this, but when you were a little baby, you had a favorite blanket that you had to have with you before you could go to sleep at night. If your mommy and daddy forgot your blankie some place or left it home, you'd cry and cry until they brought it to you."

His eyes blinked.

"Your mother said that was because you were a touching kind of person. She called you her cuddle bug. I bet she'd really like it if you took that sweater to bed with you."

He turned his head enough to look at her. The questioning look in his eyes made her nod. "Why not? Other kids sleep with stuffed animals. I used to sleep with a bear named Toby. I bet even Jake had a favorite toy that sometimes found its way into his bed."

Allison could tell the child was drained, physically and emotionally. Repositioning herself for better leverage, she carefully inched her hands under his body and lifted. She held her breath to see if he'd protest, but all he did was curl against her, as he would have in his mother's arms.

Her heart melted and she might have started crying again if not for the strong, helping hands at her elbows. Jake provided the muscle power to get them standing then guided her to the bright red bed.

She leaned over and eased the child down. Caleb's grip on the orange chenille mock turtleneck never lessened—even when his eyes closed and his breathing turned to a sweet, rhythmic flow.

Allison's knees buckled, but Jake was there to catch her. He pulled her back against him, and wrapped his arms around her middle. There wasn't anything romantic about the pose. Well, there might have been had the circumstances been different. But, this was the comfort of one friend to another after a brutal day.

"A rabbit," he whispered in her ear. "Patchwork. My mother made it when she was young and functioning."

There was a bittersweet quality to his voice that made her wish things were different between them. But they weren't.

"A-hem." A pointed cough came from the doorway.

Allison's stomach fell to her toes. She would have jumped away if Jake hadn't tightened his hold—just for a second, then let her escape. She spun to find Gayle looking at them. Was that a gleam of speculation in her eyes or compassion?

Before Allison could say anything, Jake put his finger to his lips and whispered, "The poor kid is finally asleep, and neither Allison nor I are doing much better. I don't want to be rude, but…"

Allison nudged him aside. "I'm feeling okay now that I've taken off my panty hose." Forcing a smile, she said, "You can crash if you want. I saw those piles of cards and I don't want to do anything to discourage our helpers."

His momentary look of bafflement was replaced by one of pure fatigue. "Okay, then. I'm going to bed."

Allison and Gayle walked together as far as the guest room. "I'll be right there, Gayle. I think sweats are in order."

She slipped inside before Gayle could reply and leaned against the door, her heart pounding. Ridiculous as it sounded, Allison felt as giddy as she had the first time a boy kissed her. "Cats," she said, quickly changing her clothes. "Your owner is crazy."

Cleo lay curled up on the bed. Her tail flicked in greeting. Rom was nowhere to be seen. He could be hiding, Allison thought. Or, he might have escaped while she'd been busy with Caleb.

Oh, well, she thought, leaving the door ajar in case he came back.

She stiffened her shoulders and went to join the others. *I can do this,* she repeated over and over like a mantra. *For Pam.*

And she did. Two hours later, the last stamp had been applied to the last envelope. The women had gone through two bottles of chardonnay and who knew how many packets of postage stamps? Jen, a substitute letter carrier, took the pile of completed thank-you notes and promised to mail them in the morning. A precise list had been compiled of every gift and donation. A stack of checks and a thick wad of cash were in the manila envelope in Allison's hand.

"Call me if you need any help tomorrow." Gayle picked up her oversized purse. She was the last to leave. After checking her cell phone for messages, she said, "You know, Ally, I think what you and Jake are doing is incredibly selfless. You've virtually put your lives on hold to help a child who isn't even yours."

Suddenly, Allison felt an urge to hit something. Or someone. She spun toward Gayle and said, "Actually, he *is* ours now. Does that mean I wouldn't sell my soul to have things back the way they were? No. But that's not an option. This is how it is. And Jake and I are going to do what is best for Caleb."

Gayle looked momentarily surprised by Allison's outburst, then she smiled and gave her a hug. "My point exactly. You're both amazing. Now, if you'll excuse me, it's been a day from hell and I'm ready to crash. But I'll be right next door if you need me. 'Bye." She picked up her coat and disappeared before Allison could apologize for overreacting.

Emotionally drained, Allison grabbed the finished edge of the marble countertop and leaned forward until her cheek was pressed flat against the cool, smooth surface. The solid permanence of the rock comforted her. Pam had handpicked every element of her kitchen, including this unique piece. Allison closed her eyes. She could almost imagine her friend standing beside her, stroking her exposed cheek.

"Hungry?"

It took Allison a few seconds to realize that the voice—a masculine one— didn't fit in the picture. She lifted her head. Jake stood in the doorway, hands braced against each jamb.

"What?"

"I fell asleep but woke up starved. I don't think I ate more than two bites at the reception. How 'bout you?"

"What are you having?"

"Scrambled eggs."

Her stomach answered for her. "Okay. I might be able to muster enough energy to chew, but I know I don't have the strength to cook."

His sinfully appealing grin was unlike any Allison had seen before—a mix of devil and angel. "Sit down and watch a master at work."

Allison's brain had reached the point where following orders was all she could do. She drew up a stool and sat down, finally releasing her grip on the envelope.

"How much money was donated?"

Ally heard his question, but the smell of butter in the

frying pan made her mouth water and she couldn't answer. He cracked two eggs into the skillet then walked to where she was sitting and put his face directly in line with hers. "How much money?" he asked, emphasizing each word.

"I can't remember exactly. But it was quite a lot."

He returned to his cooking and moments later placed a plate with a mound of dry scrambled eggs—just the way she liked them—in front of her, along with a piece of toast in front. Allison raised her head. She'd practically fallen asleep with her cheek resting on her hand. "Thank you."

He cocked his head. "Now, eat. You can sleep later. I promise."

She silently repeated the directions in her head. "Ummm," she mumbled between bites. "Tasty."

He pulled a stool around from the counter area so he could face her, then he started eating, too. "If you think my eggs are good, wait till you try my beef stroganoff."

There was definite humor in his voice. Allison decided she liked the sound of his voice—almost as much as she liked his touch. He had kind hands. Useful for picking up small children and holding on to when your heart was breaking.

Her eyes filled with tears and her throat closed tight. The bite of toast in her mouth turned to sawdust, and she couldn't chew any more. She spit the half masticated morsel into her napkin and slipped from the stool. "Bed. Gotta go now."

Jake must have sensed her meltdown. He was at her side before she could take a step. When she tried to protest, he linked his arm through hers. "I'll clean up this mess in a minute. I want to talk to you and you're obviously ready to pass out, so at least let me walk you to your door."

She didn't have the energy to argue. Besides, she liked the feel of his strong upper arm brushing against hers. "Talk about what?"

"First thing tomorrow, I want to call a therapist."

"What changed your mind?"

"You mean besides the teeth marks on my hand? I decided I shouldn't let my experience influence what we do. Caleb isn't me."

Allison found this admission intriguing but she was too tired to ask for details. "Okay. I met a minister at the hospital the night Cordelia was admitted. He told me he works with kids. He and Caleb seemed to hit it off. His card is around here somewhere. Maybe in my jacket pocket."

They'd arrived at her bedroom. "Fine. Tomorrow. It's late now. You need to sleep."

He opened the door, but Allison balked. "Gotta check on Caleb."

"I will before I go to bed."

That wasn't the same. She brushed past him and walked to Caleb's room. In the muted light, she saw the race-car bed, a child's body hugging a bulky orange sweater, and Rom curled up near his feet like a panther on guard.

"That's one cool cat," Jake said from over her shoulder.

Allison sagged against the door. Jake's broad hands gripped her shoulders and turned her around. "Go to bed, Allison. Before I carry you."

Picturing herself in Jake's arms was an image Allison found way too tempting. Sleep, she thought. Sleep would provide the antidote for this crazy attraction. She hoped.

CHAPTER EIGHT

THE FOLLOWING MORNING, Allison awoke feeling so rested and refreshed she momentarily forgot where she was—and why. Her bedroom door, which she'd left open in case Rom got tired of watching over Caleb, was closed. Neither cat was in sight.

She sprang out of bed and quickly showered and dressed. Her watch read ten o'clock when she finally hurried into the kitchen. The low drone of the television pulled her to the family room, after she filled a big mug with strong, black, butterscotch-scented coffee.

"I must have overslept," she announced.

Jake and Caleb were sitting side-by-side on the sofa, each holding a cat. The scene was so charming Allison felt a fresh wave of tears start to build. Quickly turning around, she went in search of food. Something sweet, she decided.

"Banana bread," she murmured, spotting an aluminum foil-wrapped loaf that she remembered seeing a gray-haired woman—the neighbor across the street — drop off. She retrieved the tub of whipped butter from the refrigerator and was about to carve her first piece when Jake joined her. He refilled a cup from the carafe and sat down.

"How'd you sleep?" he asked. "You looked so peaceful, Caleb and I decided not to wake you."

"I appreciate that, but I do have a bunch of calls to make today. Business-wise," she added. "I haven't been in my office for a week. Has it only been seven days?" she mused, slathering butter across the moist brown treat. "What about you? What are your plans?"

"Well…" he dragged out the word as if reluctant to tell her. "I didn't realize you had a separate agenda. I called the counselor you suggested last night. His card was by the computer. Father Raymund Avila. Priest *and* therapist, apparently. He said he could see us at one, so I snapped up the appointment."

Allison couldn't argue with that—it had been her idea. "That will work. It's three hours away. No problem."

"And I promised Caleb we'd go to a matinee afterward."

"Promised or bribed?"

"Is there a difference with a four-year-old?"

"Good point. I'll probably pass on the movie, but you can drop me off at my office then pick me up afterward, if that works. Or we can take two cars into town, and I'll meet you at his office."

She took a bite of banana bread, closing her eyes to savor the delicate blend of cinnamon and clove. "Oh, yum," she said, chewing. "Whoever made this is a culinary goddess in my book."

When she opened her eyes, she caught Jake looking at her. An element of chemistry sparked between them. Undeniable, but not unavoidable, Allison decided. She buttered a second slice and turned away. "I'd better make those calls. We have to factor in travel time to Fresno."

She paused at the doorway and looked back. "Would

you do me a favor? Call Gayle and ask if she could return all of those bake dishes and plastic containers by the back door. I have no idea where the owners live, and she did volunteer to help."

"No problem," he said his tone slightly sardonic. Allison knew that asking for help wasn't something any man relished, but Jake was a good sport. So far, he'd been conscientious, supportive and generous to a fault. She was still trying to figure out a way to pay him back for her share of the flowers.

Money. She came back into the kitchen. Jake was still sitting where she'd left him, staring into his mug. He lifted his head to look at her. A lock of sun-kissed blond hair dipped over one eye in a puppy-dog fashion. Her heart did a pirouette. *No. I won't fall for him. I refuse.*

In as businesslike tone as possible, she said, "We need to discuss the donations. If I remember correctly, the checks and cash totaled nearly two thousand. Some were earmarked for the volunteer fire department and quite a few to the food bank, but what do we do with the rest?"

He perked up. "Invest it for Caleb? I've already set up a college account, but if we add some slow-growth mutual funds to the portfolio, it could easily pay for the college of his choice. What do you think?"

"Perfect," she said, then added without thinking, "where were you when I was investing in the stock market?"

He rose and walked toward her. "Did you lose money?"

Allison regretted the slip. "I'm embarrassed to admit this, but when I was married, my ex-husband handled our finances. When we divorced, Dean made sure I got my fair share of our stocks, but to be honest, I haven't looked at them in ages. I have no idea where I stand."

"Would you like me to check them out for you? If things are tight for your business right now, you might be able to unload some slow movers and use the money to tide you over."

"Really? I had this on my to-do list, but there's never enough time. Plus, I didn't know who I could trust to steer me right."

"You can trust me."

"I know that." Suddenly feeling as if she'd shared too much, she pivoted. "I think the folder is on my laptop. I'll e-mail it to you. But if you find out they're all bogus junk bonds or something, don't tell me."

He gave her a cheeky grin. "Turning a sow's ear into a silk purse is my specialty."

Kind and generous, Allison thought, as she walked to her room. Damn. How was a person supposed to maintain a safe distance from that?

After sending her financial files to Jake, she checked her e-mail. Page after page of messages filled the screen.

"Good grief," Allison muttered. Most were from her employees. Jeffries Computing was still afloat, but the ship was taking on water. Fast.

She was about halfway through the list when she sensed a presence in the room with her. When she looked over her shoulder, she spotted Caleb standing by her bed, petting Cleo, who'd finally started to warm to the child. "Good morning, sweetie. How are you today?"

He shrugged but didn't speak. Allison motioned him closer. "I could sure use a hug to get my day started."

His little arms went around her neck and he squeezed tight then let go, but he didn't back away. She sensed that he wanted something. "I'm not playing a game or anything fun right now, hon. Just boring old work. Maybe Jake has a game you could play on his computer."

Caleb shook his head. "I wanna send an e-mail."

Allison's hands hovered above the keyboard. "You do?"

He nodded vigorously.

They teach keyboarding in preschool? Man, I really don't know anything about this parenting business. "Well, okay. Do you know how to type?"

He shook his head negatively. "You have to do that for me."

"Oh," she said, getting the picture. "You want me to send an e-mail for you. To whom?"

"Mommy."

Allison's heart stopped. "I…you…what?"

He looked at her with complete trust. "Sometimes when Mommy and Daddy go away, Grandma and me send them e-mails. And Mommy writes back. And sends pictures."

Allison tried to work up enough spit in her dry mouth to respond. She had no idea what to say. Should she try explaining that as far she knew there was no e-mail in heaven? Or should she listen to the voice that cried, "What can it hurt? Let him get what's troubling him off his chest."

She made space for him on her lap. After a little wiggling, they managed to find a comfortable position. Allison looped her arms around him to reach the keyboard. She selected the New Message page and said, "What do you want to tell them?"

He cleared his throat. "Dear Mommy and Daddy…" He paused to let her type. "I miss you. Come home soon." Allison's fingers were shaking but she somehow touched the right keys.

She was about to remind him of the finality of death when he went on. "Jake is here. I bit him yesterday, but he forgave me." This came out muffled.

"You did?" she asked, leaning to one side to look at him.

He nodded, his bottom lip quivering. "At the park. I wanted to swing. He said maybe we could swing today. Can we, Ally?"

Shifting into the crook of her left arm, he looked at her, but Allison ducked the other way. She didn't want him to see her tears. "A movie and swinging in the park?" she tried to make her tone skeptical. "I don't know…maybe we could for a person who doesn't bite."

"I don't. It was an accident."

"So you're not going to bite people anymore?"

He shook his head.

"Then, I guess it would be all right. Weather permitting."

He let out a whoop of joy and slipped off her lap—his letter apparently forgotten. "I gotta tell Jake you wanna come, too." He was two steps out of the room before he turned around and said, "I'll finish my letter to Mommy later, okay?"

Allison nodded, but he'd already disappeared. She stared at the screen. *Dear Mommy and Daddy…* "Oh, Pam," Allison softly cried. "Why me? What if I screw up?"

The cursor kept blinking. No answer appeared on the screen. With a sigh, she closed the letter and went back to answering her e-mails. The living demanded her attention.

"WELCOME TO MY HUMBLE ABODE," said the sixty-something man in a black jogging suit and well-worn running shoes. His thick silver hair was worn in a stylish cut that made him look younger than his years. "Forgive my attire, but I help on the playground at lunch and those kids play rough."

Jake had noticed a sign in front of the nondenominational church that mentioned a Christian school.

"Jake, nice to meet you," he said, shaking Jake's hand heartily before bending over to give Caleb a friendly wink. "Good to see you again, Caleb. Do you remember me? My name is Father Avila, but, like I told you at the hospital, the kids all call me Padre."

Caleb nodded a greeting, but refused to release the death grip he had on Jake's finger.

Father Avila smiled and lightly touched the boy's shoulder before turning to Allison. He took both of her hands in his. "A pleasure to see you again, Allison. I've been praying for you. I'm happy to know that you made it through this traumatic time. And Caleb's grandmother? How is she?"

"A little under the weather at the moment." Allison filled him in on Cordelia's post-surgical infection as they walked down a narrow hall to a brightly lit multipurpose room that smelled of spicy cooking. Jake missed out on what was being said because the scent immediately transported him to his childhood in the mostly Hispanic neighborhood on the outskirts of L.A.

"Have a seat," the priest said, gesturing toward a serving table around which six molded plastic chairs were grouped. "I thought this would be better than my office, which gives me claustrophobia anytime two or more people are in it." Before joining them, he asked, "Would anyone like coffee or a soft drink?"

Jake and Allison both shook their heads. When the man looked at Caleb, the little boy's thumb disappeared into his mouth.

"You know, Caleb," Father Avila said, "the church preschool is having story hour right through that door. Would you like to go?"

Caleb shook his head.

"No *problema*," the minister said, smiling broadly. "Sister Maria is probably going to sing 'Ten Little Monkeys.' I don't imagine you know that song, do you?"

Caleb's eyes widened. "Uh-huh."

"The one where you pretend to jump on the bed?" Father Avila asked with mock surprise. "Really? Can you jump? Let me see."

Caleb let go of Jake's hand and demonstrated his jumping ability.

"*Ay caramba*, you're good. You're probably the best jumper I've seen all day. Are you sure you don't want to check out Sister's class? She'll bring you back here any time you ask her to, and I promise these good folks aren't going anywhere without you."

Caleb considered the offer, and after checking for reassurance from both Allison and Jake, nodded. Padre took his hand and led him toward the schoolroom door.

Jake raked his fingers through his hair. "Wow. Do you think he gives lessons?"

Allison let out a sigh. "I don't know, but I'd be the first to sign up."

Jake hated the way she constantly underrated her

mothering instincts. In the past week, he'd seen Caleb turn to her time and again for comfort or permission to do something. Before he could say anything, Father Avila returned.

"Please, sit. We won't have long. A child Caleb's age, who has been through a traumatic loss, needs constant reassurance that his world isn't going to continue to disintegrate."

Allison and Jake sat opposite each other, the priest at the head of the table. Father Avila spoke first. "So, let me guess. Caleb is acting out in atypical behavior. Hitting, biting, sleepwalking, night terrors, bed-wetting."

"He had a few bad dreams, and twice he wet bed. But last night—"

Jake interrupted Allison. "It happened again. We let you sleep in this morning, and Caleb seemed embarrassed so I decided not to mention it. But he did tell me that you said these things happen when people are really, really sad."

"Good explanation," Father Avila said. "Always try to keep things simple. Use terms he'll understand. We've all heard detailed insights on the grieving process, but none of those theories mean squat to a four-year-old. He just wants some assurance that whatever bad thing happened to change his wonderful, happy life and steal his mommy and daddy from him isn't going to happen again."

"And how do you suggest we do that?" Jake asked. "We all know life doesn't come with any guarantees."

Both Allison and Father Avila looked at him curiously. Apparently his tone had been more revealing than he'd intended.

"This morning, Caleb asked me to help him send his parents an e-mail," Allison said. To Jake, she added, "I didn't have a chance to mention it to you before we left and I didn't want to bring it up in the car."

"What did you do?"

"I helped him write the letter. Mostly, I think he wanted to get off his chest the fact that he bit you yesterday."

Padre said, "Biting, hitting and thumb-sucking are not uncommon responses in a child Caleb's age. Neither is wanting to call Mommy or go see Daddy at work. E-mail is a first for me, but most of the children I see aren't that familiar with technology."

"I felt like I was taking the easy road out by helping him type his message," Allison said. "I don't want to give him the impression they're vacationing in heaven and can't be bothered to come home."

Jake knew what she meant. "After my brother died, so many people told me that Phillip was in a better place, I was tempted to kill myself to go there, too," he said, surprised to find himself sharing the memory.

Allison looked at him, her eyes filled with compassion.

"Children this age have a difficult time comprehending the finality of death," the counselor said. "You might suggest he speak to his parents in his prayers at night. But be sure to stress that this is pretty much a one-way line of communication. His parents can hear him, but they can't speak to us the way we're used to hearing."

Allison nodded. "That's a good idea. Pam and Kenny weren't regular churchgoers, but Pam always made Caleb say his prayers at night. Jake and I haven't had a chance to establish much of a schedule, yet, but I'd like to include that in his nightly routine."

Her gaze met Jake's briefly, asking if he concurred. He wasn't sure, but he nodded all the same. She smiled sweetly then looked away when the minister continued speaking. "Fortunately, as with physical pain, the brain helps diffuse the sensation of loss as time goes on. Eventually, your presence will crowd out the memories Caleb has of his parents."

Allison's expression turned to one of alarm. Father Avila reached across the table to squeeze her hand. "I don't mean that he will forget them completely. I'm sure you and Jake will do everything you can to keep their memory alive for Caleb, but the harsh fact is life goes on for those left behind. Caleb is your child now."

She lowered her chin to her chest. Jake knew he had to say something. "Until Cordelia is back on her feet, you mean."

The minister gave a puzzled frown. "I'm sorry… what?"

Jake explained that theirs was a temporary arrangement. Once Cordelia was well, she'd take over. Jake would then return home.

"I see," the priest said. "Well, I'm sure the grandmother's intentions are sincere, but given a choice, don't you think Caleb would be better off with someone younger and in better health? After all, that's usually why parents choose contemporaries to be their child's godparents."

Allison looked at Jake. "We want to do what's best for Caleb," he said. "But we're both single. My home is on the other side of the continent. Allison has a demanding business. Neither of us has ever been a full-time parent. And Cordelia feels very strongly about raising Caleb herself as soon as she's able."

Father Avila leaned back in his chair. "Well, you obviously care a great deal about his future. Perhaps we should put the long term in God's hands and worry about getting Caleb through the holidays. You did say you planned to stay here until after the first of the year, right?"

Jake nodded.

"Good. I'd be happy to work with him if he continues to act out, or I can recommend a group session for children who have experienced traumatic losses. But, basically, keep doing what you're doing. Give him as much time as you possibly can.

"Your job, your routine, your life is going to be there when you get back to it. Caleb's future, on the other hand, hinges on how well he adapts to this unthinkable change. His future will reflect the care you give him now."

Allison looked miserable. "I feel guilty even bringing it up. Jake has relocated across an entire country and he isn't complaining, but…" She let the word drag out.

"But what?" Jake prompted. "Is it work? Your company?"

She nodded. "My employees are mostly young Hispanics who came to me through a job placement agreement with the state. Last year, the government subsidized my payroll so I could give them on-the-job training.

"It worked out great, but they're still relatively new to the field and inexperienced. After a week without me, they're stretched thin and my clients are getting testy. If I don't get back on the scene, there will be six families struggling to pay the rent, let alone celebrate Christmas."

Jake sat forward. "Year-end is a crummy time for me to be away, too. My assistant has been up to his eyeballs in calls."

"Neither of you should be penalized for doing good," Father Avila said. "A child isn't the only aspect of one's life that requires time and nurturing. Is there a possibility you could both work half days?"

Allison frowned in thought.

"I remember you telling me Caleb's mother—while ostensibly a stay-at-home mom—was actively involved in the community and her husband's business."

Allison smiled. "Especially at this time of year."

"So Caleb is used to having busy, hardworking parents. He'll adapt to your schedules just fine, as long you're consistent."

"Should we send him back to preschool?"

"Ask him. He'll let you know when he's ready."

Allison fiddled with her purse strap. "What about Christmas? Is there any way we can keep him from feeling the loss of his parents?"

The priest rocked back in his chair and let out a sigh. "No. But that's not necessarily a bad thing. Try to celebrate the holidays the way his parents would have. Same decorations. Same traditions. But don't expect it to be perfect. The poor little guy's got a lot to process— and some of it will be painful."

Allison looked at Jake. He could see her second-guessing her ability to pull it off. "We can do that," Jake said firmly. "Allison has spent the past few Christmases with the Rydells, and I've seen every holiday video Kenny made."

"And if you get stuck, just ask Caleb," the priest said with a chuckle. "He doesn't seem shy about expressing his needs."

Father Avila smiled. "Is there anything else you'd like to talk about? As I told Allison when we met, I'm a family counselor, not a psychiatrist. But I have a background in child development. I used to be a teacher until I decided I could reach more people through my ministry."

"What grade did you teach?"

"Second, first and kindergarten, successively," he said with a rueful grin. "The kids kept getting smarter at a younger age while I just got older."

Jake chuckled. "I understand completely. Sometimes Caleb will say something that just blows my mind. I'm pretty sure I wasn't that savvy when I was his age."

The man looked at him intently. "I'm not sure I believe that. I have a feeling you grew up in a hurry, Jake."

Jake's mouth dropped open. He looked at Allison, who was busy hunting for something in her backpack. When she came up with her cell phone—which apparently had been set to vibrate, rather than ring out loud—he could tell that she had no idea what the two men had been discussing.

Father Avila lowered his voice and said, "You have old eyes, Jake. I see it all the time in people who come to me. Maybe I'm wrong, but you look to me like a person who has suffered great losses in his life. And I don't mean this recent one. From before. In your childhood."

Allison had turned her back to them and was talking on her phone. Jake saw no reason to lie. "My younger brother died when I was fourteen. We were in separate foster situations because our mother took off and our father was an alcoholic loser who couldn't keep food on the table—or buy medicine for my brother whose lungs never quite developed right."

The minister let out a knowing groan. "Fourteen. That's a particularly rough age. Children in their early teens often take on the role of parent. When their younger sibling dies, they blame themselves."

Jake knew who to blame for Phillip's death, but before he could say so, a door opened and the sound of children's voices filled the hall. Allison finished her call and put her phone away.

"Sorry," she murmured, glancing at Jake before turning around.

Caleb trotted at the side of a smiling woman dressed in a gray-and-white habit. In her midtwenties, the woman moved as gracefully as a dancer. She called to Father Avila in Spanish, her tone apologetic.

"Come. It's okay," Father Avila said, motioning them closer. Caleb's feelings were clearly telegraphed on his face. He dropped the nun's hand and ran straight to his godfather.

Jake scooted his chair back and went down on one knee to pick him up. "Hey, buddy, did you jump and sing?"

Caleb nodded but didn't look up from Jake's chest. Beneath the child's head, Jake's heart swelled. Suddenly the thought of leaving seemed inconceivable. But he'd promised to do whatever was in Caleb's best interest, and he would—even if that meant giving him up when it was time to return to Miami.

"WHAT'S IT SAY?" Caleb asked, trying to look over Allison's shoulder.

Jake was in the driver's seat of her car but hadn't started the engine. The plan had been to drop her off at her office after the counseling session then Jake and Caleb would go to the movie. But a quick scan of the theater listings told her that wouldn't work.

"The next show isn't until four."

Jake frowned. With his sunglasses in place it was impossible to read his eyes. "Well, I suppose Caleb and I could visit Cordelia. The hospital is close by, isn't it?"

Yes, but my office is clear across town.

"No way," Caleb said, his tone belligerent. "I wanna go to the park. To swing. Ally said I could swing today."

"But you didn't see your grandmother yesterday, and I'm sure she's missing you," Allison argued.

"No, no, no," he cried, kicking his feet against the back of the driver's seat.

Jake reached behind him to catch one foot. "Enough," he said, sternly.

Caleb's bottom lip poked out, and he turned his face toward the window to pout.

Allison's hope of getting work done appeared doomed. She couldn't justify dumping a grumpy kid on Jake just so she could juggle a few unhappy customers. "I believe I said we'd go to the park if you were cooperative and if the sun was shining," she said, stressing the word *if.*

"It's sunny," he crowed triumphantly.

"But are you being cooperative?"

He nodded—even though she was sure he didn't know what the word meant. "You'll have to prove it to me. If you're a perfect angel for one hour at the hospital, then we'll stop at the park on our way to the theater. Okay?"

He thought a minute then nodded.

"Good," Allison said.

"What about your office?" Jake asked, starting the engine. He'd seemed uncharacteristically somber since their meeting with Father Avila.

"I'm compromising, too," she said. "I'll go there at four. No Disney for me."

As he was looking over his shoulder to back out of the parking spot, he made eye contact with Allison and mouthed the words, "Thank you."

A funny feeling blossomed in her chest. Gratitude was one thing. The effect his sexy smile had on her female hormones was quite another.

Ten minutes later, they walked into Cordelia's room. Five elaborate flower arrangements, which had graced the altar of the funeral home the day before, now brightened the window ledge. "Hi, Grandma," Caleb cried, racing to the chair where Cordelia was sitting.

Allison was pleased to see Cordelia out of bed. The past two days hadn't been easy for her—emotionally or medically speaking. A blood test had shown a post-operative infection, which meant more intravenous antibiotics.

But Cordelia smiled and opened her arms to her grandson. "What a pleasant surprise," she exclaimed. "I just tried calling the house and no one answered."

"We went to church," Caleb said, guilelessly. "I jumped and sang with a bunch of kids."

Cordelia directed a questioning look at Allison. "We spoke with Father Avila. He visited you the day of your surgery. He also works with grieving families."

Allison could tell she had questions, but the moment was lost when a nurse popped her head in the door and said, "Hey, I thought I saw a person under the age of ten come in here. There's a visiting clown in pediatrics and Grandma hasn't had her walk today. Sounds like serendipity to me."

"Awesome," Allison exclaimed. "Why don't you all go? I have a few calls to make."

"No," Caleb said. "You have to come, too."

Jake helped Cordelia to her feet and smiled at Allison. "One go, we all go."

She swallowed her impatience. Work wasn't the only reason she didn't want to accompany them, but she told herself it was ridiculous to feel weird about entering a pediatric ward after all these years. People who had abortions weren't automatically banned from that floor of the hospital for life.

The performance was being held in a small multipurpose room. Since there were only enough chairs for Cordelia and Caleb, Allison and Jake stood at the back wall. Allison watched the children laugh and clap at the clown's antics. A part of her tried to smile, but so many other emotions were churning inside her—loss, grief, despair.

"Cup of coffee?" Jake asked. "Caleb looks happy with his grandmother. I'll tell them where we're going. Wait here."

He whispered into Caleb's ear, then signaled Cordelia that they'd be right back. Leaving the noise behind, they walked in silence toward the waiting room.

When they were both seated with two cups of hot coffee, he said, "What's going on? You look like you're going to splinter into a million pieces."

"You can see that?" she asked, amazed by his perception.

He nodded.

She took a sip of coffee. "Old stuff. The kind you share with your best girlfriend," she said.

"You know, Ally, we're fighting to survive here. That makes us comrades in arms. If you feel like talking about whatever's bothering you, I'm here for you. And you can be sure I'll never repeat it—even under torture."

Allison laughed, drawing the attention of the room's solitary occupant—a man who was wringing his hands like an expectant father. He got up and left.

Sinking back into the molded seat, Allison sighed. "Ten years ago I was happily married to a terrific guy I met in college. We were both techies. Had great jobs in the computer industry. Bought a home before the market skyrocketed. Figured it was time to start a family."

She looked at Jake who was listening attentively.

"I got pregnant right away. No problem. Everything was fine until the fifth month. I started having sharp pains on the left side of my belly and there was some spotting.

"We ran every test imaginable. An ultrasound eventually revealed that: one, my baby was a little girl and two, there was a growth on my ovary. A tumor. Malignant. Growing at an alarming rate, in part, they theorized, because of the pregnancy."

She studied the neutral carpeting. "My parents flew out. My in-laws came from Washington State. A second specialist was called in. Everyone agreed that the best course was to abort the pregnancy, treat the cancer then try to get pregnant again after I was healed."

He didn't ask what had happened, but since she'd revealed this much, she said, "I told them no. I refused to consider it. The baby was alive inside me. Safe. Tr…trusting." Her stomach clenched and her hand started to shake so badly she had to set her cup down on the floor. "Pam was the only one in my corner. My sisters and brother all called and told me I had to do what the doctors said. Everyone cried—even my father. My husband told me he couldn't face the possibility of raising a child alone, and might be forced to give our daughter up for adoption."

Jake reached out and took her hand. "You did it."

She nodded, squeezing her eyes tight to keep the tears inside. She couldn't admit how bitter she still felt even after all these years. She'd put her trust in others, and betrayed her child. "They treated me with radiation and chemotherapy. It was bad. There were times I wanted to die. Pam made me fight. She bullied me back to life. But in the end, she was the only person I wasn't angry at.

"My marriage dissolved. Ironically, I'd done what Dean had wanted, but we grew apart anyway. My relationship with my parents and siblings suffered. I turned into a workaholic—with cats," she added, striving for a lighter note.

"The cancer is gone?"

"It wasn't as bad as they'd thought. Nothing in the lymph nodes, although my oncologist is certain it would have spread had they failed to initiate treatment when they did. But we'll never know, will we?"

"What about your husband? This couldn't have been easy for him, either."

Allison smiled for the first time since entering the room. "The poor man didn't have a chance. Even though Dean felt he was saving my life, I blamed him for not backing my choice. It was a lose-lose proposition."

"Where is he now?"

"He still lives in our house in San Mateo. He and a partner have a software company and are making oodles of money. I see him once in a great while when I have to make a run to the city. He has a live-in girlfriend." She stood up, suddenly anxious to check on Caleb.

As they walked back to the common room, Allison glanced into the nursery. Only four baskets contained babies. She felt a twinge of sadness, but not the usual pain. Maybe Jake was right. Perhaps she needed a new keeper of secrets now that Pam was gone. Whatever the reason, she did feel better.

CHAPTER NINE

JAKE'S EARS WERE RINGING and his nerves were shot. No adult of the male persuasion should ever be forced to endure an hour plus at a preschool Christmas party, he decided.

Today was Friday. Two weeks since their meeting with Padre Avila. Two weeks into his and Allison's plan to work half days and give Caleb a "normal" family life and holiday.

She took charge of getting Caleb up and dressed in the mornings, so Jake could get up before dawn and talk to people whose day was well underway on the east coast. Then he'd do a few household chores before picking Caleb up from his preschool.

Happy Hearts Children's Center was a small, cinder-block building with a large fenced yard and an abundance of playground structures. This was the first time Jake had made it past the sign-in desk. Usually Caleb was waiting at the door, with a worried look in his eyes, clearly anxious to leave as soon as Jake signed his name on the line beneath Allison's.

But today marked the last school day before the holiday break, and a special party and gift exchange had been planned. Caleb had insisted Jake needed to attend. With Allison.

"The decibel range is worse than at a rock concert," he said, leaning close enough to Allison to be heard over the hubbub.

The necessary proximity meant he was forced to breathe Allison's scent, which tantalized him in a way he knew wasn't healthy. No matter how many times he reminded himself they were only together because of Caleb, Jake couldn't help feeling drawn to her. If not for the crowd of rowdy children, he might have been tempted to nibble on her pretty, perfect earlobe.

"Bah humbug to you, too," Allison said, tapping his nose with the paper wreath Caleb had handed her the moment she walked in the door. The elliptical, mostly green object had been constructed with obvious care using paper plates, Dixie cups, tempera paint, silver tinsel and red berries, which on closer inspection turned out to be some kind of puffed cereal that had been painted, too.

Allison wasn't the only person who'd received a holiday decoration. Ringing the circumference of the plush orange sunlike center rug, parents—predominantly mothers—sat on tiny chairs, knees to chest, clutching similar wreaths. Jake and Allison had arrived a few minutes late, thanks to Jake's final trade of the day, and had missed out on seating. Fortunately, the Christmas program had been geared to the attention span of children—brief.

Once the formal presentation was over, the place had erupted into bedlam. Jake had a hard time making out Caleb in the swarm of small bodies swamping the refreshment table, which he noticed was manned by Gayle.

"Are we supposed to line up for punch and cookies?" Jake asked.

Allison's lips—sporting a shiny, red-tinted gloss—
curved into a knowing smile. "Didn't I suggest a snack
before we left?"

Jake let out a muffled growl, which only made her
grin grow. Before he could say anything, a small mis-
sile crashed into his legs, just above his knee caps. He
took a step backward but bumped into a low bookcase
that wobbled slightly. Allison grabbed the sleeve of his
navy corduroy shirt, her knuckles firmly pressed against
his upper arm.

He liked her touch.

She looked at him and her cocky smile faded. She
let go and quickly glanced down. "Caleb, I love my
wreath. I will keep it always."

Caleb looked pleased. "We cut 'em out a long time
ago 'n painted 'em. Mine was going to be for Mommy
but since you're my mommy now, you get it."

The wreath slipped from Allison's fingers, and Jake
had to make a lunging catch to keep it from hitting the
floor. When he handed it to her, he spotted unshed tears
in her eyes. Jake knew that she was troubled by Caleb's
occasional references to her as his mommy. The little
guy still asked about his parents. He cried at least once
a day—often right before bed. But they'd found that encouraging him to address his concerns—his sadness
and anger—in his prayers seemed to help.

Jake couldn't predict how Caleb would do in the
long term. He tried to focus only on the day at hand. To
plan ahead meant facing the fact that the more comfortable Caleb became with Jake in his life, the harder it
would be on him when his godfather had to leave.

Jake was also having difficulty picturing Allison
handling the situation alone.

In addition to playing mom every morning, running her business and checking on Cordelia, who continued to battle a persistent staph infection, she'd decided to go ahead with Pam's annual charity food drive at Rydell Motors. Some days, their paths didn't cross until she returned home after dinner.

Although Allison insisted she could do it all, Jake could tell the punishing schedule was taking a toll. And the weather wasn't helping. A week of steady, cold rain had been followed by dense fog—something most people said was a rarity at their elevation. Rare or not, the continuous gray was depressing.

"Hey, I've got an idea," he said, recalling a weather report that mentioned how beautiful the weather was on the coast. "How 'bout we escape to the beach tomorrow?"

Caleb let out a squeal that made Jake's ears ring. "Yeah," he cried before sprinting about the room to share his good news with his classmates.

Allison frowned. "Jake, I have to work tomorrow. I can't go."

"You have to," Jake said, his tone pleading. "The idea just popped into my head. But it's a good one, Ally. We all need a break, and I desperately need a fix of sand and sea."

"Then you take him," Allison said, her tone obviously displeased. "I don't like being put on the spot. I've just about got my crew caught up on installations, but we have a backlog of minijobs that we're never going to get through before Christmas. No work, no money to make payroll."

Jake frowned. This wasn't the place to talk business, but… "Since you brought it up, I've got a proposition for you. I'm working on a stock sale that will make you a lot of money, but it's going to take time. Which I know you don't have, so how about I make you a loan using the stock as collateral?"

She started to protest, but he cut her off. "This is good business, Ally. Good for you. Good for the economy and good for me." Less good for Jake because he wouldn't charge her interest, but she didn't have to know that.

"Is it legal?"

"Of course," he said, a bit irked. "You could do the same thing at a bank, but that would take too long. You need the money now. Right?"

She nodded. "What's in it for you?"

"Peace of mind? I'm scared spitless that one of these nights you're going to be so tired from trying to handle everything that you'll fall asleep behind the wheel."

She frowned, but after a few seconds, a smile turned up the corners of her lips. "I'd have to see this deal on paper, but if you're sure this isn't just some magnanimous charity on your part, I'd consider it."

He was relieved to know they were on friendly terms again. *What would it be like to be on kissing terms?*

Breathless, Caleb raced back to join them. "Can we go to the place where all the fishes are?" he asked. "Mommy and Daddy took me there. They said we'd go back, but we never did." His bottom lip started to tremble.

Allison reached down and picked him up. "I want to go, honey, but tomorrow is a work day. My employees need me." Big tears rolled over the rims of his eyes. "And tomorrow is also the big gala at the canned food drive, remember?"

He blinked, his look turning pensive.

"If I remember correctly, you and your daddy used to drive the car with all the cans they'd collected to the food center, right?"

Sniffling, his head bobbed slightly.

"I thought so. You know that food helps a lot of people. You don't want them to be hungry at Christmas, do you?"

His mouth twisted, obviously torn by wanting to do the right thing and wanting to go to the beach. "Uh-uh."

She hugged him tight and said, "Good boy. Your mommy and daddy would be so proud of you. So how about we stay home and work tomorrow then go to the beach on Sunday?"

Caleb's head popped up, his eyes huge. "Mean it?"

Allison looked at Jake. "Works for me. Can you fit it into your schedule, money man?"

Jake wasn't a fool. He knew when he'd been outmaneuvered. And in this instance, Allison was by far the smartest. "As a matter of fact, I like that idea better. I forgot about the food drive. Richard told me we're going to have to use the biggest truck on the lot this year because so many people have stopped by to drop off food and money."

Caleb wiggled to be set down. "I gotta tell Bradley. His family is going to the mountains, but we're going some place better."

The word *family* echoed in Jake's head. He used to believe the term would never apply to him, but lately, he'd started to feel a lot like a father. And, even though she still professed doubts about her fitness as a parent, Allison was very much a mother. Together, they had a son. The only thing missing from the equation was love. Which shouldn't surprise him, since it had always been in short supply in his life.

"IN SOME WAYS, Jake's a better businessman than Kenny was," Richard Marques told Allison the next morning at Rydell Motors. She'd planned to give half an hour of her time to the canned food drive, then head to town to sort out the mess in her accounts receivable ledger. "Look at how he works the crowd. Shaking hands, greeting strangers. Kenny once told me that dealing with people was the hardest part of the job."

Allison didn't try to dispute that. She'd spent enough time with Kenny to know that he'd been basically very shy, which she'd found ironic considering he'd once toured with a rock band.

"So how has business been?" she asked, more to make conversation than out of any real curiosity. Allison knew that Jake had been working with an accountant and a real estate attorney to complete the sale of the business.

"Pretty darned amazing," Richard said. "Some sympathy and goodwill after the funeral helped, but we also have a dynamite sales staff and a great product. How's your Subie doing? Or are you driving Pam's SUV?"

Something about his tone gave Allison the impression that he thought she might be benefiting from her friend's death. Allison wrestled with guilt every day—she was alive and Pam wasn't. She was enjoying Caleb's childhood and Pam never would. Richard's subtle innuendo—if that's what it was—made her immediately defensive.

"I only drive the Explorer when I need to transport Caleb. My car gets better mileage and feels more solid on the road."

Kenny's cousin beamed. "We like those kind of testimonials. Maybe you could post something on our Web site." He puffed up slightly. "The electronic bulletin board was my idea. I'd suggested it to Kenny about a month before he died, but he didn't do anything computer-wise without your approval."

"Hey, Ally, what are we doing with checks and cash donations?" Jake asked, walking up to join her and Richard. Caleb, she noticed, was sitting on the parts counter flirting with two adoring secretaries. His mouth was glossy from the giant candy cane someone had given him. "Perhaps a quick trip to Tahiti?" he joked.

"Sorry, Charlie, that money buys turkeys."

"Ah, shucks, I was really looking forward to a piña colada."

She patted his arm as she might comfort Caleb. "How 'bout if I buy you one tomorrow in Monterey? Not tropical, but there should be sun."

Jake grinned. "I can't wait." He extended a hand to Richard. "You've done a great job, Rich. Kenny and Pam would be pleased."

Richard beamed. "Thank you. We couldn't have pulled it off without Allison. She contacted the newspaper and radio stations, plus she handled the arrangements with the local food bank."

Both men looked her way, and Allison felt her face heat up. She wondered if her complexion clashed with the glitzy red sweater she'd borrowed from Pam's closet. She'd felt guilty about doing so, but she hadn't had time to restock her wardrobe from home and she'd wanted something festive for the day. Fortunately, Caleb hadn't seemed to notice.

"It was no big deal," she said. "I just tried to remember what Pam did last year. She complained about it often enough, how could I forget?" Realizing that her statement cast a disparaging light on her friend, she added, "Not complain exactly. Pam loved supporting this cause, but Kenny wasn't much help a lot of the time." Her blush intensified.

Jake cuffed her shoulder lightly. "Hey, I understand. Kenny was a great guy, but he hated this kind of touchy-feely thing. I'm sure he ducked out any time he could get under his wife's radar."

Richard laughed. "That's true. Ken stayed in the background as much as possible while Pam worked the crowd. Kinda the reverse of you two," he noted. "'Cept you and Allison make a better team."

Allison quickly said her goodbyes. As she drove down into the valley, Richard's comment came back to her. *A better team. Teammates. Mates.*

She turned down the heater and opened the window to let in the brisk, moist air. Her mind had been wandering down strange paths lately. At odd moments, she'd find herself in the middle of daydreams that didn't belong in a rational brain. This attention deficit had created all kinds of havoc in her business, which is why she needed to redo the recent statements. Somehow, she'd neglected to include service hours in the invoices.

Good thing I'm too exhausted at night to dream, Allison thought with a sigh, or I'd probably screw that up, too.

"I'M HOME. And I have pizza."

Allison's cheerful greeting made Jake want to crawl under the table. She'd been working in Fresno all day while he and Caleb had delivered canned goods, done a little Christmas shopping and taken a nap. Now, instead of giving his partner some much-needed down time, he was leaving her alone to care for a rowdy little rascal who refused to bathe.

"Ummm, pizza," Caleb cheered, racing past Jake to meet her at the back door. "I want pizza. I want pizza."

Jake hurried after him. Even though he felt guilty about leaving, Jake rationalized that this outing wasn't entirely his fault. He'd been coerced by Richard, who wanted to introduce Jake to the volunteer firemen. The group planned to honor Kenny at a memorial next month and needed Jake's input.

"Let me help," Jake said, hurrying to relieve Allison of a plastic bag obviously filled with a six-pack of cans.

"Thanks," she said. "The handle was cutting off circulation to my fingers." She shook her hand then walked to the kitchen counter where she placed a large cardboard box and a paper sack. "So how did we do today?" she asked, stealing a piece of pepperoni off the pie. "Cans galore?" she asked.

"We topped last year's total by how much, Caleb?"

"Six million," the little boy said, taking the paper plates and napkins out of the sack.

"Six hundred," Jake corrected, trying not to laugh.

"Wow," Allison exclaimed. She hung up her coat and washed her hands. "That's impressive. How 'bout money-wise?"

"Eight trillion dollars," Caleb said his eyes aglitter.

Jake loved to see his godson joke. This was the child

he remembered from summer. Jake extended his arms in an impression of Frankenstein and ambled toward the little boy. "How much?" he roared.

"Eight thousand," Caleb squealed, dodging left when Jake lurched right. Napkins flew into the air. Allison tried to catch them and wound up tripping over Jake's foot. His only recourse to prevent her from falling was to snatch her into his outstretched arms, which curled backwards without conscious thought.

"Oh," Allison said, with a small exhale. Her face was close to Jake's. Her breath carried the tangy scent of pepperoni.

"Eiou," Caleb cried, ducking behind the paper plates he still held. "Kissing. Just like Mommy and Daddy."

Allison righted herself almost immediately and stepped back. "Sorry."

"No apology needed. It was my fault."

Caleb yanked on Jake's pocket. "You didn't kiss her."

"Well, no...I...um." Jake felt his face heat up. He was rarely speechless, but this was definitely one of those times.

"Shall we eat?" Allison asked, her voice wobbly. "I'm starved."

Caleb tugged again and motioned Jake to bend down for a private chat. In a loud whisper, the child said, "You have to kiss her. Girls like kisses. We can't lose another mom, Jake."

Jake's breath left him. He put his hand to his face and squeezed the bridge of his nose to keep his tears at bay.

Suddenly, he sensed Allison's presence. She picked up Caleb and put her free arm around Jake's back to pull him into a hug. "Everybody likes kisses," she said softly. She pressed her lips to his cheek, and then did the same to Caleb.

The child hugged her fiercely then wiggled free. "Can I have chocolate milk with my pizza?"

Allison smiled. "Sure. There's a carton in the door of the fridge."

Her arm was still touching him. Her warmth enveloped him. Her scent made his mouth water. Girls weren't the only ones who liked kisses. He lowered his head and touched his lips to hers. She gave a startled peep but didn't move away. He kissed her again, his tongue teasing her lips that parted hesitantly.

The whooshing sound of the refrigerator door closing made her jump back. Her expression was unreadable, but her blush told him she was embarrassed and regretted the kiss. Jake wished he did, but in all honesty, he wanted more.

"We'd better start eating before the pizza gets cold," Allison said, turning toward the counter.

Jake couldn't postpone telling her. "I can't stay," he said. Her eyes went wide with alarm until he added, "I let myself get talked into attending the local volunteer firefighter's Christmas party. I should have called and told you so you didn't buy such a large pizza."

She transferred a slice to Caleb's plate. "No problem. Leftovers never seem to go to waste around here. We could wrap it up for tomorrow." She looked at Jake. "We are still going to the ocean, aren't we?"

"Absolutely. Caleb and I have everything packed—a blanket, warm jackets, sand pails and shovels. Right, buddy?"

Mouth full, the child nodded. "Beach," he mumbled.

"Chew, don't talk," Allison cautioned. "One of my

employees had a close call the other night when her little girl choked on a piece of meat. It suddenly occurred to me that I don't know CPR. Do you?" she asked Jake.

"For adults. My gym was sponsoring classes so I got certified, but I've never tried it on a child."

Allison's serious look had returned. "I'll add that to my to-do list."

Jake thought about Allison's list as he drove to the firehouse. *Did it include falling for your godson's other godparent?*

He knew the answer. Undoubtedly not. Granted, the idea held a certain appeal, but proximity and need didn't constitute the basis for a healthy long-term relationship. Did it?

That was the problem. Of Jake's many friends and acquaintances, only one, Kenny, had been involved in a happy, loving relationship of ten years or better. Now, Jake was up to his eyeballs in his best friend's life—sleeping in his bed, raising his child, lusting after Caleb's new mother. But he wasn't Kenny.

ALLISON USED THE REMOTE control to lower the sound on the television. Caleb was asleep. Finally. Sprawled on the sofa, his cheek resting on a pillow near her thigh. She knew she should get up and carry him to bed, but she needed a few minutes to recoup.

They'd had a difficult night. Whether that was due to Jake's absence or because Caleb was upset from seeing her and Jake kiss, she wasn't sure. She'd tried playing games with him, but Candyland had turned into I-hate-you-land when he didn't win—even though Allison had tried her best to lose. A foray into the world of Lego blocks had nearly reduced her to tears when he scattered a hundred little pieces in every direction in a fit of temper.

Finally, after a messy, contentious bath, he'd agreed to watch a movie, although *Charlotte's Web* wasn't the title Allison would have picked. She loved the story but always cried when Charlotte died and her children flew away. Ally was tired of crying.

Then, to top off the night, her mother had called while Caleb was in the tub. They didn't talk often—partly because Allison was so busy and partly because of the past. Her relationship with her parents had changed after her abortion. Pam had scolded Allison for being too hard on them. "Cut your mom some slack, Ally. A mother will do anything to protect the life of her child." Allison understood that on an intellectual level, but, emotionally, she couldn't forgive them completely.

Their chat included an update on Allison's father's health—better, her sister's pregnancy, still problematic—and a heads-up on a package her mother had mailed for Caleb. Allison knew her parents worried about her. But after a day like today, she was too tired to care.

Allison let her head sink into the plush cushion. She'd just closed her eyes when she heard the sound of the automatic garage door opener. She glanced at her watch. *Nine-thirty?* Jake was home early.

She still hadn't mustered the energy to move when Jake walked in. He locked the kitchen door then headed straight to the couch where she and Caleb were sprawled. "God, that looks comfortable. I wish I'd stayed home and watched a movie with you two."

Allison could tell he meant it. "No fun?"

"Not bad. They're a great bunch of guys, but the night was nonstop Kenny stories. I gotta tell you. I loved the guy, but he wasn't a saint."

"Revisionist history," she said, stifling a yawn. "I can't keep my eyes open. Would you help me with Caleb?"

Jake moved to pick up the sleeping child but hesitated. Bent over he looked at her and said, "I feel like I should apologize for earlier. Are you okay with what happened?"

Okay? Maybe not okay. Her body wanted a heck of a lot more than just a kiss, but her mind knew that was a very bad idea. "Yeah. Sure. It was just a kiss," she forced herself to say.

He looked unconvinced, but he let out a sigh that sounded almost as tired as Allison felt. "Good. Then tomorrow should be a breeze."

Three hours on the road with a four-year-old and the man she found too sexy for her own good? *Yep, just what Santa ordered.*

Once she was free of Caleb's weight, she sat up and stretched. Taking a deep breath, she rose and looked around to find the stuffed alligator Caleb had begun insisting he needed in bed with him. It was wedged between the cushions of the couch, but after a brief tussle, she pulled it free.

When she turned around, Jake was still standing there, watching her. They looked at each other a moment—an exchange that seemed familiar, yet more intense. Then she handed him the stuffed animal and hurried away.

Allison could no longer pretend she wasn't attracted to Jake. Post-traumatic shock seemed as good an excuse as any. Her non-traumatized self would never fall for Jake-the-Rake. She was too smart for that. Pam had told her so many times.

"If Jake weren't Jake and you weren't you, the two of you would make a great couple," Pam had said as recently as September.

The family had just returned from their vacation in Florida, tanned and relaxed. Allison had been lamenting the fact that she'd missed out on yet another great trip with the fabulous Jake Westin.

"Don't get me wrong, Ally. Jake's an amazing guy. And you're the best person I know. But somehow I can't picture the two of you together."

Allison hadn't bothered asking why not. Long-distance relationships never worked out, and she was locked into a long-term lease with her business. Maybe if she were the type of woman who could handle a fling, she'd have asked more questions. But she wasn't.

Since Jake intended to leave once Cordelia returned home, Allison had to make darn sure he didn't take her heart with him.

CHAPTER TEN

THE FOG PARTED as if a giant hand had pulled aside a thick gray cloak revealing sky so blue Allison, in the seat beside him, commented, "I'd practically forgotten what that color looked like."

Jake reached for the visor, where he usually kept his sunglasses when he wasn't wearing them. They weren't there.

"Oh, nuts. I think I left my shades at home."

"Do you want mine?"

"No, thanks. Too girlish. Although they look very nice on you," he hastily tacked on.

A low chuckle made him glance her way. "Good save," she said with a wink.

"I can afford to be generous," he returned, keeping his tone light. "Someone let me sleep in this morning."

Allison turned sideways in the tan leather seat. Instead of jeans, she wore black slacks made of a stretchy material that fit sinfully well. A purplish-blue cardigan sweater was tossed in the back seat beside Caleb. Her starched white shirt with cuffs was unbuttoned low enough for Jake to see the scalloped lace of her body-shaping tank top.

"It says a lot about a person when they consider 6:00 a.m. *late.*"

Jake had always thought of himself as a night owl. Since he'd moved into the Rydell home, he'd found himself retiring earlier and earlier. Even last night, after a few hours of male companionship, he'd been anxious to return home. And when he thought about it, as he had that whole first hour of tossing and turning, he realized he didn't miss his old habits.

As if reading his mind, Allison asked, "How are you holding up? From what Pam used to tell me, this schedule has to be quite a change for you."

Jake glanced in the rearview mirror to check on Caleb who'd fallen asleep just past Casa de Fruta. "True," he admitted. "And I expected to miss my former lifestyle, but I don't."

"Not even the bikini-clad beauties in Rollerblades?"

Her tone was light, but the question irked him. Ignoring the implication, he said, "I'll tell you what I miss— the food."

"You mean pizza three nights a week isn't your normal fare?"

Jake sighed. "I live in walking distance of five-star restaurants. The last night I was there, I ate rosemary salmon in parchment, roasted red potatoes served with yellow pepper aioli sauce and caramel apple soufflé."

"Amazing you stayed in such great shape. If I ate that kind of rich food, I'd blow up like a puffer fish."

Jake laughed, pleased to know that she'd noticed his body. He'd had to work a little bit harder to stay in shape since he arrived in California, but fortunately, the home gym in Kenny's office helped.

"What's a puffer fish?" a voice asked.

Allison leaned toward Jake so she could peer into the back compartment. "Hey, you're awake. It's a very peculiar fish that blows up like a balloon when it's afraid. Maybe we'll see one at the aquarium.

"I'm embarrassed to admit this," Allison said, "but in all the years I've lived in California, I've never been to the Monterey Bay Aquarium. I went to one in New Orleans, though. It had a great gift shop."

"'Nawlins is my second favorite town. When were you there?" Jake asked. He could picture her on his arm, strolling among the vendors and artists in Jackson Square, then stopping by an outside café for coffee and beignets. He'd become quite addicted to the powdered sugar treat.

"On my honeymoon."

"Oh." *Talk about a conversation killer.* He didn't like thinking about her ex-husband. The guy must have been an idiot. How could anyone expect Allison to give up her child without a fight? Jake might not have agreed with her decision, but he would have supported her choice.

Even if it meant losing her? He didn't want to think about that. He was going to lose her. And Caleb, too, once Cordelia was healthy enough to move home.

Yep, before long, he'd back in sunny Miami. Sand, surf, and a hole in his heart big enough to Rollerblade through.

CALEB LIKED the tidal pool display best. The wall was low enough that he could look over and touch the water. Cold and kind of slippery feeling, he scooped up a palm full and started to lift it to his mouth when Allison stopped him. "It tastes like salt," she said. "Take my word for it."

Jake, who was standing on the other side of him,

laughed. "A little sip won't kill him. I've swallowed gallons."

Caleb looked at Allison, who gave Jake a look Caleb's mommy used to give his daddy lots of times.

"Sweetie," Allison said in a voice that told him she wasn't mad at him, "do me a favor and go wash your hands. The rest room is right over there. Take Jake with you. It never hurts to be on your toes."

Caleb knew that wasn't exactly what she meant. His mommy had taught him not to talk to strangers, and Caleb didn't. But yesterday a whole bunch of strangers talked to *him* at his daddy's car lot. And some of what they said made his stomach hurt. So later, when Jake said they should do some Christmas shopping for Ally, Caleb hadn't wanted to go.

"Caleb?" Allison said, looking at him. "Are you okay?"

Before he could answer, a kid across the tank from him pointed excitedly and said, "Look, Mommy. That fish is dead."

Caleb craned his neck to see. The water was clear and it moved back and forth over the rocks, making the grassy stuff wave. Caleb couldn't see what the kid was pointing at. Taking advantage of an opening in the crowd, he dashed through it and made his way around the pool, hoping to get a look at the dead fish.

Dead. He'd heard that word a lot lately, but he didn't completely understand what it meant. Maybe if he touched the fish...

"Caleb."

Jake's voice rose above the noise of the crowd, but Caleb ignored it. He squeezed around a lady and her kid—the boy he thought had pointed out the dead fish.

The wall of the exhibit seemed higher here, and Caleb struggled to pull himself up on the edge. Excited and a little scared, he almost lost his balance, but a hand caught him.

"Caleb, what—"

Before Jake could finish talking, Allison grabbed Caleb by the tops of his arms and made him look at her. Her face was almost the same color as her shirt. "Don't ever run away like that again. Do you hear me, young man?"

Caleb nodded. Her voice was sharp, and her hands were tight on his arms. He squirmed, not from pain but because people were watching and he knew he'd done something he shouldn't have. His mommy would have spanked him—even in public.

Caleb started to explain that he'd only wanted to see what dead meant, but Jake spoke first. "Relax. He's okay."

"Relax?" Allison repeated, her voice louder. "He could have been abducted. It only takes a few seconds for a child to disappear."

Caleb tensed. He didn't like it when adults argued. His mommy and daddy used to argue sometimes and now they were gone. He looked at Allison. Her face was red. "He needs to understand that the world isn't a safe place."

"You don't think he *knows* that?" Jake asked.

Allison didn't answer. Instead, she dropped her hands and looked down. Caleb wanted to say he was sorry for running off and making Allison mad, but he was afraid to speak. What if she went away, too? The way his mommy did.

Jake picked Caleb up. "There's a movie about sea otters starting in ten minutes. Shall we go watch it?"

Caleb's heart was still beating too fast for him to answer. He looked at Allison. She gave him a pretend smile and said, "You two go ahead. I want to check out the Cannery Row display, which I'm sure wouldn't interest Caleb in the least. Why don't we meet by the gift shop in forty-five minutes?"

Jake didn't say anything at first, but then he nodded. "Okay."

She turned away and walked to the stairs. As soon as she was out of sight, Jake looked at Caleb and said, "Ally's right, buddy. You scared us by running off. Promise me you won't ever do that again."

Caleb felt tears form in his eyes. "I'm sorry."

Jake gave him a squeeze then set him on the floor. "I know you are. So, how 'bout we skip the movie and go shopping, instead? Christmas is only five days away, and I need to buy something for Allison."

Caleb frowned. Everybody was talking about Christmas, but it wasn't the same without his mommy and daddy. His grandma was still sick in the hospital. And no decorations were up at his house, except for his wreath. Nothing was the same, and thinking about that made his tummy hurt.

JAKE IGNORED the looks from other parents as he led Caleb away from the tidal pool exhibit, but his gut was still churning. He'd never seen Allison react that strongly to anything, and it had unnerved him when she'd grabbed Caleb by the shoulders. Jake's mother had been a screamer and she'd tended to get physical—very physical—with her eldest son.

Allison's reaction to Caleb running away wasn't something Jake could just ignore, even if the little boy didn't seem bothered by what had happened. Jake had always known his and Allison's parenting styles were different, but he hadn't expected her to freak-out so easily. Would her overprotective nature stifle Caleb in years to come? If Caleb rebelled, would she resort to a stinging backhand or verbal abuse to make him feel small and worthless?

After a stop at the rest room to wash hands, he and Caleb walked to the glass-walled gift shop. "How 'bout those?" Caleb asked, pointing to a pair of mother-of-pearl earrings, which were in a case at his eye level. "They're pretty. Like Ally."

Jake leaned over. Delicate. Unusual. And expensive. "Perfect choice, Caleb. I'm taking you with me every time I go shopping."

Caleb visibly perked up. "Really?"

The clerk arrived, distracting Jake from Caleb's odd response. What about that vow could make the boy look so cheerful? Was it the suggestion that Jake might be around in the future?

Jake wasn't sure what was going to happen. And after the episode by the tidal pool, he was even more conflicted. Being a single parent—even with Cordelia's help—might be more than Allison could handle. But what choice did he have? He could try splitting his time between two coasts, but would a part-time dad be enough? Or did Jake need to seriously think about petitioning for sole custody? And what did any of this mean to the growing attraction he felt toward Allison?

"How 'bout this for her, Jake?" Caleb asked, tugging on Jake's sleeve. "I got money. I could buy it."

Jake examined the picture book on sharks—which would be a perfect gift for a four-year-old—and steered Caleb toward some inexpensive ankle bracelets that resembled colorful sunfish swimming in a circle. Their purchases were safely stowed in Caleb's backpack, which Jake was carrying, when Allison joined them.

"So, when's lunch? All this walking has made me hungry."

They'd booked a table at a popular spot overlooking the bay before heading to the aquarium. "Our reservation is in half an hour," Jake said, surprised to see that Allison had apparently put the incident behind her. He wished he could.

They were a block from the aquarium, when Jake said, "I think we need to talk about what happened."

Allison nodded. "I agree, but not now. See that sign?" She pointed to a sandwich-type billboard announcing Visit Santa—Today. "Why don't Caleb and I meet you at the café? This might take a little while, and I know you have your heart set on sand dabs."

Her tone was pleasant but firm. The sunlight sparkled in her hair. She'd shed her sweater, which was tied at her waist. She looked surprisingly carefree for a woman who worried more than anyone he'd ever met.

Feeling utterly confused—was it possible to love a person even if you didn't think she was the right mother for your godson?—he addressed Caleb. "Do you promise to stick like glue to Allison, buddy?"

The little boy nodded seriously.

"Then, I'll see you there."

As he walked away, the sounds of "Jingle Bells" piped over a loudspeaker made him cringe. He'd never felt more like a grinch.

ALLISON LOVED THE FEELING of Caleb's hand in hers. The sensation bordered on bliss. Why hadn't Pam told her how special it was to walk with a child, knowing he trusted you completely?

The only thing marring the moment was knowing that Jake undoubtedly regarded her as an over-reactive nut. Her panic by the tidal pool—and his somewhat cavalier attitude toward Caleb's running away—had nearly ruined her morning. But this trip wasn't about her. She'd vowed to make this a happy memory for Caleb and that's what she intended to do. "Let's hurry, honey. I hope the line isn't too long."

Picking their way through the crowd inside the converted cannery that was now filled with shops and shoppers, it suddenly dawned on her that Caleb didn't seem very enthusiastic about her idea. As they joined the line, she said, "Is something wrong? Don't you want your picture taken with Santa Claus?"

He wouldn't look at her, but his head wagged from side-to-side.

"Really? Why not? You look awfully cute today and we could give a copy to Grandma Cordelia to cheer her up. I bet Jake would like one, too."

Allison could see him hesitate. "Okay," he said, with more enthusiasm than he'd shown before.

Each step forward brought them closer to the elaborate Santa's village, where a large elf played carols on an electric keyboard. They were about four spots away from the white picket fence when Allison realized Caleb was crying. Tears, no sniffles.

"Sweetheart, what's wrong?"

The crowd noise was almost as loud as when they were at the preschool party. Caleb shook his head.

"Oh, honey, something's bothering you. Can't you tell me?"

He shook his head again. The furrow in his brow could have belonged to a very old man.

The person behind them coughed, and Allison rose to move forward. She picked up Caleb. He dropped his head to her shoulder and put his arms around her neck. In a very tiny voice he said, "Santa's not gonna come this year."

Not certain she'd heard him right, she pulled back slightly. "Sure he is, honey. Why wouldn't he?"

Caleb shook his head.

Allison's gut told her this was an issue that she couldn't simply ignore. She motioned for the young girl in a sprite costume to come to her.

"My little boy needs to use the bathroom. Can you save our place?"

The girl smiled broadly. "Of course. We certainly wouldn't want him to have an accident on Santa's lap."

Several people chuckled and Allison quickly left the line. Instead of locating the rest rooms, she found an out-of-the-way spot where she and Caleb could face each other.

"Okay, kiddo, fess up. What's going on?" She'd heard Pam talk to her son like this before—frank and to the point. "Something is bothering you and I want to know what it is."

Caleb's eyes went wide. He swallowed then said, "We don't have a tree. How will Santa know where to put my presents?"

Guilt overwhelmed Allison. How could she not have realized Caleb needed to see all the familiar decorations up? She'd been too busy to give that chore the attention Pam would have given it, but that was no excuse. "Jake and I are a little slow about some things, Caleb.

You need to tell us when something is bothering you. How 'bout you and Jake go pick out a tree tomorrow? Then we'll all decorate it when I come home from work."

"Really?"

"Absolutely. And you need to help Jake put up the outside lights. He doesn't know where everything goes. If he doesn't start soon, he could still be up on the roof when Santa comes."

Caleb smiled. "Okay. I'll talk to Santa."

"And you'll ask him for a present?"

He nodded. "Maybe some new cars for my race set. Bradley broke one. And a dump truck. And a bike. And—" He paused, his lips moving back and forth as if working up the courage to say something else. She held her breath until he added in a near whisper, "I want him to make you and Jake stay with me forever and not go away like Mommy and Daddy."

Allison had to reach deep to keep from breaking down. She took his hand and started back to the North Pole. "That's a long list, but you've been such a great kid, I'm sure Santa will do his best to fill it."

Caleb looked so full of hope. If there was a Santa, he'd be leaving a lump of coal in Allison's stocking for lying. She planned to stay, but she couldn't speak for Jake.

Caleb probably wouldn't believe in Santa after this Christmas, but what Allison found even more discouraging was he probably wouldn't believe her again, either.

HOURS LATER, Allison nibbled on a hunk of sourdough bread as she stretched out on the patchwork quilt Jake had brought from the house. Allison and Pam had used the blanket many times when they'd taken Caleb to the park or the lake. Pam always kept it in a big beach bag, right beside the sand chairs and a mesh tote with Caleb's toys in it.

Their impromptu picnic had been a stroke of genius on Jake's part. By the time Allison and Caleb had finished with Santa, they'd had to race to the restaurant. Jake had been pacing, but instead of being upset over their missed reservation, he suggested a stop at the deli so they could eat on the beach.

Allison liked this idea much better. With Caleb on his hands and knees digging in the sand a few feet away, she and Jake might have a chance to talk about what was bothering him.

Jake was helping with the elaborate sand castle. His sleeves and pant legs were rolled up, but both showed signs of encounters with waves.

The hubbub that had surrounded them along Cannery Row was practically non-existent on this stretch of beach near Pacific Grove. Pedestrians strolled along the walkway above the cove. Several other families with small children were scattered around them. For the first time since her divorce, Allison felt at peace. She suddenly realized that the quiet, underlying yearning she'd felt for years was missing.

But she knew she couldn't put off this conversation any longer. "Jake," she called. "Got a minute?"

Jake brushed the sand from his pants and sat down on the quilt. "What's up?"

"I think we should talk about what happened at the aquarium."

"Fine. Can you tell me why you over-reacted?"

"Is that what you think I did?"

He nodded. "Caleb was never completely out of our sight. Well, maybe for a second or two, but you can't keep a child his age on a leash."

Allison took a deep breath. "I agree, but the parenting books I've been reading stress that you need to impress on your child the importance of safety in a crowd situation. It only takes a second for a predator to swoop in and steal a child. When Caleb melted into that group, I panicked."

He didn't say anything.

"Couldn't we chalk it up to a rookie mistake and move on? Caleb seems to have forgiven me, how come you can't?"

Jake combed his fingers through his hair—a habit she'd seen before when he was nervous or uncomfortable. "I remember what it's like to be on the receiving end of a parent who couldn't control her feelings. My mother, when she lived with us, was always yelling and always very—physical. My brother was kinda fragile, so I usually got most of her attention when she was upset."

Allison closed her eyes, trying to block the image that sprang to mind. "And you think I'm that type of person?"

"I don't know. Are you? I hadn't seen evidence of it before, but stress can do weird things to people. My mother seemed like a normal person most of the time, but when life got complicated—my brother was sick and colicky as a baby and my father drank too much— she'd snap."

Allison didn't know what to say. She suddenly understood how her reaction this morning must have looked to him. And why he'd put this distance between them that hadn't been there before.

With tears in her eyes, she looked at the little boy digging in the sand. "I would never do anything to hurt Caleb. I love him with all my heart."

Jake made a rough sound. "My mother used to say that, too—right before she'd hit me so hard that sometimes my shorts would have blood on them. And then she'd complain about the stains."

Allison reached out to touch him, but Jake scrambled to his feet. "I'm sure you're not the kind of person to intentionally hurt a child, Ally, but I also know that sometimes people can't handle all the demands that are made of them. You have a lot going on in your life right now, and that makes me nervous for Caleb's sake. And, frankly, I don't know what to do about it."

"What does that mean?"

"I think he might be better off with me. In Florida."

Allison's mouth dropped open. "Are you out of your mind? You can't take him away from here—his home, his grandmother, his life." She stood up, too. "I didn't grab him and shake him like a rag doll. I took his shoulders between my hands—" She demonstrated by doing the same thing to Jake. "To make him look at me."

She waited until he made eye contact.

"I did it to get my point across. And I want you to listen clearly, too. I love that boy and would never hurt him. And if you think I'm going to let you waltz away—"

"Ally? Jake?"

Allison's heart stopped. She dropped her hands and turned to face her godson. "What, honey?"

Caleb stood a foot away, a sand-filled plastic bucket

in one hand and a shovel gripped in the other. "My tummy hurts."

She was furious at herself—and Jake—for adding to Caleb's worries. She looked skyward and noticed the pink hues on the clouds. *What was a trip to the beach without experiencing a Pacific sunset?* "Ohmygosh," she said, dropping to her knees to face Caleb. "Do you know what time it is?"

He shook his head.

"It's almost time for the green flash."

Caleb looked at Jake. "Huh?"

Jake put out his hands, indicating he had no idea what she was talking about.

As she hustled them into packing up, she said, "Actually, your daddy is the person who told me about this, Caleb. He said when the sun is sinking under the horizon—at the very last second—you'll see a green light. He didn't know what caused it but apparently people see it when conditions are just right."

Jake and Caleb exchanged a look that made her laugh out loud. "Come on, you two skeptics. There's a great place to watch the sunset just up the road."

"These waves are incredible," Jake said a few minutes later. "Look at that spray. Wow. I'd forgotten how impressive the Pacific could be."

Half a dozen cars were parked around them. Some people braved the strong, chilly wind to wander along the rocks. Most, like Jake and Allison, remained in their vehicles.

"Aren't we gonna get out?" Caleb asked.

"Not me," Allison said. "Once that sun starts to set, it gets cold. I'm content to watch from here."

Caleb made a huffing sound. Jake released his seat

belt and turned sideways to look in the back seat. His knee bumped Allison's thigh. She felt the tingle all the way to her toes.

"Do you want to sit up front with us? So you can see better?"

"Sure."

Caleb clambered between the seats and settled in Allison's lap. His small body was warm and cuddly. His hair smelled of salt spray and wind. Her arms closed around him automatically. She could feel Jake's gaze on them, so she turned her head. His tender smile almost stopped her heart.

"Nice picture," he said. "Better than any sunset I've ever seen."

Allison felt a flood of emotions—hope, joy, love, fear—rush through her. She closed her eyes to keep the tears away. Caleb fidgeted a moment later and scooted forward to lean against the dash. "Look how red the sun is, Jake—like Santa's belly."

Jake laughed and leaned forward, too, resting his arms on the steering wheel. He'd left his jacket in the back and Allison's gaze was drawn to his broad shoulders clearly outlined in the camel-colored shirt. What would it feel like to skim her hand across the soft material and explore the muscles beneath the fabric?

Absorbed in her fantasy, she missed what Jake was saying, until he turned her way. "Sorry, what?" she mumbled, finding it hard to swallow.

"I said, Caleb and I are supposed to help Cordelia move into a new, private room at the rehab hospital tomorrow. It's in a different wing, I think she said. Do you want to meet us for lunch?"

Allison's stomach produced an unpleasant grumble. "That's right. I forgot. But I promised Caleb you'd take him to buy a Christmas tree tomorrow. It seems he's a bit worried about Santa not knowing where to put his gifts."

A look of comprehension appeared in Jake's eyes.

"No problem. We can do both."

As Caleb and Jake talked about what kind of tree to buy, Allison recalled her last visit with Cordelia. The poor woman was anxious to get home, but every time her doctor seemed close to releasing her, her white count would spike, indicating the persistent infection wasn't quite beaten. Since all she could do was sit and fret, she spent a lot of time worrying about what would happen after she was released.

"You'll stay, won't you, Allison? I know Jake wants to get back to his life in Florida as soon as possible, but you're not going anywhere, are you?"

Was Jake in a hurry to leave? He never acted that way around her. In fact, until the incident today, Allison had been under the impression that Jake might even be interested in exploring the attraction between them. Or was she being naive? Maybe his issues with his mother explained why he was still a bachelor. He didn't trust women.

Allison didn't know why she was so surprised—and disappointed. After all, Pam always had maintained that Jake and Allison would make a poor mix.

"Look, Jake, look. It's sinking fast," Caleb said, his pitch an excited squeal.

Jake reached out to take Allison's hand as if linking the three of them in the shared moment. She sat forward, too, peering through the windshield at the shrinking red-orange ball. Caught up in the moment, she squeezed his hand.

His answering caress made her glance sideways. Instead of watching the sunset, Jake was looking at Allison with a message that clearly telegraphed want and desire—a longing Allison recognized because she felt it, too. Her throat contracted and her breath stopped.

"I saw it, Jake," Caleb cried, bouncing up and down. "Right there. Did you see it, Ally? Did you?"

The excited child crashed into her chest, making Allison expel the breath she'd been holding. "Wow," she exclaimed. "That was awesome."

Which wasn't a complete lie. She'd missed the green flash, but she'd witnessed magic of another kind—the kind that fed her soul. If she believed in Santa Claus, Allison knew what her wish would be: Let Jake stay.

CHAPTER ELEVEN

CHRISTMAS EVE, Jake thought, closing the rear hatch door of Allison's station wagon. Where did the week go?

He knew the answer without looking over his shoulder. The proof of his activity was on the lawn, windows and roof of the Rydell home. Jake—along with his helper, Caleb—had found a spot for every single decoration Pam and Kenny had collected over their years of marriage.

Allison threw herself—heart and soul—into everything she did. Her example, along with the good feelings he'd felt after delivering the Rydell Motors' bounty to the food bank, had made him want to do more.

On Tuesday, he and Caleb went shopping. Jake had withdrawn four hundred dollars from a cash machine and told Caleb that they were going to buy presents for kids they'd never met. Padre Avila had supplied the children's names, ages and general preferences in toys and books. Allison and her office staff volunteered to wrap and deliver the gifts.

Afterward, they'd eaten dinner—homemade tamales and all the trimmings—at the home of her assistant manager, the person who planned to rent Allison's home after the first of the year. Jake had been impressed with Ernesto Flores's intelligence and drive, and his wife's cooking was some of the best he'd had since arriving in California.

The following day, Jake and Caleb had helped Cordelia move into her new, temporary quarters at the cardiac rehabilitation center. Although she'd preferred to come home, her doctor was concerned about her persistent infection and sporadic bouts of dizziness.

Cordelia wasn't happy. "I want to be in my own home for Christmas," she complained to anyone who would listen. "My grandson needs me. How hard is that to comprehend?"

The physician refused to release her, although he did agree to let her go home for the day—if her temperature was normal.

That meant Jake would have to pick her up early in the morning so she could be there to watch Caleb open his gifts. But right now, he and Caleb planned to bring a little Christmas cheer to her.

He leaned in the open door of the Subaru and asked, "Ready?"

A none-too-happy "Meow" was his reply.

"Rom won't keep his antlers on," Caleb complained.

"Yeah, well, he's a spoilsport. Look how nicely Cleo is waiting," Jake said, peeking through a slit in the large plastic animal carrier. "Maybe she thinks the antlers are a crown and she's a queen."

Caleb laughed, and Jake shut the door.

Thirty minutes later, they were approaching the postsurgical center. Jake was grateful to see Pam's red SUV in the parking lot. He'd traded cars with Allison because he'd needed the flat cargo space her station wagon afforded. He hadn't told her that.

All Allison knew was that they were meeting here to sing Christmas carols with Padre Avila's youth group. Jake hadn't mentioned the potted plants that he intended to give to every patient and to every nurse. A florist had delivered the majority of the pots earlier in the day, but Caleb had picked out a couple of special arrangements he wanted to deliver personally.

Jake backed the car into the receiving bay usually reserved for deliveries. As arranged, an orderly was waiting with an empty gurney to help unload the cellophane-wrapped gifts. Jake reached into the plastic bag he'd brought from home and pulled out a wad of red fleece, which turned out to be three plush Santa hats with fuzzy white balls on the tips.

After tugging his own on, he looked at his godson. "Ho, ho, ho. Ready, Santa?"

"Yup," Caleb said, scrambling to his knees.

Jake hadn't been able to find a child's size cap, so the hat was too big. It drooped over one eye. "I never been Santa before." Caleb tapped on the plastic cat carrier. "And Rom and Cleo are our reindeer."

Jake wasn't sure the cats would cooperate, but the administrator had told him that animals were always welcome to visit. "Many of our residents are elderly. Pets are a wonderful healing tool," she'd said. "Especially during the holiday."

Jake had his digital camera ready. He planned to take photos of each patient with the cats to give to them as keepsakes. Allison was supposed to be bringing a printer that could hook up to his camera.

"Okay, Mr. Junior Claus, let's get this show on the road."

Caleb exited the car and hurried to the door. Jake directed the unloading of the flowers then picked up the cat carrier by its handle and touched Caleb's shoulder. "Are you ready?"

Caleb nodded, but stopped suddenly and asked, "Is Ally a Santa, too? Or an elf? She's a girl, you know."

Jake knew all right. She'd been in his dreams for the past two nights. "We're all Santas today," he said, his voice gruff. "I brought her a red hat, just like ours."

"Good," Caleb said. "I didn't want her to feel left out."

Jake's heart swelled. *Did you hear that, Kenny?* You raised a pretty great kid who thinks of others. That's your doing, my friend. Yours and Pam's.

"WHAT'S THIS ALL ABOUT, Allison?" Cordelia asked.

Allison's heart went out to Cordelia. Her recovery seemed a jerky dance of forward and backward steps. Even two rounds of intravenous antibiotics hadn't completely cleared up a persistent infection. And a new course of stronger drugs had made her nauseous. She'd lost weight she couldn't afford to lose and struggled with shortness of breath and dizzy spells.

"I don't know, exactly," she answered, striving for a light-hearted tone. "Jake asked me to meet him and Caleb here, and bring a printer."

"Sounds rather bossy. Doesn't he know you have work to do?"

"I let everyone go home at noon today since it's Christmas Eve. I'd planned to do a little packing at my house, but I'll have time this weekend. Ernesto and his family have until the middle of the month to move. His landlord is going to do some work on the place before he rents it for almost double what Ernesto is paying now."

Cordelia moved restlessly between her chair and the window. "Are you sure you want to do that? Rent your place to someone else? What if they trash it?"

Allison frowned. "Ernesto is a great guy. His wife is one of the sweetest people I've ever met. I'm not worried. They'll be great tenants."

Allison had made the decision to rent her home as a way to save money. Plus, it was increasingly obvious that even when Cordelia returned home, she wouldn't be able to handle Caleb without help. Privately, Allison was worried that Jake could be right. Maybe *she* wouldn't be able to handle Caleb without his support. But she didn't tell him that.

Cordelia took a seat in the cushioned rocker facing the window. Her sigh sounded as if it carried the weight of the world. Allison walked to her and squeezed her shoulder. "Thanks for your concern. My parents were worried, too. They'd heard horror stories about how difficult it could be to get renters out, if things turned ugly. But the Flores will probably take better care of the place than I did." She laughed ruefully.

"So you're planning to stay at Pam's then? Even after I move home?"

They'd been over this a dozen times. Why the questions? "Yes. Jake will be here until you're completely on your feet, then he'll return to Miami. And you and I will take care of Caleb."

Cordelia sighed. "You're a young woman, Allison. Things change. People fall in love—"

Her words were cut off by the sound of footsteps coming from the hallway. Before Allison could give the woman's comment much thought, Jake and Caleb walked in, both wearing red hats. An orderly paused outside the doorway beside a gurney loaded with poinsettia plants. "Jake," Allison exclaimed, "what's going on?"

"We're here to spread some holiday cheer. You two ladies need to accompany us to the reception hall. We have goodies, gifts and song. But first—" Jake set down the animal carrier in his hand and walked to Allison "—you need your hat."

Allison laughed out loud. She would have clapped, but her hands were hampered by Jake's proximity as he tucked her hair behind her ears and placed the fuzzy cap on her head. His breath was sweet and warm. His eyes twinkling. Allison wanted to kiss him, but she knew Cordelia was watching. Maybe this closeness, this attraction, was what the older woman sensed…and feared. Was she worried that Allison would fall in love with Jake and go back to Miami with him? Impossible. For one thing, Allison's closest friend, the person who'd known her best, had insisted that Ally and Jake would make a lousy couple.

"You're crazy, but in a good way," she said, stepping back. She faced the mirror above the dresser to adjust the little white ball so it was hanging to one side instead of down her back like a ponytail. As she pivoted, she spotted the carrier. "Please tell me those aren't my cats."

Caleb rushed forward. "They are, Ally. Only really they're our reindeer. Look."

He dropped flat to the tile and peered sideways to look at Cleo and Rom. "Caleb, get up off that dirty floor," Cordelia cried.

Caleb ignored her. "Cleo's still wearing her antlers, Jake."

Jake hefted the boy to his feet. "That's great, champ.

But your grandmother asked you to stand up. Remember this is a hospital. Why don't you wash your hands before we go to the community room?"

Caleb made a face, but a second later dashed into the adjoining bathroom.

"Antlers?" Allison asked, holding her hat on her head as she leaned over to peer inside. She opened the little door, half expecting Rom to bolt, but the animal—sans antlers—merely looked at her. "Did you drug them?" she asked suspiciously.

"No, of course not. Caleb and I introduced them to the antlers this morning. Rom wasn't wild about his so I took them off, but Cleo seemed to like hers. I'd planned to ask you if it was okay to bring the cats, but Caleb wanted to surprise you. Was that a mistake? They are your cats, of course, but they seem to have gotten quite close to Caleb."

Allison agreed. For the past week or so, both cats had taken to sleeping with the little boy. Even though she paid the vet bills, Allison knew that cats set their own rules. If they weren't bothered by this little excursion, why should she care?

"No, I'm fine with it. But…" She looked at Cordelia and winked. "Jake's obviously never heard of payback. I hate to think about the little gift Rom is going to leave in his favorite loafers tonight."

Jake laughed and picked up the carrier by the handle. "Let's get this show on the road. Who wants to take photos and pass out plants?"

"I do. I do," Caleb shouted, racing back into the room.

"Do you have enough of those for everyone in the place?" Cordelia asked.

"I sure hope so. And you get a special one that Caleb picked out just for you." The attendant who had been waiting patiently beside the gurney handed Caleb the largest plant, dense with ruddy red and off-white leaves. The shiny foil and gold bow around the pot looked festive.

Since the child couldn't see over the top of the vegetation, Allison steered him to a low table. "Merry Christmas, Gramma," the little boy said, rushing to give her a big hug once his arms were empty.

Tearfully, Cordelia hugged him back. "Thank you, dear."

"We knew you felt bad about not being home and we were hoping this might brighten your day," Jake said. "Here's to a happier new year."

Allison was all for that—even though this was shaping up to be one of the most memorable Christmases on record.

"Coming, Ally?" He offered his free hand to her. Allison was powerless to resist.

"Cordelia?" he asked, pausing in the doorway. "Will you join us? Father Avila will be here with a choir to sing carols. And we ordered refreshments."

Allison could see that the woman was trying hard not to cry. She dabbed her eyes with a hanky and nodded. "I need a few minutes to freshen up a bit."

"Don't be too long," Jake warned. "We need you to sing. Caleb says you know all the Christmas carols by heart."

Cordelia waved them on then slumped back in her rocker. Allison didn't want to cast a pall on the festive occasion by expressing her worries, but she felt compelled to say, "I'm worried about her, Jake. I think

Cordelia might be slipping into depression. Do you think it would be okay to ask Father Ray to talk to her?"

Jake stopped abruptly and stepped to one side so the cart could pass them. "Hang on a sec, pal," he told Caleb. "I want to adjust Allison's hat before we make our grand entrance." He set down the cat carrier. "Why don't you see if you can interest Rom in wearing his antlers?"

Allison glanced up at the white fabric resting just above her eyebrows. "What's wrong wi—?" Her words faded away when Jake moved closer, positioning himself so his back was to Caleb.

The look in his eyes made her throat dry up, but she tried to swallow anyway. She licked her lips for some moisture, and Jake's gaze dropped to her mouth.

He put his hands on either side of her temples and adjusted the hat, but at the same time he leaned in and said softly, "I just wanted to tell you that you're not only the cutest Santa I've ever seen, you're quite possibly the most compassionate person I've ever met."

Allison had no words—even if she could have found her voice to speak them. Completely nonplussed, she somehow managed to smile.

Jake gave her white tassel a little tug, then said, "Okay, felines and fellow Santas. It's showtime."

CALEB WAS HAPPY, and he wasn't sure that was okay. Normally, he'd ask Jake, but Jake was busy pouring punch into little cups.

Ally was standing in the corner alone, so he could have asked her, but Ally was like his mom. They'd both just tell him whatever he was feeling was fine. Mommies were like that. They didn't want you to feel bad about anything.

But Caleb needed to hear the truth, so he turned to the minister Jake and Allison called Padre. The silver-haired man laughed a lot, but Caleb trusted what he saw behind the smile.

Today, Padre was wearing a long black dress with a pretty scarf that hung around his neck almost to the floor. Caleb had seen ministers in dresses before, and it didn't bother him because he knew they wore pants underneath.

"Hello, young Caleb," the man greeted him, motioning Caleb to come closer to the chair where he was seated. "Merry Christmas. This is some party you and your godparents have thrown."

Godparents. Caleb had heard the word, of course, but he'd never really thought about it. He knew who God was—the biggest person in the world. The One who took his real parents away.

"Don't call them that," Caleb said. "God is mean. Can't they just be my parents, without God?"

The man's thick brows flickered the same way Rom's whiskers moved. "That's the term given to the person or persons who look after a child if anything happens to his family. I think God would be proud to have His name associated with Jake and Allison."

"Will God take them away, too?" He voiced the question that made his stomach ache.

Padre put down his coffee and helped Caleb climb up on his knee. "Caleb," he asked gently. "Do you know the story of Baby Jesus?"

"Sure. That's why we have Christmas. Ally read me the story last night before bed."

"Then you know that Jesus was God's son. And millions of people celebrate his birth. He was God's gift to us. A very generous gift, considering he died, too. Just like your parents."

Caleb didn't answer. He didn't like thinking about his parents. He wasn't mad at them any more, but he missed them very much.

"Caleb, what happened to your mother and father was a really sad thing. When something bad takes place, it's natural to blame God. But I want you to think about this—He lost a son, too. He knows how you feel and He made sure that you have good people in your life to look after you. That's not mean, is it?"

Caleb thought for a minute. If Jesus was God's son, did that mean Mary and Joseph weren't his real parents? Maybe they were godparents—picked special to care for His little boy.

"I don't want Jake and Ally to go to heaven," Caleb said. "Or anywhere. I want them to stay with me."

"Have you told them how you feel?"

Caleb looked around. Ally wasn't in the corner anymore. And Jake was looking down the hallway toward Caleb's grandma's room. He was frowning. "Should I?" he asked.

Padre smiled. "I think being loved by a neat kid like you would make them both very happy."

"Okay," Caleb said, sliding to the floor. "I gotta go tell them I want them to be my mommy and daddy forever. 'Bye." He took a step, then stopped. His mother would have scolded him if he forgot his manners. "Thank you."

"You're welcome. And Merry Christmas."

As he raced away, Caleb heard the man laugh. It

sounded a lot like Ho-Ho-Ho. Caleb grinned. Maybe Padre was the real Santa Claus. He wasn't fat, but he did make Caleb feel better.

ALLISON'S PLEASURE in the Christmas party ended the moment a nurse gave her the message that Allison's mother was on the phone in Cordelia's room.

Anticipating news about her sister, Allison started to follow, but paused to make sure Caleb was okay. Her godson seemed engrossed in a conversation with Father Avila. She made eye contact with Jake, who was serving punch to the carolers, and mouthed, "Cordelia's room," to let him know where she was going. His brow cocked in question, but she didn't have time to elaborate.

"Callie just got back from the doctor's," her mother said the minute Allison took the line. There were tears in her voice.

"Is she okay? Is the baby okay?" Since Cordelia was still sitting in the chair by the window, Allison sank down onto the bed.

Her mother gave a little twitter. "Turns out she's going to have twins. That's why she's been so sick and run-down. Keeping up with a six-year-old and a toddler, plus dealing with double-whammy morning sickness just did her in. She's doing better now and the ultrasound shows that the babies are fine, too."

The delicious punch Allison had just drunk threatened to come back up. "Twins? Really?" Her mouth went dry. "Wow."

"I tried your cell phone, but when you didn't answer, I called your office. Ernesto gave me this number. Cordelia said you're having a party so I won't keep you, but I knew you'd want to hear the news."

"You were right. Thanks. Give Callie a big hug for me."

"I will. I have to run, honey. Merry Christmas, dear. We love you."

"Me, too. Merry Christmas."

Allison took a deep breath before hopping off the bed. The first thing she saw was Jake, looking at her with concern in his eyes.

She swallowed and pretended to smile, but apparently she didn't pull off the nonchalant look she'd been trying for. He removed his silly hat and walked directly to her. "What's wrong?"

"Nothing. Absolutely nothing. In fact, my mom just called with good news. I told you my sister's been feeling lousy with this pregnancy. Turns out she's having twins."

Her voice gave out on the last word. Her sister was going to have two babies, and Allison couldn't even carry one child to term.

Jake wrapped his strong arms around her and pressed her face to his shoulder. "I'm glad she's fine and the babies are healthy, and I know you are, too, but I understand, Ally."

He did. She could tell. She knew that he wouldn't judge her for feeling sorry for herself in the face of her sister's happiness.

"I'm an idiot."

"You're human. That's what makes you so special. You're a real person who doesn't pretend not to feel."

Allison pulled back. "Lately, it's been impossible not to feel things."

Her tears returned. Allison no longer knew what she was crying about, but it felt good to weep. To know that someone cared enough to listen, to comfort. "I'm sorry." She hiccuped as the wave passed.

She moved back and noticed Cordelia staring at them. Although there was nothing suggestive in Jake's hug, Allison quickly stepped away. She grabbed a tissue from a box on the dresser to wipe her eyes and blow her nose, then picked up her purse. "Would you mind if I skip the carols? I should get going. I have a mountain of presents to wrap, including the bike."

Jake's eyes still showed concern, but he nodded. "Okay. Why don't you take the cats and I'll bring Caleb? I could pick up Chinese, if they're open."

"We always have lasagna on Christmas Eve," Cordelia said, her tone oddly desperate. "Ask Allison. She'll tell you. Pam traditionally made vegetarian lasagna because she said people got enough meat the next day."

Jake glanced at his watch. "Well, I'm not much of a chef, but I do know that's one pasta dish you don't just whip up in an instant. Plus, Allison has been working since dawn. She's too frazzled to cook."

Cordelia started to say something, but Jake didn't give her the chance. He turned to Allison and said, "Go home and take a hot bath. I'll help you with the bike after Caleb is in bed. The squirt and I will bring dinner when we come. There must be one Italian restaurant in town with takeout. If lasagna is tradition, then lasagna it is."

Allison would have protested, but she was too tired. And a bath sounded heavenly. But before she could reply, Caleb bounded into the room. "Jake. Jake. Padre said to tell you—"

Jake put a hand to the little boy's head. "Tell me what, buddy?"

"I want you and Ally to be my new mommy and daddy. Forever."

Allison couldn't completely process her emotions, they hit so fast. Joy, fear, pride, love. She stood rooted, wondering—of all things—how someone would wrap such a gift. A smile grew so wide it threatened to break her cheek muscles...until she spotted Cordelia's expression. *Stricken* was the only word that fit.

CORDELIA ENDURED Allison's attempt to downplay the significance of Caleb's plea, but after a few minutes, she asked them to leave. She claimed her head ached, which wasn't total fabrication.

To put it mildly, life hadn't been kind to her lately. First, her husband passed away suddenly. Then, her daughter and son-in-law were gone in a split second. If anyone was entitled to self-pity, it was Cordelia. And now she seemed to be becoming an invalid. What if she never got better? Who would care for her grandson?

Jake and Allison had done a good job so far, but she knew Jake planned to leave, and her fear was that he might try to take Caleb back with him. Up until today, she'd been confident that she could count on Allison to stand up to him. Until she'd seen the look that passed between them.

They cared for each other. Maybe they were in love. He was a handsome devil and Allison could do worse than a man who was rich, good-looking and adored the child she'd promised to care for.

Cordelia had been in love once. George Wells had taken her breath away the very first time she'd met him at a coffee shop in Detroit. Their life together hadn't always been harmonious, but he'd adored her and spoiled her rotten. Losing him had almost killed her. She'd just begun to recover when tragedy struck again. She'd lost the ones closest to her, not once but twice. She couldn't lose Caleb, too.

"Knock, knock," a voice said.

Cordelia startled, her heart thumping erratically against her chest. Although the doctor assured her that he'd repaired the damage caused by her heart attack, she wasn't sure she believed him. Anytime she felt nervous or upset, her hands would turn clammy and her breathing shallow. Twice she'd nearly passed out.

"Hello," she said, as graciously as possible.

"I was looking for Allison and Jake," the Hispanic minister—Father Avila, she believed his name was—said. "Have they left?"

"I think Jake and Caleb are loading things up. Allison is gone."

He came into the room without her invitation, his hand extended. "I'm Father Ray…or Padre, if you prefer. The last time I saw you, you were pretty sleepy from the pain medication. It's a blessing to see you looking so fit and lovely."

Cordelia felt her cheeks flush. She'd missed the attention she once received from her husband. "Thank you."

"Jake tells me you'll be with the family tomorrow for the festivities. That's wonderful. I'm sure Caleb will be excited to have you there."

"I hope so. I'm beginning to think they might be just as happy to leave me here forever." Cordelia knew that wasn't true, but her fears were making her bitter.

The minister pulled up a chair beside her. He leaned forward and took her hand. "I'm certain that isn't true,

Mrs. Wells. Have you talked to Jake and Allison about your feelings?"

"No," she murmured, suddenly ashamed. What was wrong with her? She wasn't normally this bleak and mean-spirited.

"Mrs. Wells. May I call you Cordelia?"

She nodded.

"I've spoken to Jake and Ally. They came to me with concerns about how best to help Caleb through this terrible loss. They were both hopeful that you'd be well enough to return home by the first of the year. How has that changed?"

"Jake is a smooth talker—just like my husband, who passed away four years ago. He could sell coal in the Kalahari. But Jake's business is in Miami. He can't stay here forever. What if Allison falls for him and wants to move there, too?

"Her sister just found out she's having twins. A childless woman Ally's age might feel the need to produce a family. How better than to start with an instant child? My grandson. Caleb."

She pictured the moment Caleb had run up to Jake and Allison and told them that he wanted them to be his parents forever. Jake had laughed and pulled Allison into a one-armed hug. The three looked like a family, and Cordelia was left on the outside. She couldn't sit by and let that happen.

"Maybe I need to contact a lawyer," she said. "I'm still Caleb's grandmother, and I'll fight for my rights, if I have to."

CHAPTER TWELVE

ALLISON GLANCED AT the clock on the family room wall. Almost midnight. Pushing back from the square glass-and-oak coffee table at which she and Jake had been working for the past several hours, she dropped to all fours and arched her back, like a cat.

She'd changed out of her dressy slacks but still wore the festive red sweater Pam had given her last Christmas. The neckline and cuffs were edged in white and three snowflakes made a design in the wool.

Jake's low chuckle made her lift her head. "My lower lumbar is killing me," she explained. "Do you realize how long it's taken to wrap presents for *one* child?" She pointed at the pile of boxes stacked in the corner. "Even he'll think we've lost our minds."

"Caleb's an only child. He's used to being spoiled," Jake said from a foot away where he was trying to attach a pair of training wheels to a flashy purple bicycle. "Besides, half of this stuff is from Cordelia. She had three pages worth of items circled in the toy store flyer. I just picked them up."

Unwrapped, Allison thought, immediately ashamed of her grumpiness. She was tired and it was past her bedtime.

As if reading her mind, he said, "If I'd known gift-wrapping was this much work, I'd have paid to have it done. But this is my first hands-on Christmas in I don't know how long."

Intrigued by the comment, she moved closer. Still in the clothes he'd worn at the hospital, a fine wale corduroy shirt of muted gold that had come untucked from his waist, he looked both classy and huggable. He sat cross-legged with tools and instruction sheets spread in every direction.

"What do you mean by 'hands-on'?" she asked.

He glanced up from the diagram he was studying. "I usually order everything online and have the gifts sent directly to the person. No stores, no canned Christmas music, no hassle."

"That works for adults, but having a little kid to shop for is half the fun of Christmas. I used to buy things for my nieces and nephews until they got older and pickier. Now, I send them money. But with Caleb, Pam always gave me a list of the things he wanted two months in advance.

"Who else do you buy for?" she asked, her gaze fixed on his hands as he turned the wrench around the nut holding the metal bracket to the bike.

"This year, my assistant sent baskets filled with champagne, caviar and truffles to my bigger clients and gift certificates at the Disney Store to everyone else. One year, I gave coupons to a day spa for couples."

"Do you exchange gifts with other friends?" she asked, recognizing a striking similarity in their lives.

"Only the Rydells."

"Me, too."

Neither spoke for a few minutes, then Jake made an exasperated huffing sound. "Does this look right? I warned you when the guy at the store said they couldn't assemble it in time, that I'm not mechanically minded."

Allison had supported Jake's purchase of the compact motocross-styled bicycle only because she knew Pam would have loved it. But privately, she thought it looked like a broken arm waiting to happen.

"At least you're not afraid to read instructions." Smiling at a memory that popped into her head, she said, "My ex and I almost came to blows while trying to build a bookcase in our first apartment. It was funny."

"Funny?"

"Well, not at the time, I guess, but in hindsight... pretty funny."

"By that standard, we're doing pretty well. Not a single cross word or temper tantrum. We make a good team."

Allison returned to her seated position and started gathering the little bits of paper and ribbon that were scattered across the table. "Richard said the same thing the other day. I took it as a compliment."

He looked up sharply. "That reminds me. Fenniman called while I was picking up the lasagna. He said Rich's loan was approved. The sale should close escrow early next year."

"That's great. Richard will do well with it. I'm really pleased that you made him keep the Rydell Motors name."

"It made sense. Customers know the name so there's goodwill associated with it. And it will keep the memory of Pam and Ken alive."

Jake moved to the other side of the bike. With his back to her, Allison could see his muscles flex with each movement. She remembered feeling that strength when he held her. She closed her eyes and let herself fantasize for a moment what it would be like to make love with him. A sigh slipped from her lips.

"Go to bed, Ally," he ordered. "I'll straighten up after I finish."

Although tempted, she wasn't the type to leave a job half-done. Nor did she waste time fantasizing about things that couldn't be. "I'm just about finished. Maybe I need another sip of that yummy liqueur you brought. What's it called again?"

"Tuaca. One of my Italian friends introduced me to it. I thought it would be nice after dinner." He rose gracefully and filled two tiny glasses that were sitting beside a slim bottle on the nearby counter. "Do you think Pam will forgive me for buying lasagna with meat filling? There were no vegetarian ones left."

Allison stretched out her legs, resting her back against the sofa. She pulled a throw pillow from the couch and tucked it under her bottom. "Pam wouldn't care. She introduced vegetarian dishes into the family's diet because she thought her behind was too big." Rubbing her belly, Allison said, "Personally, I think Papa Joe's makes the best pasta I've ever tasted." Looking upward, she added, "No offense, Pam. Yours was good, but this was to die for." A second later, she slapped her hands to her burning cheeks. "Well, that was a stupid thing to say."

Jake handed her a glass then dropped to a squat in front of her. He waited to make a toast. "To Pam. She might not have made the best lasagna in the world, but she knew how to pick friends—loyal, generous and devoted."

Allison's cheeks turned hotter. "I can't."

He leaned closer. "It's true. Drink."

She took a sip. The sweet, nutty-tasting liquid warmed her mouth and throat as she swallowed. She lifted the remaining portion. "And to Kenny, for choosing a godfather who knows his liquor."

Jake's wry hoot sent a shiver of awareness through her. With a rumbling chuckle, he polished off the gulp. "Okay, enough mutual admiration. Let's finish this."

Allison reached behind her to set the glass on the end table, then swept the last of the trash into a plastic bag and carried it to the kitchen. She crossed wrap presents off her list. When she returned to the family room, Jake was kneeling beside the bike. "Ta-daa. All done."

She held out her hand to help him rise and they stood side-by-side admiring his masterpiece. "Wow," Allison said. "I'm actually starting to feel like Santa Claus."

Jake's chin turned her way. "But you look like a sleepy elf."

"An elf who's stiff and grouchy, with a cold butt, but, hey, it's Christmas Eve—pass the Tuaca."

He wiped his hands on his jeans. "How about a cup of my special cocoa instead? It'll help you sleep and no headache in the morning."

Allison couldn't argue with that. "I'll take the bike into the living room." She stopped. "Or, should I hide it in the garage?"

Jake paused with his hand on the refrigerator door handle. "It's pretty cold tonight. Let's keep it in the house. Maybe just tuck it behind the chair or something. Do you have a ribbon for it?"

"Yes. In fact, I bought a special one. Thanks for reminding me."

Allison parked the bike in a strategic spot near the

tree but slightly hidden by the rocking chair before walking to the linen closet where she'd stashed a red felt bow that fit perfectly between the handle bars. She affixed it with tape then stepped back to eye the bike critically. Would Pam and Kenny approve?

Trust your instincts, Ally, she heard a voice say. Pam's voice.

Allison squeezed her eyes shut. *Oh, Pam, I'm so sorry I'm here and you're not. This isn't right.*

But it's the way it is, girlfriend.

"Here you go," a masculine voice said. "Liquid comfort."

Allison spun around. Jake stood by the fireplace, a Christmas mug in each hand. The gas flames behind the glass doors danced with quiet grace. Allison moved closer to the heat and accepted the cup, which she noticed included a candy cane stir stick. "Thanks."

"You're welcome. You look sad. Thinking about Pam and Kenny?"

Instead of answering, she lifted the mug to her lips. The smooth, rich drink tasted like a melted candy bar with a hint of peppermint. The flavor was so decadent she almost moaned with pleasure. "This has twelve million calories, doesn't it?"

"Not on Christmas Eve," he said with a wink.

She took another sip. "I feel better already. Are you sure there isn't any alcohol in it?"

"Chocolate soothes and comforts all by itself. You've been on edge all night. Does this have to do with Caleb asking us to be his parents?"

Allison wanted to deny his observation but couldn't. "Do you think he noticed? I tried to be upbeat during dinner and the movie." They'd watched *It's A Wonderful Life* until Caleb fell asleep.

"No. You were great. I'm sure he didn't sense anything out of the norm, but I could tell you were preoccupied. I assumed that was the cause."

Allison sat down on Pam's red leather sofa. Jake joined her, sitting close enough that they could speak softly. "I expected him to bring up the subject in the car. But he didn't."

Allison hid her frown in her cup. "He will, though. And we should have some kind of answer prepared. But I'm too tired to discuss it tonight."

"I know you are. Unfortunately we won't have much privacy tomorrow. Cordelia will be here."

"*If* her doctor okays it. She didn't look too hot today."

Jake nodded. "The nurse told me they're worried about pneumonia. Apparently, she has some lung damage. Did she smoke at one time?"

"For years and years. Pam made her quit before Cordelia moved out here. She didn't want Caleb exposed to second-hand smoke."

"Well, even if she doesn't come, the day will be hectic. I'm sure these new toys will occupy Caleb for a while, but eventually, he's going to repeat his question. What do we tell him?"

She settled back against the cushion. The subtle lighting from the tree, the outside decorations and the fireplace gave the room a romantic feeling. *Too bad we're just...* She didn't finish the thought. "Unless you were serious about pushing for sole custody, I say we stick to our plan."

Jake set his cup on the coffee table then turned sideways, his knee touching her leg. "Plans change. But I'm not thinking of Caleb at the moment. I'm thinking about you and me."

Allison felt a flutter in her chest. "Jake, given our proximity and day-to-day contact, it's normal to feel a certain attraction toward each other, but we can't trust—"

He cut off her sentence with a kiss. A kiss that demanded her full attention. His tongue didn't ask for permission, it simply took. His hand cupped the back of her head and pulled her closer. Their chests touched.

Her empty mug tumbled to the carpet. The wide, rolled arms of the sofa provided a backrest when they eased into a reclined position. He was heavy against her, but in a comfortable way. Her limbs craved warmth, the kind only Jake's body heat could provide. Too long without a loving touch, she wanted it all. Now. Here. Fast.

Jake rose up on one arm and looked down at her. His lips were slick from her lip gloss. He wore a bemused look. "It must be after midnight because my Christmas wish just came true."

His tone was teasing but heartfelt. His words were the wake up call she needed. "Jake, we can't do this. It isn't fair—to Caleb."

He hesitated a moment as if trying understand her meaning. "You're right. He might wake up." A second later his moccasins were flat on the floor. "Let's go to my room. Or yours."

Once free of his weight, Allison sat up and drew her knees to her chest. "I meant that we can't do this, period."

His brows furrowed. "Why? We're consenting adults. Both single."

"Not exactly. We have a child."

"And how does our making love hurt him?"

Allison stifled a groan. She was positive she'd regret what she was about to say for the rest of her life. But better her regret, than Caleb's. Or Jake's. "Jake, I've never been the kind of girl who can handle casual sex. I know that about myself. If we made love, it would be admitting to myself that I love you. And I can't do that. Not when I know you're going to leave as soon as Cordelia moves back."

He drew in a deep breath and slowly let it out. "Ally, nothing is written in stone. But if you're asking me to commit to something long-term…well, I'm not sure I can do that."

Allison heard something new—and raw in his tone. She'd never seen this side of him. Self-doubt. Fear.

He sat forward, feet flat, shoulders hunched. "Affairs of the heart and I don't mix, Ally. I've come close twice. In the end, I failed to commit both times."

"You left two women at the altar?"

He shook his head. "It never got that close, but I almost had a china pattern with my name on it, once."

His attempt at humor didn't affect her. She scooted closer and put her hand on his back. "Pam never told me."

"Both happened when I lived in New York. Kenny knew, but I asked him not to talk about it."

"Well, I think we should. You know about my failed marriage."

He flopped backward into the cushions. "Can't we just agree that when it comes to long-term relationships, I have a miserable track record?"

"I think Kenny would have disagreed with you," she said. "And I know Caleb would."

He started to reply, but she added, "And your clients. People who trust you with their retirement, their dreams."

He made a dismissive gesture. "That's just money. I have a knack for numbers. Buying and selling stocks is a game to me, and I like to win, but when it comes to the intangible…" He let out a long, deep sigh.

"Does it have something to do with your childhood? You told me about your mother, and Kenny mentioned once that you had a rough time growing up. That you'd spent time in an orphanage."

He snorted. "Nothing quite so Dickensian. After my mother left, my dad managed to keep things together for a while, then he lost his job and started drinking full time. Eventually the state got involved."

"Are your parents still alive?"

"No."

"Tell me about Phillip."

He made an offhand motion. "I already told you, he died when I was fourteen. We'd been in the system for a couple of years. I had a new, court-appointed advocate. A gung-ho college type who had big plans to get the two Westin brothers reunited with an adoptive family. It almost happened, but then Phillip got sick.

"He'd always been small for his age. He caught every cold that went around. I figure our mother's smoking and drinking the whole time she was pregnant was to blame. But he was a feisty little runt. And he never let things get him down—even when he was sick."

Allison could tell this was painful for him, so she moved closer and put a hand on his shoulder. The muscles beneath her fingers were bunched. She massaged the kinks. "What happened?"

"The family who was interested in us backed out because they said their insurance couldn't handle the health risk. I was really, really pissed off. Not for my sake, but because I knew Phillip had been counting on us being together. He said his foster mother had it in for him."

Allison massaged a little harder. "Did he get sick?"

"A cold turned to bronchitis. By the time his foster mother took him to the doctor, it was pneumonia. My caseworker drove me to the hospital to see him. Phillip had a plastic tent around him. He was so drugged up, he didn't even know me."

He grabbed her hand and held it tight between them. Looking straight into her soul, he said, "Our father was there. In the hallway. He told me that Phillip was going to die and it was my fault."

"Yours?" Allison cried. "You were just a boy. How could that be?"

"Apparently, the family felt guilty about turning us down and was reconsidering until I got in a fight at the group home. A kid I'd been having trouble with from the very beginning said something about my faggot brother, and I went ballistic. I broke his nose. Naturally, a mark went on my record. The people decided a sick kid and a violent one was definitely more than they could handle."

Allison heaved a sigh. "That was unfortunate, but your reaction was understandable. You weren't to blame for their decision. It sounds to me like they were looking for an excuse. Where was their compassion? Didn't anyone care about what you were going through?"

His snicker was anything but humorous. "Apparently not. Phillip passed away a few weeks later. On Christmas Eve. The night attendant at the home woke me up early just so he could give me the news."

Jake would never forget the look on the sadistic bastard's face when he said, "Hey, loser, your pissant brother is dead. Merry Christmas."

At fourteen, Jake had mastered the stone cold stare. He never gave the man the satisfaction of seeing his heart break into little pieces. Instead, Jake got out of bed and went to the bathroom. But he didn't cry. He waited until he was sure he was alone then punched his hand through the drywall in the linen closet. Afterward, he rearranged the stacks of towels to keep anyone from seeing it. His knuckles bled, but blood was a common sight in this group home. Nobody asked.

"To be honest," he told Allison, "I knew Phillip was going to die, and I didn't blame him. Life pretty much sucked. Our mom was history. Our dad was a loser. And society was made up of a bunch of psychopaths and pedophiles. He didn't have a chance."

She sighed. "Turn around. I wasn't finished massaging your shoulders."

"I'd rather you didn't."

She looked hurt. "Why?"

"Because your touch makes me want things you told me can never happen. I appreciate the comfort, but it's damn hard to be *friends*—" he emphasized the word so she'd get his meaning "—when you want to—"

He didn't have a chance to finish the sentence. She kissed him. Her taste was sweeter than the chocolate bar he'd melted into the cocoa. Her lips were soft and warm and her arms a balm to the pain he'd just recalled. Jake was always melancholy this time of year. The bitterness and futility he'd felt in his youth came back to him no matter where he was—St. Barts or Switzerland. Or even California.

But those feelings were pushed aside like a curtain parting when Allison put her hand under his shirt. "Do you know what I want for Christmas?" she asked, rubbing her nose along his jaw.

"What?"

"Us. To be together. Tonight."

He shook his head. "No. I don't want you to make love to me because you feel p—"

She put her hand over his mouth. "Say the word, and Santa will definitely not bring you any presents. This isn't about pity. It's about honesty. Do you remember at the wake when you said you'd learned at a young age to show people the image they wanted to see?"

Jake nodded, the tightness in his throat preventing him from speaking.

"This is what *I* needed to see. The real you behind the facade."

"The damaged little kid?"

"The survivor who never gave up."

He might have argued, but it was late and her lips were sweet. And some gifts were best opened on Christmas Eve.

ALLISON STRETCHED, slowly coming into awareness. The messy sheets of her bed were a clear reminder of her impulsiveness. Her naked body and satisfied feeling further proof that she'd spent the night in Jake's arms, making love to the man she'd vowed not to fall for.

How did this happen, she silently asked herself?

She knew what Pam would have said: "You're a sucker for vulnerability. Look at your cats. Perfect example. One was chewed up and limping when you found her, and the other hissed at you for six months before you tamed him enough to get him to the vet. You insisted that beneath that angry bluff was a desperately lonely soul."

Maybe Pam was right. Jake's story of his childhood leveled the playing field in a way she couldn't explain. She'd grown up safe and provided for, but there were times when she'd felt overlooked. Could that explain why she identified so strongly with the lost little boy Jake had been? She didn't have an answer, but she did know one thing—just as she'd predicted, making love with Jake had sealed her fate. She loved him. Period.

Her foot inched to the left, looking for the warmth of his body. Her eyes popped open. He wasn't there.

"Jake?" she called softly, sitting up.

Chilly air poured under the down quilt.

He didn't answer, but the door leading to the hall was open. The soft, colorful glow of Christmas lights was visible. Lights they'd turned off before coming to bed.

She found her robe and slippers and quickly dressed. Did he have regrets? She had to know.

His back was to her as she approached. He appeared to be hanging ornaments on the tree, but whatever he was putting up was so small she couldn't make it out clearly.

"Jake?"

He spun around. "I didn't mean to wake you," he said apologetically.

"You didn't. I missed you and figured it was almost morning, but it's still dark outside. What are you doing?"

"Penance."

Penance? "For making love?"

"No," he said, his tone tender. "That was a gift. This is about Phillip."

Allison walked to his side and looked at what was in his palm. "Jacks?" she asked, hesitantly touching one. Seven or eight were jumbled together, their tiny points interconnected like some kind of science project. Threaded into the mixture were loops of yarn—the kind she'd seen in Pam's sewing basket.

Jake took a deep breath. "When the attendant came to tell me Phillip was dead, I was mad. Furious. But I couldn't let him see that. So I took the dumb gift I'd bought for my brother—" He presented his open hand in a way that made the little objects sparkle. "And tied pieces of thread that I pulled from the hem of my jacket and hung them on the artificial tree at the group home."

"As a tribute to Phillip?"

"Or a reminder that everything good in my life would eventually wind up in the garbage."

"You don't really believe that," she told him, "or you would have given up. Which, obviously, you didn't do."

She reached out and touched one of the pieces. "May I?"

He frowned and it took a heartbeat for him to answer. "I guess," he said with a shrug that reminded her of Caleb.

The metal playing piece was cold and spikey but seeing the neatly tied yarn almost broke her heart. She let it dangle from her fingers against the light. "Have you done this every year since he died?"

"No," he replied. "There were years when I couldn't

even afford the price of a set of jacks. But every once in awhile I'd be in the toy aisle at the grocery store and if I saw a bag, I'd think of Phillip." He finally smiled. "Poor little guy was almost always sick around the holidays, but, dang, he could play jacks. He had the most amazing eye-hand coordination. Quick as a flash."

Allison took her time finding just the right spot to hang the first jack. "I haven't played for years. I remember beating my brother one day, and that was the last time I ever saw our set. He hated to lose—especially to a girl."

She reached for another piece, but his fingers curled into a fist. She looked up.

"I love you, Ally."

Her heart stopped beating. Neither had spoken the words aloud at any point of their lovemaking. "You do?" she asked, barely able to get the words out.

He nodded. "I don't know what that means to our plans—"

She cut him off by putting her finger to his lips. "Don't ruin the moment by being pragmatic." She laughed lightly. "That's my job."

His arms went around her, crushing her to his chest. He bowed his head but didn't kiss her. When their cheeks brushed, she felt a dampness she knew didn't come from her. She was moved beyond words, and the love she felt but couldn't confess, almost burst from her lips. Suddenly she felt a velvety softness rub against her bare ankles.

"We have company," she whispered into his hair.

Jake stiffened.

"Merry Christmas, Rom," she said, glancing down. "Where's Cleo?"

Jake stepped back and turned her around, still keeping an arm around her shoulders. A little boy in red pajamas stood four feet away, his arms overflowing with white cat.

Caleb blinked sleepily. He apparently didn't see anything wrong with his godparents hugging in front of the Christmas tree. "Did Santa come?" he asked, yawning.

Jake tightened his hold on Allison and answered, "Oh, yeah. Big time."

The innuendo went right over Caleb's head, but Allison knew what he meant and stepped down solidly on his bare insole. "Ouch," he cried, a laugh in his tone. "That was my foot you accidentally crushed. Let's get some lights on and find the video camera."

Allison started to protest—they couldn't open gifts until Cordelia arrived, but she lost her train of thought when Jake opened her hand and dumped the remaining jacks in it. He closed her fingers around them and said, "We'll play later."

The promise invoked images of a different kind of game. "Wh…what about Phillip?" she finally managed to ask.

He grinned and dropped a quick kiss on her lips. "If you beat me, I guarantee he'll be watching from heaven, laughing his butt off."

She stumbled to the closest chair and sat down. Rom joined her, landing solidly in her lap. He sprawled lengthwise on her chest, his whiskers just inches from her nose. With the faintly crossed-eyed look that made her think he must have had some Siamese in his gene pool, he studied her. "Meow."

She used her free hand to pet him. "Yes, you're handsome and I love you, too."

His purr hummed through her. *I love you, too.* How come she could say those words to a cat, but she couldn't tell Jake how she felt?

CHAPTER THIRTEEN

"YOU'RE DOING GREAT, buddy, but it's almost time to leave for your grandma's," Jake called to the little boy testing out his new bike.

Their plans had changed radically when Cordelia called, in tears, to say that her fever had spiked in the night and she wasn't well enough to join them. Jake had promised to videotape everything. "Then we'll come to you—loaded with gifts," he'd told her. "Right after we dig into the feast Allison is preparing."

The morning had disappeared beneath an avalanche of crumpled wrapping paper. But each joyful exclamation and tender moment was tempered by a bittersweet feeling that every second of personal joy had come to him by way of his best friend's death. Were he and Allison pretending to be happy for Caleb's sake or were these genuine happy memories he would carry with him forever? He didn't know the answer.

As he watched his godson ride in circles in the driveway, Jake sensed an air of caution about the boy that hadn't been present in August. Maybe with time, that carefree, rambunctious child might return. Or would he? As much as Jake admired and appreciated Allison's devotion to Caleb, he also knew that she tended to be overprotective, like Kenny. That wasn't necessarily a bad thing as long as Caleb had a risk-taker like Pam for counterbalance.

Allison, who was taking advantage of the mild weather to water the three leftover poinsettia plants, rose from her stooped position. Dressed in tight black slacks, boots with heels and the new white sweater Caleb had picked out for her online, she looked like a gift he wouldn't mind opening. She caught him staring and waved.

His heart gave a corresponding answer that seemed almost cliché. Good lord, was this what the poets talked about? Had he finally experienced the real thing? He was afraid to examine his feelings too closely. As Allison had pointed out, theirs was a complicated relationship, with other people's feelings to consider, as well as their own.

"Look at me, Mommy. I mean, Ally. Look how fast I can go."

Allison put down the hose. Instead of applauding as Pam would have done, she stepped forward with a frown on her face and said, "You're doing great, but be careful not to shoot into the street."

Jake almost rolled his eyes. This was a cul-de-sac. Any approaching car could be heard making the grade to reach the summit. But he said nothing. Did his opinion matter if he was leaving soon?

Allison turned off the water and joined him. Although the air temperature was only in the midforties, the sun warmed his head and shoulders, reminding him of the Christmases he'd spent on a surfboard.

"I think the bike is a real winner," he said when she neared. "He's going to be able to ride it without training wheels in a couple of months."

"Not on my watch," she said, apparently without thinking. A second later, she tried to wave away the words. "I meant I'm not in a big hurry to take them off. I was in the E.R. when Caleb broke his finger. That's one ordeal I'd like to avoid going through again."

"Where was Pam?"

"In the waiting room. The doctor sent her away after she almost passed out. She never handled pain well." Allison folded her arms around her middle. "When she went into labor, Kenny and I were supposed to be her coaches. She managed about half an hour of contractions before demanding a C-section.

"Thankfully, Caleb came quickly. He's always been sensitive to other people's feelings."

They watched the little boy ride back and forth, singing a silly, made-up song. Jake wondered if she was thinking about the accident. Every once in awhile, out of the blue, he'd find himself trying to imagine what happened that morning. He prayed that his friends had died swiftly, without suffering.

"Where was Kenny when Caleb fell off the scooter?" he asked.

Allison shrugged. "I don't remember. I got Pam's call and raced to the emergency room. She was borderline hysterical. She was sure he was going to be crippled for life." Allison shook her head. "We're talking a broken finger. I told her she was crazy. That Caleb was too young to let any kind of handicap scar him— especially not a broken digit."

"What did she say?"

"That I wasn't a mother. I didn't understand."

Jake pulled her into a one-armed hug and leaned his cheek against her crown. "That was a bit harsh."

"She was upset. Pam could be a little insensitive at times, but I let it slide because she was worried about Caleb. Besides, she was absolutely right. The past month has proven that there's a big difference between being a pseudo aunt who pops in for parties and an occasional baby-sitting gig, and a mother who is on duty twenty-four-seven.

"I used to be able to maintain a certain emotional distance. Now, I'm right here in the trenches, feeling every smile and tear."

"And you love it."

"I like parts of it," she equivocated. But, in response to the skeptical look he gave her, added, "Okay, I love it, but let's not forget. Caleb is four. His mother got him through the baby stage."

He let his hand fall to her waist. He liked her figure—trim and fit but not waiflike. "Does that mean you don't want any more kids?"

She turned sharply, her expression aghast. "We both know that isn't going to happen." For the length of a heartbeat, she paused. "Don't we? You took precautions last night."

"Of course." Jake could have put more oomph in his reassurance but he hadn't cared for her vehement denial. "But no method is foolproof."

Her pensive frown made him sigh. "I wasn't talking about last night, Ally. I meant in the future."

"Then the answer is no." Her bottom lip disappeared again and she shook her head. She was lying. He knew it as surely as he knew his computer password.

He drew her into his arms and whispered against her hair, "Liar."

She tried to pull away, but Jake kept her arms pinned.

He nuzzled her cheek until she looked up, then he kissed her. Her skin smelled of fresh air and rosemary, which she'd snipped from a plant in Pam's herb garden to sprinkle on the turkey. He couldn't remember ever desiring anyone more.

A honking horn made them jump, then spring forward in a reflex response. "Caleb," Allison cried, her tone pierced with fear.

Jake's heart raced off the charts until he spotted his godson safely in the driveway, waving to a little boy in the window of a passing sedan. Bradley and his family had returned. Weren't they supposed to be skiing until after the new year?

Allison's cheeks were flushed with embarrassment—no doubt realizing they'd been caught in a public embrace. She turned away, but he blocked her escape. "We're grown-ups, Ally. Mutual affection is allowed. Come on, they're waiting with the windows down."

He pulled her with him to the curb. "Merry Christmas, everyone," he called. "Aren't you folks home early?"

Marc, who was driving, leaned around Gayle, who looked wrung out, and said, "Had to cut it short. Brad has chicken pox. We wanted to warn you. He probably caught it at preschool, so you all have been exposed."

Exposed. Perfect word. That's how Allison felt. To avoid the question she was sure to see in Gayle's face, Allison stepped to the rear passenger window and tapped on the glass. "Hey, cutie. Not feeling so hot, huh? Got spots?"

Bradley nodded solemnly, then lifted his Spider-Man T-shirt. His chubby white belly looked like a connect-the-dot puzzle that had been slathered with some kind of flaky pink residue. "Poor baby. When did it start?"

His father answered. "He had a fever all day yesterday then broke out this morning. He's so miserable, we decided to come home."

"Although if I'd known the resort would refuse to give us even a partial refund, he could have been sick there as well as anywhere," Gayle said, obviously at odds with her husband about the decision. "I'll tell you this. We're never going back there again. Come on, Marc, let's get our son to bed." As the car pulled away, Gayle leaned her head out the window and called, "You guys are probably next. I hope you're both immune—adults get this a lot worse than kids. Brace yourselves."

Caleb got off his bike, but didn't remove his helmet. "Is Bradley sick? He didn't even look at my bike."

Jake tapped on the sleek and stylish molded plastic shell that Allison had insisted they buy, along with knee pads, elbow pads and gloves. Jake didn't comment on the gear at the time, but Allison was sure he thought she was a neurotic, overprotective mother. "Yeah, pal, he feels real crummy. But you can show him next week, when you're better."

Caleb gave him a stern look. "I'm not sick."

"But you probably will be, sweetie," Allison said, wracking her memory to recall if he'd ever had the disease. "You and Brad were both exposed to the germs at preschool."

Jake looked at Allison and groaned. "You realize we're not going to be able to visit Cordelia, right? We probably put the patients at risk yesterday when we did the Christmas party. Darn. I wish I'd known."

"It's not your fault," Allison said. She prayed Cordelia was immune; the poor woman couldn't take another setback, medically or emotionally. "Have you had it?"

He shook his head. "I have no idea."

Allison pictured all the people they'd been in contact with the past week. "I'd better make a few calls. The rehab center, Padre Avila, my mother."

"Good lord, you mean it's contagious over the phone?" he quipped.

Allison grinned. She loved his sense of humor. "Hopefully, Mom will tell me that I'm immune," she said. "I can't spare a single day this week. It's make or break time for Jeffries Computing."

Jake looked as if he might say something—probably some supportive platitude, but he never got the chance. The house phone rang and he dashed inside to answer it. She was glad. If it was Gayle wanting to know if Allison had lost her mind by falling for Jake the Rake, Ally needed time to think of an answer. *Why, yes, Gayle, thank you for asking. My mind is on vacation. It's lovely here in paradise. Warm sands, still water and a hunky cabana boy who thinks I'm great.*

"Ally," Jake hollered, interrupting her silent soliloquy. "That was the padre. He called to wish us *Feliz Navidad* and wondered if we could meet with him next week. I told him about the chicken pox threat and that we'd have to play it by ear. That work for you?"

Allison nodded. "Fine. And while you're on the phone, would you call Cordelia? She's going to be upset. Poor woman. She'll probably think we planned this as a way to steal her grandson's affections."

Jake frowned. Instead of going back inside, he walked to where she was standing. "I'd be happy to call her, but first explain what you meant by that comment."

Allison groaned. Maybe she was reading too much into the alarm she'd seen in Cordelia's eyes yesterday. "I was looking at her when Caleb said he wanted us to be his parents. She wasn't happy. If Cordelia knew we'd…if she knew about last night, it might add to her paranoia, which is totally understandable given all that's happened," Allison quickly added. "She's trapped in the hospital and has had to give up control of every-thing in her grandson's life. If she thought something had developed romantically between us, I'm sure she'd feel threatened."

Jake ran a hand through his hair. "Would it shock you if I told you that I've been trying to figure out a way to take you and Caleb back to Miami with me?"

Allison felt a shiver pass through her, but she refused to acknowledge the cause behind it. "Yes," she lied. Then, because of the skeptical look he gave her, con-fessed, "Okay, I might have given the idea a nano-second of consideration, but when I wake up out of my daydream, I remember that I'm locked into a thirty-year mortgage and a five-year business plan. I'll be paying off loans till I'm gray if I backed out, now."

"So moving to Miami is not an option, but what if I moved here? Part-time, at least. Two of my clients are in the movie industry. It's very hip to lead a bicoastal life."

Allison was momentarily speechless. Jake, here. And there. With the Rollerblading bombshells and five-star restaurants. Something about the image made her stomach turn over. "Naturally, you'll be welcome here any time. It would be great for Caleb if you could visit often."

A cloud passed by overhead, turning his eyes a troubled gray. "I wasn't just thinking about Caleb when I suggested that, Allison. I was thinking about us."

Us. Allison wasn't ready to delve into that topic. One, because she knew she wasn't cosmopolitan enough to handle a long-distance relationship, and two, because she couldn't get past Pam's conviction that Jake was wrong for Ally.

Fortunately, Caleb came zooming past at that moment, picking up speed as the driveway sloped down to the garage doors, which were closed. Allison and Jake both turned to watch. Ally held her breath, hoping the brakes worked. They did. He tottered to a stop and waved in triumph. "Did you see me? Did you?"

Tears threatened. *Did you see him, Pam?*

Jake answered since Allison couldn't. "We sure did, pal. You're phe-nom-e-nal. Now, can you pump all the way back up the hill?"

Caleb's lips set and he nodded. "I can do it."

They watched him try, but it was soon obvious that he didn't have the steam to make it. Before going to his godson's aid, Jake said, "We'll talk about this later. We're going to do what's best for Caleb, but that doesn't mean we're not entitled to a life, Allison."

She agreed. But whether they had any hope of making their lives mesh was another question. And how would Cordelia fit into the picture? The woman had suffered enough. Allison would do anything to avoid causing her more pain.

As she watched him push Caleb up the incline, she

decided the metaphor fit. The next couple of weeks were going to be an uphill battle for them all.

ALLISON WAS SEATED at her desk in her office five days later, when a knock on the door made her look up. "Padre," she said, rising. "Good to see you. And without spots."

He laughed good-naturedly. "As a child, I contracted every childhood disease known to man. One time I was so sick, my mother promised me to the church if I kept breathing. And here I am—a priest that breathes."

"Is that a true story?" she asked, motioning him to come in. Her normally pristine workplace was still showing the effects of her month-long neglect. Boxes topped boxes. Files were scattered everywhere. Her checkbook and ledger lay open on her blotter.

"Mostly," he said with a wink. He moved a box of modems from the room's spare chair and pulled it opposite her. "I'm just glad that my early problems left me fairly immune. Good thing, since I'm around children every day. And you, Ally? All clear?"

"So far, so good," she said, pushing back the sleeve of her black cashmere sweater—Jake's gift to her, along with the most beautiful earrings she'd ever seen. "Caleb helped pick out the earrings. I chose the sweater," he'd explained when she opened the gift bag. "It looked perfect for the successful executive who wants to stay warm without sacrificing her femininity."

Allison loved the decadently rich feel of the fabric, but next time she'd wear a slip, since the wool was a little bit itchy. She absently scratched the inside of her wrist then sat forward. "Plus, my mother is positive I had them. With three older siblings, it stands to reason."

"But Jake and Caleb weren't that lucky?"

She shook her head. "Caleb had a fever last night, but so far, no spots. And Jake has felt crummy for three days—joint aches, slight cough. He's trying to convince himself he's coming down with a cold, but according to my mom, people often experience flulike symptoms before breaking out in a rash."

"Although it's never fun to be sick, Caleb is better off getting it now. Children his age usually have mild cases, compared to adults. If Jake has it, he'll probably be miserable. Doesn't he know if he's immune?"

"Apparently not."

The priest gave her a knowing look. "When your family is gone, there's no one to connect you to your history."

"He told you about his youth?" Allison asked, surprised.

"A bit. But he has the look of a man who's survived hardships at a young age. I see it in his eyes. He feels responsible for much of his loss."

Allison agreed. "I told him he has nothing to feel guilty about. His parents failed him. The system failed him. Why should he take the blame for things that weren't his fault?"

"Because he's Jake. People can point out the facts—as I'm sure Kenny did many times—but self-forgiveness can be very difficult for some people."

Allison wondered if he meant that comment for her benefit. To change the subject, she asked, "What brings you here today? Jake couldn't remember what you said when you set up the meeting. And, don't take this the wrong way, but you look more like a distinguished lecturer than a priest."

His laugh didn't sound offended. "A dear friend's daughter's wedding is later this evening. When not on duty, I try to blend in to put the other guests at ease."

She could understand that. "I've known several people who waited till New Year's Eve to marry—for tax purposes."

He chuckled. "In this case, they are simply a young couple who wanted to take advantage of a long weekend before they both have to return to work. Their employers have given them Friday and Monday off."

"I did that, too," she said. "Most of my crew has already left, in fact."

After a slight pause, the priest said, "I was hoping Jake could be here, too, since this concerns you both."

He sounded serious. "We could reschedule."

"No. Things happen for a reason. Besides, I get the feeling you're closest to Caleb's grandmother so you might be able to assuage her fears."

"Cordelia? We talked on the phone this morning. She seems fine. A little…distant, maybe, but no chicken pox, thank God."

"I just left there. She's worried and upset. Her doctor is concerned that her mental state might be hampering her recovery."

"How? Why? I thought she was doing better," Allison exclaimed.

The priest sighed. "I spoke with her on Christmas Eve, after you left. Apparently something Caleb said upset her. Then she heard a rumor that convinced her you and Jake are going to get married and take Caleb to Florida."

Allison groaned. "It's my fault. I told Jake she was upset." She explained about Caleb's Christmas wish that Allison and Jake be his parents for good. "I should have stopped by to see her this week, but we were worried about being contagious."

That was the truth, but not the *whole* truth. Allison was also afraid that her emotions would be apparent to Cordelia. She'd slept in Jake's arms every night this week. He continued to wake up before dawn to start his calls, so there was little chance of Caleb catching them together. But nothing could diminish the happiness she was feeling.

"I'll go see her today. I don't know how else to reassure her except to say that our plan is still the same. Nothing's changed."

He gave her a penetrating look. "Nothing?"

She sank back in her chair. "I won't lie to you. Jake and I have feelings for each other, but we're adults. We'll do what's best for Caleb."

"What if the best thing is two parents who love each other? You and Jake would make ideal parents. I simply want to be sure that Caleb's grandmother isn't overlooked in the equation."

Ideal parents? She rubbed at the pinprick between her eyes. All morning the idea of her and Jake together for the long haul had bounced around her head, but there were so many obstacles. Her business, for one. And his.

Because her head ached and her stomach felt like a war zone, she answered more sharply than warranted. "Jake and I have divergent lives. His business is three thousand miles away. And I'm stuck here for as long as I can make my payments."

Which, thankfully, she should be able to do for a bit longer, she thought, glancing at the order form she and

Ernesto had been discussing earlier. A new investment firm was moving to the area. The purchasing agent wanted Jeffries Computing to install an integrated computer network for them as soon as they could acquire a suitable building. For year-end tax benefits, they'd included a very healthy retainer.

He reached across the desk and clasped her hand. "I didn't mean to pry. I'm not a social arbitrator. I'm your friend, and although I would never betray a confidence, I think you should know that Cordelia hinted about contacting a lawyer."

"Are you serious?"

"I believe she will fight for custody if she feels threatened."

The throbbing between Allison's eyes intensified. "But we've done everything we could to include her. It's not our fault she couldn't leave the hospital on Christmas Day."

"I know. And I reminded her of that this morning, but she has a valid point. If you and Jake married and tried to adopt Caleb, you'd look very attractive to the courts. You're young, with ample means to provide for him, and, theoretically, your claim is supported by Caleb's birth parents' wishes."

Allison looked down at her hands. The only ring on her finger was a cheap mood ring that "Santa" had left in her stocking. She and Jake hadn't discussed marriage. In fact, Allison wasn't sure the word was even in his vocabulary, but there was no denying the intensity of the feelings they had for each other. "Even if—someday—Jake and I got together, we'd never exclude Cordelia from Caleb's life. He's already lost so much. How could she think we'd take her away from him, too?" Allison asked, her eyes filling with tears.

He nodded, his expression filled with sympathy. "I knew that would be your answer. Unfortunately, I'm not the person you have to convince. Cordelia has worked herself into quite a state. Some of this might be from the medication she's taking."

Allison hadn't thought of that. Both were silent a moment, then Allison said, "I feel badly for Cordelia, Padre. And if I thought Caleb would be better off with her alone, I'd bow out of the picture in a heartbeat. But in all honesty, she couldn't keep up with him. There are times when I'm ready to throw in the towel and I'm thirty years younger and in good health."

She forced herself to add, "As much as it kills me to admit this, at times, I've wondered if Caleb wouldn't be better off with Jake in Miami then staying here with me and Cordelia."

"Why is that?"

"Simply put—one Jake is better than two of anybody else. He's a great dad. Patient. Calm. When they're together, Jake gives Caleb all his attention."

"And when you and Caleb are together?"

Allison made herself answer honestly. "Part of my brain is thinking about laundry, groceries, what to fix for dinner. And another part of me is focused on Jeffries' Computing."

The priest smiled but said nothing.

"We just received a commission for a new installation. It's a big job and will allow me to meet my payroll for several months. I'm ashamed to admit I was so excited that I dove right into work—making calls, setting up job orders. I completely forgot to call Jake and

Caleb to share my good news. What does that say about me?"

The priest reached across the desk and squeezed her arm supportively. "It says you're human. Allison, it's okay to revel in your success without feeling guilty. Male business owners have done it for years."

She tried to smile. "You're very kind, but I still feel bad. Of course, my role in Caleb's life might be nonexistent if Cordelia goes ahead with some kind of custody complaint. I'd better go talk to her."

"What will you tell her?"

Allison thought a moment. "If she's feeling threatened by my relationship with Jake, then maybe I should move back to Fresno until she and I can return to the house together. Jake can manage alone till then."

"Don't you think you should run that by him, first?"

She did, but she also knew that she couldn't face him right now. Her emotions were too jumbled. A part of her wanted to be with him more than anywhere in the world, another wanted to make this whole thing go back to the way it was. But one truth was irrefutable. "Jake knows firsthand what happens to a child when the courts get involved. He'll do anything in his power to protect Caleb from that."

JAKE HUNG UP THE PHONE with great care. It was either that or lob the receiver across the room.

He couldn't remember the last time he'd been this furious. Possibly the moment he learned that his best friend was dead, but even his shock and dismay at that news paled in comparison to his current sense of rage, because Kenny's death had been an accident—a random act of fate. This was outright betrayal.

"Jake, my tummy hurts. I don't wanna watch this movie any more. Can I have a Popsicle? Where's Mommy?"

Caleb's litany of wants and complaints had been nonstop ever since he'd woken up from his nap. Jake's patience was at the breaking point, but he made himself take a deep breath and let it out. "Ally just called, kiddo. She's on her way to see Grandma Cordelia." *The woman who just booted my life off course.*

"I wanna go, too. Can I go?"

"Sorry, buddy. You and I are quarantined until we stop being contagious."

Caleb threw back his head and started to wail, "I don't wanna be 'tagious. Make it go away."

Jake could think of several things he wanted to go away—Kenny's mother-in-law, for one. "She just needs some reassurance that we're not going to change the plan, Jake," Allison had explained in a coolly detached tone. "I'm going to tell her I'm moving back into my house until she's able to come home. I shouldn't be around you two, anyway. I'm worthless as a nurse and I could spread your germs to the public."

"Too bad," he muttered under his breath. He wanted Allison. He needed her. He couldn't care for a sick child alone—especially if he were doomed to catch this, too. So far, only Caleb was showing signs of coming down with chicken pox. He'd developed a fever last night and had slept off and on today, but no rash. Yet.

Jake's symptoms seemed to be diminishing rather than intensifying. His headache and sniffles still felt more like the flu than the chicken pox.

He walked to the freezer, took out a grape Popsicle and broke it in half. He carried one piece to Caleb, who was wrapped in a blanket on the couch in the family room. "Here, kiddo," he said, passing the stick to Caleb. "Try not to spill."

Caleb stared at the offering. His bottom lip popped out and he started to cry. The icy treat waved precariously like a flagpole about to topple.

"What's wrong?" Jake asked.

"You broke it…the whole thing…Mommy lets me…"

Jake got the drift. He wasn't sure which mommy Caleb was talking about, but it didn't matter. He plucked the offending treat out of the child's hand and carried it into the kitchen. He dumped both halves into the sink and went back to the box. Only one remained. Orange, of course. No grape. He carefully peeled the paper off and wrapped the double sticks in a wash cloth.

When he returned, Caleb was sitting upright, his knees to his chest. He looked more scared than sick, and Jake's anger disappeared. He sat down and looked his godson in the eye. "I think we're both a little grumpy because we've been cooped up all day. Nobody said we had to be quarantined in one place, did they?"

Caleb shook his head, although it was obvious he didn't know what quarantined meant.

"Cool. Then you eat your Popsicle—we only have orange left, and I'll go pack a bag."

"Pack? Where are we going?"

Florida. Tempting though the idea was, he pushed it out of his mind. "I'm not sure, exactly. We'll figure that out when we get there."

Actually, he did have a destination in mind, but he was hoping he could talk himself out of it. Taking a sick kid on a road trip would probably provide fuel for Cordelia's custody battle, if Allison's plan failed to appease the woman's concerns. But this would be a fast trip and he'd deal with the consequences when they came.

At the moment, all Jake could think about was Ally. Did she actually believe that their being apart was better for Caleb? Or was her unselfishness just fear in disguise? Maybe she was afraid she loved Jake enough to give up her dreams, her business, her independence.

Jake understood because he felt exactly the same. And as tempting as it was to run away from the feelings she evoked in him, Jake was ready to try something different. He'd made some changes this week—big ones. Unfortunately, he hadn't found the right moment to talk about them with Ally.

Why? Because he'd perfected the art of avoidance years ago. But Jake knew that eventually the past caught up with you. Which explained why he was now headed south to L.A., or as they said in Spanish, *La Ciudad de Los Angeles.* The city of angels. Maybe it was time to settle up with one of those angels—Phillip.

CHAPTER FOURTEEN

ALLISON SLOWLY GOT INTO her car. She hurt from the inside out.

After talking to Cordelia, Allison realized that her involvement with Jake was asking for trouble. She, Jake, Cordelia and Caleb were four traumatized souls who had just suffered a staggering loss. No doubt the natural inclination was to try to fill that void with some other emotion, but to jump into bed with a man she barely knew this soon after losing her best friend was foolish. Stupid. Crazy.

Cordelia hadn't used those words, but the implication had been there. Yes, Cordelia admitted, she was worried about being left out of Caleb's life if Allison and Jake became involved, but she also feared for Allison. "You're not the kind of girl who falls in love out of the blue," Cordelia said. "You're more pragmatic. Pam always said so. That was one of the reasons she never tried to match you and Jake. He's a footloose playboy. You're more practical."

Her words had compounded the throbbing ache in Allison's head. She couldn't disagree because Cordelia was right.

The plan. They needed to stick to the original plan. Which is what she told Jake when she'd phoned him from the lobby. Before he'd hung up on her. Or had they been cut off?

Plans meant order and stability, she repeated under her breath as she started her car to go home.

Home. And where would that be, exactly? Her heart said up the hill to the house that had once belonged to her friends. Her head—her aching head—said it was time to return to her little bungalow on the other side of town.

She was about to put the shift lever in gear when her cell phone rang. She recognized the number. Jake.

"Hello?"

"The cellular service up here drives me nuts. I didn't want you to think I'd hung up on you."

"But you *are* mad at me, aren't you?"

"Yes."

Allison leaned forward and rested her forehead against the steering wheel. Did she have a fever? A chill passed through her body. She was exhausted. Maybe that was all. Physically and emotionally exhausted.

"I can't do this, Jake. Not now. I'm just too tired."

He hesitated. "You sound it. I was going to tell you to come home. You don't have to worry about bumping into me because Caleb and I are going to take a little trip. We'll be back tomorrow. This is just something I've put off too long. But you sound ready to drop. Maybe you should go to your house, instead. It's closer."

My house. My *empty* house. "What about the cats?"

"They'll be fine for one night. Gayle was just here. I'll ask her to check on them in the morning. She also apologized for inadvertently telling Cordelia about seeing us kissing. She said she didn't realize Cordelia was worried about anything."

Allison sighed. "If *I* didn't know Cordelia's paranoia was this bad, how could Gayle?"

Jake's low chuckle made her wish she was in his arms. God, she'd miss him when he was gone. She was so tired of people leaving. But asking him to stay was not part of the plan.

"How's Caleb?"

"Grouchy, demanding, unhappy and he misses you. This road trip is partly to give him a change of scenery."

"Where…?"

Her question was lost to the loud wail of a small child in the background. "Ja…ake…"

"Listen, Ally," he said his voice suddenly low and serious. "I know you think you're doing the right thing for everyone, but playing the martyr to appease Cordelia isn't in anyone's best interest.

"I love you, and we have a lot of things to talk about, but not on the phone. I'll come see you when Caleb and I get back. Okay?"

"But you haven't told me where you're going. What if I need…" she stopped as a beep warned her that the phone's battery was low. "Jake, I'm fading here. I'll call you from my house."

She pressed End and tossed the phone in her bag.

She'd expected him to be angry, but once again he'd surprised her. He wanted to talk. After he took Caleb on a little trip. Where? Why? What was that all about?

She looked out the window. Too many questions and not enough answers. But he was right about one thing, she was too tired to risk driving thirty miles. The fog was just a few condensation points away from turning to rain. The roads would be slippery.

Despite the blast from the heater, the wet cold seemed to permeate her cashmere sweater, leaving her shivering from the bone out. She needed to lie down. Maybe this was another symptom of post-traumatic stress, she thought, as she put on her windshield wiper.

"Home," the squeaky noise seemed to say. "Home."

CORDELIA STARED BLANKLY at the pages of the book on California history that Jake had given her for Christmas. Allison had left fifteen or twenty minutes earlier. She'd caught Cordelia sneaking a candy bar when she first walked in. As part of Cordelia's new diet, she was supposed to cut back on candy, but her sweet tooth had gotten the better of her.

Allison hadn't said a word about it. Pam would have. Pam would have scolded her, as if she were the mother and Cordelia the child. It was times like that that made Cordelia understand what her friends had meant when they'd warned her not to move to California. "Living too close to your children will change your relationship—and not always for the good."

But for the most part, Cordelia's move had been good. She and Pam had reestablished a closeness that had suffered greatly during Pam's turbulent college years. Cordelia and George had been against their daughter dropping out of school to marry a drummer in a rock 'n roll band.

Pam had spurned their offers of money and help. She'd been in love and she was certain love would provide for them. She'd been right. Love had given her and Kenny a good life. That had ended far too soon.

Grabbing a dainty white handkerchief—a gift from Caleb, and of course, Allison—Cordelia dabbed her eyes. She missed her daughter. She missed her life. She was so angry most of the time she needed pills to help her sleep. She hadn't even been able to see her daughter one last time before they buried her. How unfair was that?

"Hello again," a voice said from the doorway.

Sniffling, Cordelia wiped her nose. "Oh. I wasn't expecting you."

Father Avila, the priest who'd visited her several times, walked into the room. He'd stopped by earlier looking very dapper in his street clothes. This time he carried a small paper sack.

"I thought you had a wedding to attend."

He set the package on the table and removed his long gray wool coat, which he draped across the foot of her bed. Cordelia missed men in overcoats. You didn't see that kind of outerwear in this climate much, she thought.

"I'm headed there next. But I spoke with Allison a little while ago and she said she'd be over to see you. I thought you might need a sounding board to bounce ideas off after she left."

Cordelia wasn't sure she knew what he meant, but his company was always welcome. Many of her friends visited on a regular basis, but they were mostly women. A man, even a man of the cloth, was a nice diversion. "Please, sit down. I was just thinking about my daughter."

"You miss her."

"So much I can hardly stand to open my eyes each morning. It would have been better for everyone if my heart attack had killed me."

He drew the extra chair closer to her and sat down. "You know that isn't true, Cordelia. Jake and Allison would have been lost without your advice and counsel during the funeral. And think what that additional loss would have meant to Caleb."

"He has Jake and Allison. He doesn't need me."

The father shook his head. "He had his parents for the first four and a half years of his life, but he still needed you. Grandparents are our link with a bigger world. He will need you for as long as you are on this earth, which—" he looked upward with a wry grin "—I have on good faith is going to be for quite a few more years to come."

Cordelia smiled. She couldn't help it, but any respite from grief made her uneasy. Was she a bad mother for not mourning longer? All her friends told her she needed to fight to get well, but one part of Cordelia questioned whether or not that was fair to Pam. Could that ambivalence be the reason for her lengthy and difficult recovery?

She needed answers. "Father Avila—"

"Padre," he corrected.

"Ah, yes...Padre, is it right for a mother to resume her life so quickly after losing her only child? Allison just told me that she plans to stay in Fresno until I'm well enough to move back into Pam's house with her and Caleb. She looked so sad and miserable when she said it, I'm sure I've ruined her life, too. I don't want Allison and Jake, and, God forbid, Caleb to be unhappy, but I'm afraid that there won't be a place for me if Jake and Allison become close."

Padre reached out and squeezed her hand. "Your fears are understandable. They're tied to your loss,

Cordelia. People who study these things say that three of the most traumatic losses a person can experience are the loss of a child, the loss of a spouse and the loss of one's health.

"You've just lived through all three. Plus, you're worried about what will happen when you return home. Two relative strangers are living there now with *your* grandson. How will you fit in?"

Cordelia tightened her grip on his fingers. Fear coursed through her veins like a shot of poison. Her throat was too tight to speak. She nodded.

He patted the back of her hand. "I understand. So does Allison. That's why she told Jake she wouldn't return until you were with her. She told me she didn't want to add to your pain. Do you know what I told her?"

Cordelia moved her chin from side to side.

"I said that your issues weren't with her and Jake. Love is always a good thing. You know that. And if these two young people have fallen in love as deeply as I suspect they have, then they will provide the bedrock of a wonderfully happy family life for Caleb. Knowing how much you love your grandson, I'm certain you would never view that as a bad thing."

Shame swamped her. Had her fears damaged her grandson's future?

"No, Cordelia, your fears are tied up in what you perceive as failing your daughter. If you let Allison and Jake take over Caleb's care, won't the world believe that you let Pam down?"

The pressure on Cordelia's chest intensified. She tried to breathe through it as her therapist had coached her. "Would I?" she croaked.

Father Avila shook his head. "No, *abuelita*. No. Pam

and Kenny *chose* Jake and Allison to be Caleb's god-parents. Not because they doubted that you could be a wonderful parent to their son, but because they knew you already had a job to do. You're his *abuela*, his grandmother. That will never change."

Suddenly, Cordelia felt a lightness touch her. A sense of peace and serenity so pure she knew it had to come from Pam.

Tears, healing tears, flowed from her eyes. Pulling at the corners of her wet hanky, she said haltingly, "Thank you."

The priest opened the paper sack and took out his gift. A brand-new package of men's handkerchiefs. He ripped open the plastic wrapping and handed her one. "Those delicate feminine ones never seem to do the trick."

Cordelia's laugh sounded odd to her ears, but welcome. So very welcome. When she took a deep breath to blow her nose, the bands of tightness around her chest that had followed her since that morning when she learned of the accident were gone.

She looked out the window. The sky was still gray and overcast, but she knew that brighter days were on the horizon.

JAKE WAS LUCKY. Traffic on Highway 99 wasn't bad, except for a few tricky spots around Bakersfield and over the Grape Vine. The drive took longer than it might have if he'd been traveling alone, but he didn't begrudge his passenger a few stops. Overall, Caleb had slept most of the time, his stuffed alligator under his arm.

Once the Explorer descended into the basin that made up the fringe towns of Los Angeles, Jake's memory kicked in. Images from his college days and living with the band filtered past the barricade he'd erected in his mind.

Funny, he thought, the blackout of anything that had happened prior to his leaving for New York had hidden really good memories along with the bad. He decided to swing past the apartment complex that he'd lived in with Kenny and his band mates.

The neighborhood looked much the same—a collection of cinder-block apartment buildings, each grouped around a pool. The landscaping had improved, and there were fences with locked gates now. That would have cramped our lifestyle, he thought with a grin.

"Are we there yet?" Caleb asked.

"Yep. We're in the city. Are you hungry?"

"Maybe. I guess. Can we have pizza?"

Allison would probably roll her eyes. That didn't sound like the best choice for a sick kid, but Caleb didn't seem nauseated. "Sure. First we'll find a motel, then we'll get one delivered to the room and watch a movie. In the morning, I want to visit my brother."

There, I said it. His fingers tingled on the steering wheel. In the rearview mirror, he spotted Caleb's surprised look.

"Is he my age?"

"Nope. Sorry, pal. He died a long time ago, when he was ten."

"He's dead?"

Jake nodded. "I haven't visited his grave in a long, long time. Will you go with me?"

Caleb nodded, but he didn't look thrilled.

Jake spotted a motel sign and turned on his blinker.

"Did your brother go to heaven like my mommy and daddy?" Caleb asked somberly. "They died, too."

The car eased to a stop under the canopy. Jake turned off the engine then released his seat belt so he could look in the back seat. "I know. Maybe that's why I've been thinking about Phillip so much. But the good thing about memories is that no matter how long ago someone died, they continue to live in our minds."

"And hearts," the little boy said, pressing his hand to the center of his sweatshirt. "Ally said Mommy and Daddy will always be in here."

Jake quickly turned away. "Yep, that's right," he said, his voice husky. "Now, get your shoes on. The sooner we're checked in, the sooner we can order our pizza."

Two hours later, a half-finished pizza and two empty soda cans crowded the small circular table by the window. Jake had forced himself to eat his share, but Caleb had barely picked at his.

The poor kid might not have chicken pox, but he sure isn't himself, Jake thought—just as a panicky cry rent the air.

Jake flew off the bed and rushed into the bathroom to see what was wrong. Caleb's pajama bottoms were pooled around his skinny little ankles and he was holding up his pajama top to display his midsection. "I got spots," Caleb stuttered, fat tears spilling down his cheeks.

Jake had to fight back a smile. The little tyke looked so cute. Jake would have given anything to have Allison at his side. The thought was in his head before he could block it. He missed her. He loved her, and even though he wanted to be mad at her, he wasn't. He knew how much it had cost her to put Caleb's and Cordelia's interests ahead of her own.

He dropped to his knees on the cold tile floor and helped Caleb pull up his pants, then hugged him. "It's okay, buddy. Chicken pox is annoying as heck, but you'll get over it fast. They say adults get it worse, so I'll probably be itching like a dog with fleas in a day or two. Maybe we'd better make a quick trip to the pharmacy before bed."

"What for?"

"Something to dab on the itchy places."

When they got back from the store, Jake made a game of covering each tiny inflamed spot with a pinkish liquid. A few minutes later, the little boy was sound asleep—alligator at his side. Jake changed into his sweats and crawled into the adjacent queen-size bed.

He stretched out on his back with hands linked behind his head. He wondered if Allison had decided to spend the night at her home or if she'd returned to Kenny and Pam's. He wanted to call her—just to hear her voice, but he didn't want to risk waking her up. She'd sounded so weary. This had been a tough week for her and Jeffries Computing. Jake had tried to help out, but a part of him wondered whether she would be angry when she learned what he'd done.

With a sigh, he snapped off the light and crawled under the covers. At least he felt better now than he had that morning. The flu-like symptoms had passed, and so far, he didn't feel at all itchy. But who knew what tomorrow would bring?

ALLISON WALKED INTO her silent, chilly house. It was stuffy and smelled faintly of cat. She wanted to crawl into bed and forget this day had ever happened. Tomorrow was the last day of the year, and frankly Allison was glad to see it end. She might not be bankrupt, but that was the only good thing she could say about this past month.

And you fell in love.

"Fat lot of good it did me," she muttered, hurrying across the room to turn up the heat.

One minute she was freezing cold, the next burning up. *Aspirin,* she thought. But a quick search in her bathroom produced not a single bottle. Apparently she'd packed more thoroughly than she remembered in preparation for her new tenants.

She found one crinkled package of a cold treatment that required mixing with hot water. It promised to treat symptoms she didn't have—like a stuffy nose, but at this point, she didn't care. If it masked her aching muscles and the pain in her temples, she'd be happy.

As she waited for a cup of water to heat up in the microwave, Allison checked her cell phone for messages. Just one. From her mother.

Pling. Pling. The bell let her know relief was on the way. She ripped open the package with her teeth then stirred the powder in the hot water.

She had to hold her nose to drink it. The flavor tasted vaguely like lemonade—combined with a little sink cleanser, she thought.

Ten minutes later, she was curled up on the couch in her old flannel pajamas and the thickest quilt she could find. She reached for the television remote and knocked the phone off the hook instead. With a sigh, she decided to phone her mother since it wasn't quite bedtime in Minnesota.

"Ally, I'm so glad you called. We have news. We've sold the farm."

It took several seconds for the statement to register in Allison's mind. "You can't be serious. Dad always said you'd have to pry his cold, dead fingers off the wheel of his tractor."

Her mother chuckled. "I know, but this health scare really made him think. He's farmed all his life and now, we're going to play."

Play? Allison couldn't make the word fit with the image she had of her parents. Her father with his muddy boots stomping across the yard, his hearty voice calling out to some kid, cat or cow to do what he wanted. Her mother tied to the boxy, two-story white farmhouse she decorated with crafts learned at her monthly Ladies Home Extension meetings.

"Your brother will keep the farm, but the changes he has planned would drive your father crazy. We've bought a used motor home. We're heading south in early March to visit friends in Arizona, then we'll drive over to California. I can't wait to meet Caleb and Jake."

Allison's eyes clouded with tears and she swallowed. Apparently loud enough for her mother to hear. "What's wrong, honey? You sound upset."

"I don't feel good."

"I'm sorry. It's not the chicken pox, is it?"

"A cold or the flu. Aches and fever."

Her mother made a sympathetic sound. "Well, drink lots of liquid and let Jake take care of you."

"He can't."

"Why not?"

"Because I'm at my house. I was too groggy to drive up the hill," she said, stretching the truth. She *was* groggy. Her head felt like a bowl of oatmeal. There would be time when she felt better to explain her decision. "I just took some medicine and I'm going to bed."

Her mother hesitated, as if reading something else into Allison's explanation. "Well, that's probably smart. You know your body better than anyone."

Her mother's innocuous statement made her sit upright, but lights flashed like photo strobes around her head. She sank back down. "That's true, Mother. I do know my body, but how come no one would listen to me when I wanted to save my baby? Back then, my opinion counted for squat."

"I…you…Allison, what's wrong?"

Tears filled Allison's eyes and her nose started to run. "I'm sick. And alone. And Cordelia feels threatened by my feelings for Jake. She's afraid of losing Caleb and is prepared to hire a lawyer to make sure she has some kind of custody."

"Oh, honey. I can see why you're upset. Especially since you're so in love with him."

Allison's head spun. "How do you know that? I never said it. I haven't even told Jake how I feel."

Her mother's chuckle seemed bittersweet. "You're my daughter. I know you."

A painful memory pressed upward, nearly choking her. "If you know me, then why didn't you support me when I wanted to keep my baby? You…you sided with the doctors."

There. The words were out. Allison had been holding them in all these years. Her hurt, her feelings of betrayal. Wasn't a mother supposed to support her child's decision, back her up in times of crisis?

"Oh, Ally," her mother cried, "I'd have done anything to save your life. Anything. I'd make the same decision today."

Her vehemence shocked Allison to silence.

"I know how much you wanted that baby, but I kept asking myself what would happen if the doctors' prognosis was right. It was an awful choice, but I couldn't risk losing the daughter I knew and loved to save an unborn child I'd never met. Then, if you'd died after giving birth, your child would have been left motherless. Just like Caleb. Only in this case, Pam wouldn't have been there to take care of him. You had a husband, who would have been a single father. Who would have remarried. I might have lost touch with my grandchild.

"I'd have lost you both, Allison. I just couldn't bear the thought. And I won't apologize for it," she said, her voice breaking. "You're a mother now. You should be able to understand."

Allison squeezed her eyes tight to hold back the tears. It was true. Hadn't she just proved that she'd do anything for her godson? Even give up the man she loved.

"I do," she whispered. "I'm sorry. None of what happened was your fault."

Her mother blew her nose, then said, "Well, it wasn't yours, either. Bad things happen sometimes. We can't make sense of it. All we can do is hold tight to the people we love and go forward."

Bad things happen. Like a senseless car accident on a sunny morning. Like a cancerous growth competing for space with an unborn child.

"You'd better get some sleep, honey," her mother said. "Things will look better in the morning. I promise."

Allison said goodbye and hung up. Maybe her mother was right. Maybe a good night's sleep would help. In the morning, she'd drive up the hill and wait for Jake and Caleb to return from their mysterious trip. Maybe if they both talked to Cordelia they could convince her that she would always have a place in her grandson's life. And if not, well…they'd deal with that, too.

CHAPTER FIFTEEN

JAKE COULDN'T BELIEVE his luck. A hunt through the phone directory had paid off with a voice from the past. His old caseworker, who still lived not five miles from here. The man was a teacher now, and although school was out for the holiday break, he'd been on his way out the door. "You just caught me," the man said. "I promised my wife and daughter a trip to Sea World today."

After exchanging general information about their lives, the man said, "I'm really glad you called, Jake. You and your brother were the reality check I needed to get my feet on the ground. I started out planning to save the world. After your case, I realized I couldn't even protect one little boy who just wanted to be reunited with the big brother he worshipped."

The man's voice stirred up memories that were both cruel and heartwarming. Phillip had admired Jake and had tried to emulate him—which was one reason Jake's father had been so bitter. "Don't you get it?" Rod Westin asked that day at the hospital. "Your brother thinks you're the sun and moon, and all you can do is fight. As a role model, you stink."

Jake had tried to convince himself that his father was wrong, but deep inside the words rang true. Phillip had followed Jake around since the kid had been big enough to crawl. And just as Padre Avila had once commented, Jake had started to think of the little boy as his own child. But the system that held power over them both refused to let the brothers stay together.

"I'm in town with my godson and thought I'd pay my respects to Phillip's grave," Jake explained softly so as not to wake up Caleb. "But the last time I was here... well, I'm not sure I can find it."

The man gave him directions. They chatted a few minutes more, then said goodbye.

As he stared blankly at the cars moving around the sunny parking lot, Jake thought about his early years. He pictured his mother as short-tempered and nervous, but very beautiful with waist-length black hair. She'd walk around with an ashtray in one hand, a lit cigarette in the other—no matter which of her children was in the room.

Jake couldn't recall a single time that she'd played a game with him or read him a book, the way Allison did with Caleb. Jake might never have known how *normal* mothers were supposed to act, if he hadn't met Kenny.

Kenny's birth father was a fiery-tempered Sicilian, who worked for a government contractor and had a drinking problem. His mother was a sweet woman who'd been to college. She kept their house filled with books and often took Kenny and Jake to the library.

Jake turned to look at Caleb, who was still sleeping. His hair needed cutting. He looked older than the child who had visited him in August, yet very young—and vulnerable. He needed a mother. Someone like Allison who let him snuggle on her lap while they read great adventure stories or learned about spiders.

The importance of a mother's role in a child's life—and a grandmother's for that matter—couldn't be overstressed.

Caleb let out a sharp cry, as if in pain. He wrestled with the covers until his arms were free. He shook his head from side to side, his eyes scrunched tight.

Jake rushed to the bed. "What is it, buddy? Wake up."

"Don't go, Mommy," Caleb cried, his eyes blinking against the light.

Jake shook the child gently by the shoulders and moved into his line of vision. "It's okay, Caleb. I'm here. Allison is at home waiting for us. With Rom and Cleo." He made himself add, "And your grandma."

The child let out a long, deflating sigh. "Daddy?"

Jake's heart twisted. "He's not here, pal. Will I do?"

Caleb looked at Jake, his eyes filled with tears—and trust. Jake remembered the look all too well. Phillip had trusted him but Jake had been too young, too poor and too powerless to keep the boy safe. But Jake wasn't going to fail another kid.

"What do you say we get some pancakes then go visit my brother?"

Caleb scratched at a red dot on his nose. "Okay."

"But first, you're going to swim in oatmeal."

Caleb let out a surprised bark. "Huh?"

Jake showed him an envelope. "An oatmeal bath. It's supposed to help the itching."

Caleb seemed to find that idea hilarious. He scrambled out of bed and raced to the bathroom. "Can we call Ally and tell her?" Caleb asked.

Jake looked at his watch. Not quite seven. "She's probably doing her exercises. We'll try later. Maybe on our way home, so she knows when to expect us."

Jake now had two things to tell her. One, he wasn't leaving. They'd find a way to convince Cordelia that she had nothing to fear. Jake would make sure Caleb's grandmother would always be a part of his life. And two…well, she may have figured that one out on her own if she cashed the check Matt Hughes—his assistant, who'd jumped at the chance of becoming a managing partner in Jake's new bicoastal operation—had sent to Jeffries Computing.

CALEB DIDN'T LIKE it here. There were weird sculptures all over the ground. And there were funny blocks with pictures on them. Caleb was glad the big black stone over his mommy and daddy's grave didn't have pictures. He didn't even like seeing R.Y.D.E.L.L. there. He knew that meant his name, and Caleb didn't want to be under the rock—even if it meant seeing his parents again.

"Jake, I don't wanna go any more."

Jake dropped down low so they could face each other. Caleb liked that about Jake. He took time to listen. Caleb couldn't remember if his other dad did that or not. It kinda bothered him that he couldn't remember his mommy and daddy real clear any more, but Ally said not to worry. That his head was just filling up with new stuff because he was growing and learning, but that Caleb would never *really* forget them.

"What's up, buddy? Getting tired?"

"No. I just don't like it here."

Jake nodded. "Me, either. So, I promise, I'll make this super quick. Just drop the flowers and say goodbye."

Caleb frowned. "How come you didn't tell him goodbye before?"

"Before he died?"

Caleb didn't like that word, either. "Uh-huh."

Jake put one knee on the ground and pulled Caleb over so he could sit on his lap. Jake's big body helped block the wind. Not that Caleb was cold. The new sweatshirt Allison had given him for Christmas was nice and warm, but Caleb saw a movie once where ghosts got out of their graves and walked around touching people. He hated that movie.

"He was in the hospital," Jake said.

"Like Grandma Cordelia?"

"Not exactly. She's almost well. Phillip was too sick to have visitors. And after he died, my dad wouldn't let me go to the funeral. He thought I was too young."

"I got to go to my mommy and daddy's funeral."

Jake's smile made Caleb feel good inside. And safe. He hoped Jake never left, the way his mommy and daddy had. "Exactly," Jake said. "And remember how we cried when we put flowers on their graves?"

Caleb nodded. He'd cried because everyone around him was crying, but he didn't tell Jake that.

"Then afterward, we felt better, right?"

Caleb definitely agreed with that. It felt a lot better not to cry.

"That's what I want to do this morning. Put flowers on Phillip's grave then we leave for home. Are you with me? I can't do it without you."

Caleb felt proud to be needed. "Okay, but then I want to call Mommy. I mean Ally."

Jake rose and took Caleb's hand. As they walked to a part of the cemetery where the blocks—headstones, Jake called them—were smaller and less fancy, Jake said, "You know, Caleb, I think it would be okay if you called Allison Mommy all the time."

Caleb looked up. "Really? She won't be mad?" Remembering Allison's tears the few times he'd said the word by mistake, he added, "Or sad?"

Jake shook his head. "I think she'd be very happy. And any time you feel like you want to call me Daddy, go for it."

Caleb's tummy suddenly felt kinda funny—in a good way. He knew something had happened on this trip that changed things.

They were wandering down a lane between little white crosses, when Jake stopped abruptly. "There it is," he said.

He let go of Caleb's hand and walked closer. He got down on his knees and touched the words that were written in the cross. "Phillip John Westin. Hello, little brother. Long time, no see."

Caleb looked around, but all he could see was grass. Nice, green grass. Big trees—some tall skinny ones, some without any leaves at all. Not far away sat a fence and a long row of fat bushes with pretty pink flowers.

"This is a good place," he said, hoping to make Jake feel better.

Jake wasn't crying but he looked sad.

At Caleb's words, Jake took a big breath and glanced around. "Yes, it is. I used to picture it as dark and scary, but it's not."

A fat gray bird hopped across the grass nearby.

"The birds come here," Caleb said, pointing. "We should have brought them some food."

"Next time," Jake said, getting to his feet.

He left the flowers propped against the cross, but

they tilted precariously and Caleb fixed them so they wouldn't fall down. Glancing up, he asked, "Can we bring Ally—I mean, Mommy, too?"

Jake turned away to look at the street, but Caleb heard him say, "Good idea."

Caleb knew that Jake felt sad now. He remembered leaving the cemetery where his parents were. He'd cried, then, because he wanted them to come back, but Ally said they couldn't because their souls were in heaven.

"Is your brother in heaven, Jake? Where my mommy and daddy are?"

Jake made a grunt that sounded like, "Yes."

Caleb walked to his godfather's side and took his hand. "Then, maybe he's their little boy, now. Like I'm yours and Ally's."

"Oh, Caleb," Jake said, reaching down to pick him up. "You are an amazing kid. I love you. And I am so thankful your parents let me be a part of your life."

Jake hugged him tight. Caleb couldn't see his god-father's face, but he felt him cry. It scared him a little at first until he remembered Ally telling him, "Tears of love are a good thing." Jake loved him.

He needed to tell Ally that. Right away. Caleb wasn't sure why this felt so important, but he knew he had to share his news with her as quickly as possible.

"Can we call Mommy and tell her?"

Jake swallowed and wiped his face with his sleeve. "Tell her what?"

"That you're my daddy. For good. You are, right?"

Jake's smile was better than pancakes and syrup. "Oh, yeah. I'm not going anywhere—except home." He set Caleb down and took his hand. "Come on. We'll call Mommy from the road. And Grandma Cordelia, too."

ALLISON FOUGHT HER WAY out of a deep, comatose sleep. She thought she heard a distant ringing, but it could have been a dream. She opened her eyes, blinking against the gloom.

Her nose was cold. *Am I camping?* Then, she spotted her furniture. She was on the couch in her living room, and her furnace's energy-saving setting must have turned off the unit. She didn't know what time it was, but since the sky was more gray than black, it had to be daytime.

She moved under the thick down comforter, trying to decide how she felt. Sick. Miserable. Contagious. There was no way she could go to the office today. Besides feeling horrible, she'd pass her germs to her employees. Then she remembered. Today was New Year's Eve. She'd given everyone at Jeffries Computing the day off.

Braving the chill, she snaked her arm out to reach for her purse, which had fallen over on the floor. Her phone was dead. What if Jake had tried calling her? What if Caleb was worse?

The thought provided the impetus to drive her to her feet. She wrapped the blanket around her and stumbled to the kitchen where her answering machine sat. Pulling up a chair because she felt dizzy and slightly nauseated, she sat down to check her messages.

Drawing the phone closer, she noticed a red light flashing the number eighty-seven. "I have eighty-seven messages?" she mumbled. "Good Lord, when was the last time I checked them?"

She couldn't remember. Obviously, it had been a long time ago. "Too bad. If they're this old, they can't be too important." With a long sigh, she hit delete. Or so she thought.

The machine made a clunking sound as the recorder started to play back the first message. "Hey, girly-girl. Are you at work already? Jeesch. Don't you ever sleep, oh computer-vampire-geek?"

Behind the familiar laugh was the sound of a car on the road. Allison's breathing stopped. "No, God, please no," she prayed while the message continued.

"I just wanted to tell you that Kenny and I are on the way to the snow and we've been talking. We think you should come to Florida with us over spring break to meet Jake. I know. I know. I always said the two of you are too much alike, but I've changed my mind. He may project an image that's all Jake the Rake, but deep down, he's very tenderhearted and vulnerable. Like you." Pam giggled. "There I go contradicting myself again. Sorry, but I know when I'm right. And I'm right now. You and Jake would be very cool together.

"But Kenny says he'll take away your baby-sitting privileges if you break his best friend's heart."

Allison heard Kenny's voice in the background but couldn't make out his words.

Pam let out a sigh and said, "Okay. It's been nice talking to you. I'll tell you more about our matchmaking scheme when I see you. Gotta go. White powder waits. Love ya."

Allison hit the stop button then slid to the floor weeping. She curled in a ball and let all the bottled-up grief of the past weeks spew forth. She didn't know how this could have happened. How had she failed to check her answering machine even once since the accident?

Her only excuse was that she'd left her life on hold the instant Cordelia called.

As her tears subsided, Allison wiped her eyes and nose with the corner of the blanket. She tried not to think, but her mind refused to shut down. *Why that message, Pam? Why now?*

Allison knew the answer. Pam never passed up a chance to give Allison the benefit of her opinion. Allison might be the pragmatist, the planner, but Pam was insightful, instinctual and often spotted solutions that Allison had overlooked.

Allison clambered awkwardly to her feet. She grabbed her jacket, backpack and car keys. Even though she felt horrible, she was going home. She needed to be there when Jake and Caleb—her family—returned.

The Subaru pulled into the driveway twenty minutes later—a new record. The house was warm and smelled of candles, cookies and kids. The kitchen was neat and tidy. She dropped her backpack on the hall table and wandered down the hall, looking for her cats.

Not in her room. Or Caleb's.

She found them curled up on Jake's pillow. Rom lifted his head and gave a lukewarm greeting. "Fickle beasts," she muttered. She sat down on the bed. "That's the best you can do? Meow?"

The animals looked at each other, then Cleo, by far the more compassionate of the two, rose and walked to her mistress's side. She rubbed her nose against Allison's back. Suddenly feeling too warm, Ally took off her jacket and tossed it on the foot of the bed. "I could call them," she said. "Find out when they'll be back."

She picked up the phone beside the bed and punched in Jake's cell number. A sudden chill made her kick off her shoes and dive under the covers. Eyes closed, she listened to the voice mail message. "Hi, this is Jake Westin. Leave a message and I'll get back to you." Beep.

"It's me. My cats have adopted you. Did you know that?" She took a deep breath. "And Pam thinks we'd be great together. She told me so. This morning." Allison sighed. She knew she sounded crazy, but she was too tired to care. "Could you come home soon? I…need you."

There was something else she'd meant to add but it slipped her mind. She started to hang up, then it came to her. "Oh, and my mother says to tell you I love you. 'Bye."

"She looks like Goldilocks," Caleb whispered. "Only with brown hair."

Jake had spotted Ally's car the minute he pulled into the cul-de-sac. He'd found her purse and un-charged cell phone on the floor. He knew she was here—he'd retrieved his messages as soon as he and Caleb cleared the dead zone where cellular reception was spotty. He just hadn't expected to find her curled up in his bed, with her cats standing guard.

"Is she sick?" Caleb asked.

"My guess is she feels like you and I did yesterday," Jake said.

"Can I wake her up?" Caleb's whisper came out just shy of a shout.

Allison moved her head and blinked a few times. A smile formed on her lips. "Caleb," she said releasing her grip on the covers to reach for her godson. "I missed you. Where were you?"

Caleb threw his arms around her neck and squeezed

as if he'd been gone a week. "We went to see Jake's brother. He died. Just like my other mommy and daddy."

Jake watched her smile grow, then falter as the child's words sank in. "Other?" she silently repeated.

Jake knew they had a lot to talk about—the past, the present and the future. Some of it required privacy.

"Hey, champ," he said, ruffling Caleb's blond locks, "I bet the cats missed you. Do you think they'd like a treat?"

The boy jumped back, his expression gleeful. "Oh, yeah, I know where you put the box. I'll do it. Come on, cats."

While not renowned for following orders, the two animals apparently did understand the word *treats*. They jumped off the bed and followed Caleb out the door.

Once alone, Jake didn't know where to begin. "When you told me that part of Cordelia's problem was she never got to tell Pam goodbye, it struck me that that might be my problem, too. My father wouldn't let me attend Phillip's funeral. Kenny's mom took me to the cemetery a week or so later, but it wasn't the same. I'd missed the process."

Allison nodded. "You visited Phillip's grave?"

"This morning." Jake wanted to hold her, kiss her, but he didn't know if he dared. She looked so fragile and ethereal.

She stared into his eyes for several seconds. "How do you feel?" she asked.

He sat down beside her and touched her hair. "Great. I must have had a twenty-four-hour bug, but it wasn't chicken pox. Turns out I'm immune. I talked to my old caseworker. He said he remembered me coming down with the worst case he'd ever seen. It sort of stuck in his memory and for years he told people about this poor kid with spots on every conceivable inch of his body."

Allison reached out to touch his face. She was wearing an oversized pair of flannel pajamas. The button-up V-neck offered a provocative glimpse of her chest. Her spotted chest.

"How do you feel?" he asked, putting his hand to her brow.

"Crummy." She brushed his hand aside. "You probably shouldn't get too close to me. In case I have a different bug."

"Actually, sweetheart, you don't have the flu."

"I know. It's typhoid fever or something, isn't it?"

"Have you looked in the mirror today?"

Allison pressed her hands to her cheeks. Not only had she not bothered washing her face or combing her hair this morning, she hadn't even brushed her teeth. "No," she said, holding her palm in front of her mouth. "Let me get up. I must look like a disaster. I fell asleep on my couch last night and then this morning I ran across…" She could see he was holding back a smile. "I know I look ugly, but it isn't very nice of you to laugh."

He let out a chuckle and pulled her into his arms. "Oh, sweetheart, you are beautiful. You could never be anything but beautiful to me because I love you with all of my heart."

"You do?" She pulled back to confirm his veracity.

He took her hand and pressed it to his chest. "I do. And I want to marry you, and adopt Caleb, and have a dozen more kids with you."

"A dozen?"

"We can find lost children to fill that quota. Society's cast-offs."

Allison could barely believe her ears. She felt like pinching herself to make sure she wasn't dreaming. "What about Cordelia?"

"We'll adopt her, too."

Allison's eyes filled with tears, and she had to fight to keep from crying.

"Actually, Cordelia and I had a heart-to-heart talk between Bakersfield and Delano," he told her. "She expects to come home next week, and because she doesn't want to intrude on a pair of newlyweds, she plans to do something that she intended to do ever since she moved to California."

Newlyweds? "What's that?"

"Build a house on the lot next door. She owns it. She and her husband bought it the same time Pam and Kenny bought this place. She'd always planned to build her dream home, but she got comfortable living so close, and Pam depended on her a lot."

"I kinda remember hearing about that," Allison said. "Pam thought it was a waste of money."

Jake shrugged. "I told her I thought it was a good investment."

Allison was dumbfounded. "All this happened between Bakersfield and Delano? How far is that?"

Jake laughed. "It happened because you were honest with her. Plus, Padre helped her realize that Pam had picked us for a reason. Cordelia is a cool lady, and I'm looking forward to getting to know her better once she's well enough to come home."

Allison's heart swelled. "Pam was right," she said, fighting tears.

He cocked his head in question.

"She said, 'He might look like Jake the Rake, but

deep down, he's a father waiting to happen.'" She opened her arms to him. "I love you, Jake."

"Oh, Ally, I missed you." He squeezed her tight then tried to kiss her.

She avoided his lips by ducking her head. "No, I have germs."

"I'm immune."

He kissed her soundly, but when she moved her hand to thread through his hair, the sleeve of her horribly unsexy pajamas got pushed back, exposing her arm. Her mind failed to register the image for a moment, but when Jake angled his head to deepen the kiss, she suddenly let out a yelp and pushed him away.

"Spots," she cried, clawing at her arm.

Jake sat back on the mattress and started to laugh. "I know."

She yanked up her oversized shirt. Her belly was covered in fiery red dots, which seemed to multiply before her eyes. "Chicken pox?" she gasped, looking at Jake to confirm her fear.

"Oh, yeah," he said matter-of-factly. "Looks like a pretty severe case. Someone told me adults get it a lot worse than kids."

She gave him a dirty look before demurely covering herself. "Well, this isn't possible. My mother said…"

Jake leaned close and kissed her nose. "Mothers make mistakes." He shrugged. "Who knows? Maybe mine thought she was teaching me to be strong."

Allison let out a long sigh then threw her arms around Jake's neck and kissed him soundly. "I love you, Jake. And, yes, I will marry you—even if it means having a bicoastal husband."

Jake made an odd, strangled sound. She knew him

well enough to know that this meant trouble. "What? You've changed your mind? You don't like women with spots?"

He kissed the rash on the inside of her wrist. "I would marry you if you were plaid. That's not the problem."

"Then what is?"

"I have something to tell you. You might be mad."

"Mad is better than scared. What?"

"Did a check arrive at Jeffries Computing yesterday?"

She nodded. "A new company…" She couldn't finish. Her throat closed shut.

"A new investment firm that's opening a branch office in California," he completed for her. He put out one hand in supplication. "It's my company, Allison. I offered to make my assistant a partner if he'd handle the Miami office. He jumped at the chance, of course, and has been working with my lawyer to set up the partnership."

Allison wasn't sure how she felt—elated or angry. "Why didn't you tell me?"

"I planned to—after I proposed. I was afraid you'd think I was trying to look heroic by bailing out your firm. Which isn't the case, of course. I gave you the business because Kenny always said you were the best."

Allison was touched. "Well, thank you. I promise you won't be disappointed in my company."

He started to reach for her, but paused, his attention shifting to the doorway, where Caleb stood, his arms filled with a big white cat. Allison motioned him to come closer. "We have room in this hug for you, love."

Caleb jogged toward them. As soon as he jumped on

the bed, Cleo let out a displeased cry. The surprised child opened his arms and the cat scrambled up Jake's torso for higher ground. Rom bulleted into the room and disappeared under the bed.

Allison pulled Caleb into her arms and started to laugh. She and her spotted son might make a funny-looking pair, but nothing beat the image of Jake wearing a white cat hat.

Her world was complete. Not a world she ever would have asked for—void of her two dearest friends. But she knew that somewhere in heaven, Pam was holding Ally's baby while Kenny and Phillip played jacks.

Visit Dundee, Idaho, with bestselling author

brenda novak

A Home of Her Own

Her mother always said if you couldn't be
rich, you'd better be Lucky!

When Lucky was ten, her mother, Red—the
town hooker—married Morris Caldwell,
a wealthy and much older man.

Mike Hill, his grandson, feels that Red and
her kids alienated Morris from his family.
Even the old man's Victorian mansion, on the
property next to Mike's ranch, went to Lucky
rather than his grandchildren.

Now Lucky's back, which means Mike has a
new neighbor. One he doesn't want to like…

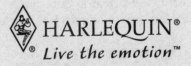

HSRH001204

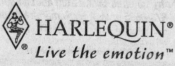

If you enjoyed what you just read,
then we've got an offer you can't resist!

Take 2 bestselling
love stories FREE!

Plus get a FREE surprise gift!

HARLEQUIN *Super*ROMANCE®

A six-book series from Harlequin Superromance.

WOMEN *in Blue*

Six female cops battling crime and corruption on the streets of Houston. Together they can fight the blue wall of silence. But divided, will they fall?

Coming in December 2004,
The Witness by Linda Style
(Harlequin Superromance #1243)

She had vowed never to return to Houston's crime-riddled east end. But Detective Crista Santiago's promotion to the Chicano Squad put her right back in the violence of the barrio. Overcoming demons from her past, and with somebody in the department who wants her gone, she must race the clock to find out who shot Alex Del Rio's daughter.

Coming in January 2005,
Her Little Secret by Anna Adams
(Harlequin Superromance #1248)

Abby Carlton was willing to give up her career for Thomas Riley, but then she realized she'd always come second to his duty to his country. She went home and rejoined the police force, aware that her pursuit of love had left a black mark on her file. Now Thomas is back, needing help only she can give.

Also in the series:
The Partner by Kay David (#1230, October 2004)
The Children's Cop by Sherry Lewis (#1237, November 2004)

And watch for:
She Walks the Line by Roz Denny Fox (#1254, February 2005)
A Mother's Vow by K.N. Casper (#1260, March 2005)

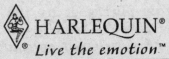

HARLEQUIN®
Live the emotion™

www.eHarlequin.com

HSRWOMIB1204

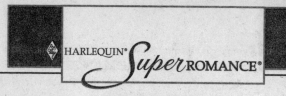

HARLEQUIN *Super*ROMANCE®

YOU, ME & THE KIDS

Along Came Zoe

by Janice Macdonald

Superromance #1244

On sale December 2004

Zoe McCann doesn't like doctors. They let people
die while they're off playing golf. Actually, she knows
that's not true, but her anger helps relieve some of
the pain she feels at the death of her best friend's
daughter. Then she confronts Dr. Phillip Barry—the
neurosurgeon who wasn't available when Jenny was
brought to the E.R.—and learns that doctors
don't have all the answers. Even where
their own children are concerned.

Available wherever Harlequin books are sold.

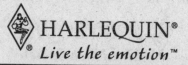

HARLEQUIN®
Live the emotion™